In sleep her lips were slightly parted and full. He wondered how they would taste against his own.

As he watched, her eyes fluttered open and her gaze met his.

"Forry . . ." She said his name on a sigh.

Desire burned hot coals low in his abdomen. Suddenly her sherry-washed eyes were full of awareness, and he knew she, too, felt the desire pulsing between them. She shivered, and shook her head slowly in denial.

"Georgina." Unwisely, he reached out to pull her into his arms, to taste those forbidden lips.

"Mama, I . . . Oh!" Sabrina's soft shriek brought them both to their senses.

Georgina, holding his eyes, withdrew into the protection of her coverlet. He couldn't seem to look away either. He jumped to his feet and backed across the room.

# *AUTUMN LOVES*

## *A Regency Anthology*

**AUTUMN GLORY**
*by Barbara Metzger*

**"SWEET CHARLATAN"**
*by Patricia Veryan*

**MY LORD'S LADY**
*by Leslie Lynn*

**PETTICOAT HALL**
*by Joan Smith*

FAWCETT CREST • NEW YORK

A Fawcett Crest Book
Published by Ballantine Books
Compilation copyright © 1993 by Random House, Inc.

Library of Congress Catalog Card Number: 93-90202

ISBN 0-449-22224-1

Manufactured in the United States of America

First Edition: October 1993

# Contents

# AUTUMN GLORY

by
Barbara Metzger

# 1

Lord Bannister hosted the hunt, Lady Bannister held the annual hunt ball. Together the events were the highlights of the fall season for the neighboring gentry. Berkshire was not Quorn territory, nor was the ball any Carlton House extravaganza. Still, the Bannister dos were enough to keep much of local society from traveling early to London for the Little Season, and even drew some of the *ton* away from London for the excellent sport and convivial gathering. Where dashing riders went, hopeful mamas were sure to follow with their unwed daughters in tow. Bannister Grange had been the scene of many a successful chase, both on the field and in the ballroom. Lady Bannister was determined that this year should be even more memorable.

"Isa," she said, addressing the newspaper across the breakfast table. "We have to speak."

Isa Snodgrass, Baron Bannister, lowered his paper an inch or two. A glimpse of his wife before luncheon was enough to turn a man off his kippers. Irene rarely graced the breakfast parlor, and only did so now, he was sure, to ruin his day with her endless nattering about assigning bedchambers and ordering wines. The house party was her responsibility, b'gad. He raised the paper in front of his face again with a grunt, hoping to block out her carping whine as well as the sight of her narrow nose, squinty eyes, and colorless cheeks.

"Isa, put down the newspaper at once, I say. We have to speak about your daughter."

Daughter? The pages rattled in his quaking hand, a kidney lodged in his throat. How the devil did she find out about the little girl in Cheriton village? He waved away the footman who came to pound on his back, and only when the room was empty did he cautiously repeat, "Daughter? Which daughter is that?"

"Iselle, your eldest, in case you have forgotten. The girl has to be married off instantly."

Lord Bannister took a swallow of ale in relief, then choked as his wife's words penetrated his brain box. "Has to? Has to, by George? I'll take a horse-whip to the bounder!" he sputtered, spewing droplets on his neck cloth.

Lady Bannister grimaced. "Don't be more of a fool than you have to be, Isa. I'll thank you to remember your daughters are ladies."

As if no lady ever found herself needing a husband in a hurry, he ruminated, mopping at his shirtfront. Then again, Irene's daughters were likely to be as cold as the hatchet-faced harridan across from him. "Well, if the gel ain't increasing, what's all the pother about? Iselle's the beauty of the family, ain't she?"

Lady Bannister's thin lips tightened into a smug smile. "All three of the girls are good-looking. The two oldest take after my family, of course. That is not the issue, however," she said, recalling herself. "Iselle is nearly four and twenty. She has had five London Seasons. Five, Isa. Why, we were engaged three months after my debut!"

Yes, and by parents who saw a perfect melding of lands, fortunes, and titles in the arrangement. Neither Isa nor Irene had been consulted. Perhaps because of their own experience, neither parent had been eager to choose spouses for their offspring.

4

Lady Bannister seemed to read her lordship's mind, for she continued: "She never seems to settle on any beau! I fear she won't ever make a choice. Why, with her face and the handsome dowry, she could have had her pick of all the eligibles. Instead she is in danger of becoming a veritable ape-leader! Well, I won't have any daughter of mine sitting on the shelf, Isa, and mean to see her engaged at our hunt ball. Yes, and the other two also."

"I thought the, ah, middle one had her sights set on young Allbright."

"What, let Inessa throw herself away on a country vicar? Never."

"Seems a good enough lad. Bruising rider, for a man of the cloth."

Lady Bannister set her teacup down with a clatter. "I am the granddaughter of a duke, may I remind you. I would not be a proper mother if I did not wish better for my children. Inessa knows her duty, she has simply not made up her mind to accept any of the many excellent offers she has received. She has had three Seasons to decide, so now I shall do so for her also, and before the ball, too."

"And the youngest? You're going to see her fired off, too? The chit's never had a Season, has she?"

Irene stiffened her already rigid spine. "You expect me to chaperon three unmarried daughters in town? Why, I'd be a laughingstock. Besides, I am not about to take that hobbledehoy child to London, even if she is eighteen. She'd disgrace us all. If Inessa and Iselle with their beauty and refinement cannot make a match, that hoyden never will. You've let her grow wild and—"

"I? I let?" the baronet shouted, growing red in the face. "Since when have I had a say in the rearing of your daughters, madam?"

"That's just like you, Isa Snodgrass, passing all the blame onto me, you heartless lout. Why, you

5

know more about your foxhounds than you do about your daughters. You—"

After the births of the two eldest daughters in quick succession, the baroness had born a son, Ira, who did not survive infancy. Then there were a series of miscarriages, and finally another daughter some six years after the first. Irene decided she had done her duty by the Bannister name and retired from what she considered an onerous, undignified exercise. With a nephew to inherit the title and entailed property, and three chits to dower with the rest of his assets, Isa was content to forego a chore he found no less appealing than his wife. They each, gratefully, took up other interests. Unfortunately, none of their interests included raising their three daughters.

Isa was a good landlord, but his first love was the hunt, his horses and his hounds. What good were daughters there? His next love was the army widow in Cheriton village.

Lady Bannister took up science. No dabbling in phrenology or magnetism or Herr Mesmer's new practice for the duke's granddaughter. No, she became a student of graphology. Irene Snodgrass was going to uncover the secrets of human nature through the study of handwriting. She studied translations of Dr. Baldi's works and everything else written over the centuries on this exacting science. She collected specimens for her extensive notebooks, and spent hours poring over her correspondence with other like-minded students of character analysis. Mostly she pestered every noteworthy figure of the age for handwriting samples. She had scrawls from everyone from Byron (lusty loops, passionate periods, inspired indentations) to Wellington (forceful finials, determined downstrokes) to prove her theories.

This last was another reason Lady Bannister was

not about to return to London in the near future, this time with not one, or even two, beautiful but hard to please daughters. There was also that small embarrassment at the War Office over her attempts to communicate with Mr. Bonaparte. Those dodderers in the government had no respect for science. No, the girls had to be married, and soon, so Lady Bannister could pursue her course of enlightenment.

"Well, madam, are you going to tell me what lucky sods you have selected to leg-shackle to your daughters, or have you ruined my breakfast for another of your megrims?"

Lady Bannister regretfully pushed back her plate with her own now-congealed poached egg; throwing food was certainly beneath her dignity. She did take a moment or two to dab fastidiously with her serviette at her pursed lips while her husband fumed. Aggravating the blockhead into an apoplexy was not beneath her, not at all. Finally, she cleared her throat and announced—in tones to rival King Louis's *"L'état, c'est moi"*—"For Iselle I have selected Viscount Wingate."

Lady Bannister had no more finished the second syllable of his lordship's name before Lord Bannister guffawed heartily. "Wingate? Why, the fellow's rich as Golden Ball, from one of the oldest families in the land, and a mainstay of the Foreign Ministry. He's a world traveler, a high-stickler, and a confirmed bachelor. You'll never bring him up to scratch."

Lady Bannister elevated her aristocratic nose. "That's what you know. He is recently returned from Vienna at the death of his cousin. A death that left him in line for the dukedom without an heir of his own. According to Sophy Melincamp, who is a friend of Margaret Hanley-Thorpe's, who is a bosom-bow of his mother's, the viscount is retiring

7

from the government to look after his own extensive properties as well as those he'll inherit. The *on-dit* is that he is ready to settle down and start his nursery. Who is more suited to be such a nonpareil's bride than our own Iselle?"

Who indeed? Iselle was a regular diamond, an exquisite willowy blonde with all the graces of a reigning toast. In her mother's eyes her advanced age only made her more acceptable to a worldly sophisticate like Lord Wingate. If Iselle didn't have two thoughts to rub together in her pretty head, Lady Bannister never regarded the lack. Surely a renowned collector of art like the viscount wouldn't either, not once he saw Iselle. Furthermore, Iselle's handwriting showed her eminently suited for such an exalted position as future duchess.

On the girl's fifteenth birthday, Lady Bannister had requested a sample of her penmanship to study, the way a gypsy might study tea leaves, although there was no scientific basis in soggy vegetation, of course. Iselle's script was everything elegant, all graceful whorls and perfect symmetry, nearly a textbook copperplate. Lady Bannister had started looking about at the royal dukes. 'Twas too bad she hadn't looked in the schoolroom, where the current governess, fearing for her position, had transcribed the passage for Iselle. Everyone but Miss Snodgrass's parents knew the gorgeous peagoose could barely read, much less copy a paragraph from Reverend Quigley's *Proper Thoughts for Proper Ladies*.

"So Wingate's home at last, and he'll be in the neighborhood, you say?"

"He'll be here, sir. Haven't you been listening? He has accepted my invitation to join the house party and hunt. That must mean he is interested." She still regretted that his reply was penned by some anonymous secretary. Perhaps while his lordship was here . . .

"And you think the wench'll have him?"

"Have him? Iselle will jump at the chance. He's said to be handsome and charming, and she's at her last prayers. Besides, she had all those years to make a choice. Either she'll have the viscount or she can go visit your Aunt Irmintrude."

"Gads, in Wales? How could she ever make a match stuck in that cold place?"

"Exactly. She'll make a perfect diplomat's wife." Lady Bannister poured a fresh cup of tea. "As for Inessa, she requires a different kind of spouse."

"She's the quiet one, ain't she?"

"She never really took in London, despite matching Iselle for looks. She seems to prefer the country and quiet pursuits. She'll be a perfect match for Mr. Frye. It's not a brilliant connection, with no title, of course. But there is all that lovely money."

"Why, Frye is forty if he's a day. And word is a lot of that blunt comes from trade. He's got the finest stud in the county, by George—what I wouldn't give for one of his Thoroughbreds—but Inessa?"

The middle daughter's handwriting at age fifteen had been painstakingly neat. Inessa truly wished to please, so copied her passage from Reverend Quigley's tome over and over until she had it perfect, though her tired hand lent a slight waver and weakness to the letters. According to Lady Bannister, the thin lines meant she was unsure of herself, but the waver meant she was easily swayed. "The gal needs an older man, a steady influence. And Frye isn't one for racketing around."

"He's not accepted in first circles, you mean."

"Country society is good enough for Inessa," she insisted. "And Frye's been a widower for four or five years now. He needs a wife, especially one whose birth will make him more welcome in polite society."

"Well and good for Frye, but what about Inessa?"

"She is biddable, I always told you, and knows her duty. Furthermore," she said through gritted teeth, "I refuse to drag that shrinking violet to one more ball. She'll have Frye or join her sister in Wales."

Isa nodded, seeing visions of one of Frye's colts being part of the marriage settlements. "What about, ah, the last one of the brood?"

Lady Bannister sniffed, that the gudgeon could hardly remember his own children's names, then she shuddered to think of seeing her third daughter making her curtsies in town. No, the chit was impossible. Where the older girls had fine spun-gold hair, this one had flyaway red curls, wild hair and wild manners. She'd be a disaster at Almack's, where one misstep set a female beyond the pale, and beyond the reach of any marriage-minded male. In truth, her every scrape and bumblebroth proved the validity of Lady Bannister's theorems. Hadn't her copied passage been full of blots and backward-leaning letters, a totally undisciplined, nearly illegible scrawl? The writing proved what Lady Bannister already knew, that the chit was headstrong and ungovernable. What she didn't know was that the girl was left-handed, forced by convention and a cruel governess to write the "correct" way, with her right hand. The governess was dismissed anyway, for Lady Bannister saw no reason to pay good money in a hopeless case. The girl's tomboyish behavior after that only reinforced Irene's findings. The chit definitely needed a husband, or a keeper.

"I fear Squire Thurkle's son is the best we can hope for in that quarter. And you'll likely have to throw in that parcel of unentailed property that Thurkle has been after to get him to bring the boy up to the mark."

"The lad's got a good seat," the baronet mused.

"He's young, but the two have been playmates for dog's years."

"Good, because he *will* marry her. Not even Aunt Irmintrude will take that hurly-burly miss off my hands."

Just then there came a thud from the room next door, as from a book dropping off a shelf.

"Blast, I told you I didn't want those clumsy maids in my library. I don't know why you cannot hire more competent servants, since you claim to know so much about human nature."

"I only claim that there are inferences to be drawn from a person's handwriting, and servants don't write."

"If they could write, they wouldn't be servants, they'd be barristers. Or poets. Perhaps you could tell if Walter Scott would make a good valet. You sure as Hades cannot keep a good cook." He pushed aside his ruined breakfast.

"At least I never judged a man by how well he sits a horse. Why, if I'd seen your miserable scribbling before we were wed, I would have—"

# 2

"Botheration." The young lady in the library stooped to pick up the fallen book, then tore out of the room and down the hall. She avoided colliding with the butler and his fresh pot of tea by mere inches, calling over her shoulder, "Hurry, Dobbs, they are at it again," before flying up the stairs. Dobbs winced and redirected his stately tread in the other direction, back toward the kitchens, shaking his head at the sight of his youngest mistress taking the marble stairs two at a time. Her muslin skirts, dusty from an early visit to the stables, swirled around her muddied half boots. Red-gold hair tumbled out of its ribbon to trail down her back and in her face, and when she brushed the offending curls out of her eyes, her hand—her left hand—deposited a streak of dirt across a cheek already afflicted with freckles.

"Botheration," she cursed again on her way to wake her sleeping sisters, to announce the disasters in store for them. Of all the dire fates, though, in a life filled with injustice and slights, Algernon Thurkle was the worst blight of all. At least Ellie, beautiful Iselle, was to get a handsome peer. And Nessie, sweet Inessa, was to get Frye Hall and those marvelous horses. She, the last child, the unwanted third daughter, was to get Algie Thurkle, with his spots and stammer and stable-centered conversation. Why, his horse had more intelligence! She'd rather wed his horse, for that matter. At least the horse did not have roving hands. Lady Bannister's youngest girl may have been without a governess for these past years, but she had the lending library and the collection downstairs to teach herself, and if there was one thing she learned, it was that there was more to life than horses and hunting. Well, she was not going to do it. She was not going to marry an unlicked cub without even making her bows at the marriage mart, and she was not going to become Mrs. Algernon Thurkle, not after spending the last eighteen years as Irmagard Snodgrass. Life could not be that cruel.

The freckles were bad enough, the left-handedness could usually be concealed, and she had long resigned herself to being the ugly duckling in a family of swans, but Irmagard! Not even Maggie, she thought with eighteen years of resentment, because Lady Bannister thought Maggie sounded common. So she was Irma to her closest associates, and more often Irm the Worm to her older sisters, who had too often found the grubby infant underfoot, asking questions, following them about. From the natural superiority of five or six years, they resented the constant shadow of a bumbling baby sister.

They did not resent her now, falling on Irma to save them from the atrocity of arranged marriages. At least they did so after Iselle roundly berated her for waking them before noon, and Inessa raised her blue eyes to heaven and clucked her tongue at the sight of the dirt tracks across her carpet.

"Oh, hush, both of you, do. Ellie, you know you don't need any beauty sleep; you're always prettiest after dancing the night away. And if you don't hurry and listen, you'll find yourself never dancing again. And, Nessie, you'll have to do more than pray over a little untidiness, unless you wish to

13

have Mr. Frye tracking stable muck through your parlor."

"Mr. Frye? Whatever are you speaking of? He would never come calling on Mama in all his dirt."

"And what do you mean, I'll never dance again? Why, there will be balls every night as soon as Papa's wretched hunt is over and we leave for London."

"We are not going to London, none of us, that's the point. We have a veritable crisis." And so she explained about their mother's plans to see each of them engaged by the night of the hunt ball, less than a week away.

Predictably, Iselle dissolved in a flutter of weepy lace onto the chaise longue, without looking one jot puffy or red-eyed or rumpled, Irma thought disgustedly as she bathed her eldest sister's forehead with lavender water.

"I made sure Mama would give up after all these years," Ellie groaned. "I'll go into a decline, I swear, and waste away from a broken heart. Viscount Wingate will marry a faded wraith, and then I'll come back to haunt him for taking an unwilling bride."

The only books Iselle ever read, nay, listened to while Inessa or Irma read aloud, were gothic romances from the Minerva Press. It showed. The handkerchief wafted through the air. "I shall die for true love."

"Don't be a cabbage head, Ellie," Irma chided. "No one dies from an arranged marriage. Just look at Mama."

Ellie moaned again. Then she sat up suddenly, tipping the basin of scented water onto Irma. "Wingate!" she shrieked, as if she'd truly seen a ghost. "Why did she have to pick that stuffed shirt Wingate?"

Irma ignored the spreading wetness in her lap.

"Oh, do you know him? Did you ever meet him in London? Mama says he is handsome."

"Handsome?" Iselle echoed distractedly. "I suppose, if you like sober-sided and stiff-rumped old men. Why, there's never been so much as a hint of scandal to his name, not a single *affaire* or gaming debt or duel, only his stodgy accomplishments at those wretched peace conventions. No, I never met him, although I did see him a few times. But, but, Irma, you were right! He never dances, just stands in corners having boring conversations when he's not at those fusty government conferences and things. I'd have to be a political hostess," she wailed, "giving those interminable dinners where no one laughs or gossips or flirts. And you know I never understand any of that other talk about excursions and excise taxes. You know I don't!"

"Sh, Ellie, don't get yourself in a pelter. Mama says Wingate is retiring from the government to take up managing his properties."

"Worse and worse!" Iselle cried. "Then I'll never get to London at all! How will I find out the latest fashions? Besides, in the country away from company, I'd have to talk to him all the time, every day!"

"Yes, dearest, that is customary among husbands and wives."

"But, but, Irma, they say Wingate speaks eight languages! Eight!"

Irma had no words of comfort for the beautiful wigeon who barely spoke one. She turned instead to her other sister, who had been quietly wringing her hands together in the corner of the sitting room the sisters shared.

"What think you, Nessie? Can you be happy with Mr. Frye?"

With blue eyes awash in tears, Inessa looked like an injured angel. Her chin trembled and her voice

15

quavered, but she managed to say, "If Mama wishes it, I shall try to make him a good wife."

"But can you be happy?" Irma insisted. "Mama doesn't have to live with him, you know."

Inessa swallowed. "A woman cannot simply follow her own heart in these things, Irmagard. You've always been too impetuous to see that there are higher goals than the mere pursuit of happiness. A daughter owes her parents obedience and . . . and deference to their wisdom."

Irma made an unladylike sound. "Is it wise to shackle you to a man nearly old enough to be your father and whose manners, moreover, smell of the shop no matter what airs he puts on for the countryside? That is not wisdom, Nessie, it's greed for all that money he has."

"Well, at least I shall be able to accomplish a great many good deeds with all that wealth."

"What fustian. The man did not get to be a nabob by giving alms to the poor. And I am certain he won't want his beautiful young bride going among the diseased and downtrodden. Can't you see, Nessie, Mama just picked him because he is well-heeled and handy. She just wants to get rid of us."

Iselle dabbed at her nose. "I cannot see what you have to complain about, Irma. Your life won't be ruined. You'll still be able to muck about in the stables and tromp over the hills to visit the tenant farmers the way you've been doing. Algie won't mind that you never learned to play the pianoforte or embroider."

"What you mean is that I can never hope for a better match."

"I never said that! It's just that you and Algie have so much in common. Your . . . your outdoor-syness, and . . . and your freckles!"

Irma laughed. "A fine basis for a marriage. You are as bad as Mama, but never mind. No one

16

thought to inquire if I might enjoy a London ball, or even an intelligent conversation. You might be resigned to the fates Mama has assigned you, but I swear to you, I shan't marry Algernon Thurkle. And no," she said to Iselle, "I won't go into any histrionic declaration that I'd sooner die. I'd more likely murder poor Algie first. But if you don't want to hear my plans . . ." And she made to leave the room, flipping her damp skirts away from her legs.

"Don't you dare leave, you little worm, without telling us your plan!" Iselle commanded. Then Inessa murmured, "Do you really think there is a chance Mama will change her mind?"

Irma grinned, showing dimples alongside her mouth. "Never, but not even Mama can make us marry gentlemen who don't ask. And I mean to make sure they never do."

Nessie worried her lip between perfect white teeth. "I don't believe I could act vulgarly enough to give Mr. Frye a disgust of me, Irma."

And Iselle fretted: "If you're thinking I can get myself up to look like a hag in order to discourage Lord Wingate, I don't think I can do it. Remember when I was supposed to be Medusa for that masquerade? Everyone laughed."

Irma drew her sisters closer. "I know neither of you is good at deception, so you'll just have to trust me. Nessie, you can be as good as ever, and Ellie, twice as beautiful, if that's possible. Just listen . . ."

# 3

His boots were dusty, by Jupiter. Dusty and scuffed and caked with mud. Damn if they didn't look good to Brigham Winn, Viscount Wingate. Here he was, alone in the English countryside, with no one to impress but the occasional sheep or cow and his own horse. And the stallion trailing behind him at the end of the reins was missing a shoe altogether, so the blasted horse couldn't complain. Winn laughed out loud with the sheer joy of freedom. He looked back along the tree-lined lane the way he had come, then forward on the leafy path, then reached up with his free hand and loosened his neck cloth. Walking one's horse for a few hours was warm work, even if the bright autumn sunshine did not carry much heat with it. The viscount told himself that it would not do to arrive at Bannister Grange looking like some kind of undergroom, but he was gambling on getting 'Ledo to the stables, then finding a servant to direct him to a side door before he had to greet his hosts. That is, if he ever found Bannister Grange at all.

Lord Wingate had been wandering these country byways for hours, it seemed, after leaving his carriage, baggage, groom, and valet at the last posting stop. The ostler had sworn he knew the best way to get to the Grange across the fields and streams, the best ride to challenge both nobleman and stallion. Master and horse had been confined too long, held to the carriage's slow pace halfway across Europe, making their way to London after three days' delay for the Channel crossing. Then they had to idle about for a fortnight in town waiting on the Cabinet ministers and doing the pretty with Wingate's mother and her friends. It was exhilarating to have the strength of the stallion beneath him as hedgerow and stone wall flew by. It was not quite as exhilarating to walk miles out of the way to find an opening in those same fences and brambles after the steel gray Toledo cast a shoe. The ostler's directions, of course, meant nothing if horse and rider couldn't take the third fence after jumping the brook, catercorner from the fallen elm, et cetera. By the time he found a low spot to lead the stallion across a fast-running stream that was strewn with dangerous rocks, he couldn't locate a fence post, fallen tree, or his hat.

So he was lost and late, damp and dirty—and he didn't care. The viscount was no longer a public figure. He was not representing England, the throne, or the entire British upper class. Negotiations did not hinge on the punctilio of his address, nations were not going to rise or fall on the height of his shirt points or the depth of his bow. Brigham Winn was a free man.

If he was about to assume another type of yoke, well, he still knew his duty to God, the king, and the family name, but, deuce take it, he was going to enjoy these last hours of liberty. Like a small boy, he kicked up piles of fallen leaves with every boot step until the stallion snorted and sidled at the end of the reins.

"Very well, lad," the viscount told the horse, "I'll stop playing and get on with finding you your supper and a cozy crib for the night. Ah, but 'Ledo, isn't England a pretty place?" Wingate paused to wave his hand around, encompassing the blue skies, the scarlet leaves, the rolling fields. The horse nudged him from behind, sending him on his way again. "Yes, yes, I am going. You have no poetry in your soul, though. Come along now, there's a hill just ahead. Likely I'll be able to spot some landmark or other from there, or at least a farmhouse where I can ask directions."

Wingate was right. From the top of the hill, he could look down to what had to be the main highway, from the width and condition of the road. On another rise across the road, he could see the chimneys of a large building, large enough to be Bannister Grange itself. He checked his watch. With any luck his own coach would be passing by shortly, and he could freshen his appearance before reaching his destination after all. Unless the carriage with his valet and clean clothes had already gone by. Undecided, Wingate looked around him while the horse cropped the still-green grass.

The viscount took a deep breath, catching wood smoke and the hint of an apple press in the air. Cultivated fields stretched in all directions, grains tied in bundles or piled in ricks, waiting for the lumbering wagons and huge workhorses he could see making their way from row to row. The windbreak evergreens made dark contrast to the orange and yellow leaves of the vines and hedges. "I cannot help it, 'Ledo," he told the disinterested animal, "I am happy to be home in England, especially at this time of year. It may be trite but no less true for all that: autumn truly is a glorious season."

Wingate turned back to gather the reins again when another splash of color caught his eye from the side of the hill he was on, closer to the road. As he went nearer, leading the stallion, the brightness defined itself into a female figure in a russet frock reclining on an undyed wool blanket beneath a small hawthorne tree. A maid on her half day off, he thought a bit enviously, waiting for her beau for a picnic in the grass. At least someone could tell him if his carriage had passed by recently and if that was, indeed, Bannister Grange.

Unfortunately, the maid appeared to be asleep. He tied 'Ledo to a nearby branch so as not to startle her, and walked quietly to her side, then silently whistled. This was no maidservant. Not in a russet velvet riding habit cut in the latest military fashion, and no child, either, judging from how the velvet hugged a delightful little figure. He looked around for the horse and spotted a dainty roan mare across the roadway, placidly cropping grass. That was no workhorse, and this was no farmer's daughter picking berries or whatever. So where was the groom who should have been in attendance? Well-bred young ladies did not loll about empty hillsides for any passing stranger to chance upon. England could not have changed that much in his absence. Gads, what if he'd been one of the roving ex-soldiers or an angry, out-of-work farmhand?

He sank down beside the foolish wench, a scowl on his face, ready to blister her ears with a few home truths, when he saw the pistol tucked under her skirts. Not quite a henwit, then, if the pistol were loaded, if she knew how to use it, and if she had the bottom to shoot a man. That pointed little chin seemed to indicate enough determination, but there was a sweetness around the lips that hinted at a tender heart. He found himself wondering what color the chit's eyes were, and if they'd be stormy if he kissed those soft lips awake. He gently nudged the pistol further out of her reach, just in case he let his baser instincts win out. 'Twould teach the girl a lesson, he tried to convince himself, and failed. He was still a gentleman, for all his release from duty. Wingate sighed and forced his eyes away from those tempting lips. The corners of his own mouth tilted up when he studied the jaunty little hat, now cocked over one brow, with a green ostrich feather resting against one creamy cheek. Fine lot of good that minuscule bonnet was doing keeping the sun off her face, about as much as the pistol was protecting her from unsought admiration. By the freckles he spotted and the warm-toned skin, Sleeping Beauty was no more caring of her complexion than she was of her reputation. And that red hair—a minx for sure.

It wasn't quite red, not carroty at all, more a mix of gold and copper, with curls that just asked a man to hold them to the light, to watch the fiery glimmers change color. Damnation, his wits must have gone begging along with his hat.

Winn looked away with a twinge of regret that the unknown miss wasn't one of the Bannister daughters, who were exquisitely fair, according to his mother. Then who the devil was she, and what was she doing out here alone on what had to be Bannister property? And with a pistol. He had not forgotten the pistol.

He moved it farther away, feeling guilty at the liberties he had taken, if only in his mind. Hell, if he gave way to even a quarter of the impulses this female was stirring, she'd have every right to shoot him. On the other hand, he couldn't just go away and leave her unprotected this close to the road. Winn started to clear his throat when a paper fluttered at the girl's other side. He moved around to see what he'd missed, a drawing pad and a set of watercolor paints together with a small jug of water and a rag. Ah, so she was off on a drawing excursion, practicing one of those paltry skills deemed so necessary among debutantes, like harp playing and batting their eyelashes just so. Winn swallowed his disappointment as he flipped back the page on her painting. Lud, she needed a lot of practice!

The view from the hill was there, the reds and golds of the changing leaves, the blue of a cloudless sky, and the greens where the grasses hadn't turned yet, even the browns of the harvested fields—except the browns came more from her reds and greens running together, and all the colors flowed and moved like leaves on the breeze. There was no recognizable feature in the whole picture, and yet the chit had captured the essence of the autumn day as seen through half-blind or squinted eyes. Winn looked around for spectacles. No. Perhaps she just saw things through a child's mind, then? There would have been an attendant here for sure if she was that much of a slowtop. With his collector's eye, Wingate decided the chit was either brilliant, doing with autumn what Turner did with fog, or she was a wretched watercolorist. Undoubtedly she was using the excuse of painting to avoid whatever duties awaited her at home, the same as he was avoiding his.

To put the moment off a bit more, he replaced the painting next to her on the blanket, only this time upside down. Not that it made much of a difference, he decided, a definite quirk in his smile. He stood back and studied the new still life he had created: the vibrantly colored girl, the vivid painting, the radiant hillside. "Yes," he said aloud, "the glories of autumn, indeed."

Green. Her eyes were bright green, and his connoisseur's heart breathed a sigh of satisfaction. "Ah."

Irma jerked herself upright and groped for the pistol. But, "Ah"? What kind of threatening sound was "ah"? The attractive stranger did not seem menacing, especially when he knelt on one knee so that he no longer loomed over her.

"I mean you no harm, miss," Irma's fuddled mind heard him saying, over the pounding of her heart. She took a deep breath and a better look at the gentleman, for such he assuredly was, even from her narrow experience with the breed. His coat and boots, albeit dusty, proclaimed he patronized the finest London tailors, and the dark gray stallion she could see tied nearby was as neat a piece of horseflesh as anything in even Mr. Frye's stable. The rider's accent was refined, his voice low and pleasant. The breadth of his shoulders and the buckskin-clad muscles on his flexed thigh showed him to be in superb condition for a man with as many gray hairs as brown.

"Do I pass inspection, or shall you shoot me after all?" Warm brown eyes flickered to the pistol, still out of her reach. But he smiled.

Irma blushed furiously to be caught staring like a gapeseed, all the while thinking that the gray hair was deceiving. He was not old at all; the boyish grin took ten years off his age. Which, she belatedly reflected, made her encounter with him on this hillside even more improper. She hurriedly got to her feet.

"Please don't let me frighten you away from your, ah, artistic endeavor," he said indicating the watercolor painting.

Irma could feel her cheeks grow still warmer. She straightened her hat and started packing up the paint box, her sister Nessie's set since Irma never possessed such a thing. She could feel his smiling regard while she folded the blanket. Then she realized the feather on her hat—why ever had she let Ellie talk her into such an absurdly useless little bonnet?—was dangling straight between her eyes. As she lowered her hand after adjusting the plume, she noticed with horror the orange streaks on her fingers, streaks which must have been transferred to her forehead. She couldn't blush any harder, could she? A quick glance at the stranger showed his eyes twinkling, but he gallantly refrained from comment, only holding out a fine-edged linen handkerchief.

"Thank you, but I have one right ..." But she'd used hers to wipe the brushes, having forgotten to bring a rag. Her own scrap of cloth looked quite as atrociously colorful as the painting. There was nothing for it but to borrow his after all, a perfect stranger's! Mama would have a spasm. "Thank you, my lord."

Then she stood looking at the cloth, already blotted with orange. No mirror, and the only water was the jug she'd used to wash the brushes. Why did these things always happen to her? Iselle could walk through a soot storm and not get smudged.

Winn took the cloth back, held it toward her mouth, and said "Spit."

"My lord?" She couldn't have heard right.

"I said spit. Or ride back to your house looking like a Red Indian on the warpath."

The earth wasn't about to open up and swallow her, no matter how Irma might dearly have wished it, so she stuck her tongue out, dampened the cloth, and permitted an attractive stranger with dancing eyes and casual neck cloth to wipe her face. In a lifetime of misdeeds, never had she done anything this far beyond the line. Never mind Aunt Irmintrude; Mama would ship her to the Antipodes.

"There," he was saying, tucking the messy linen back into his pocket. "Pretty as a picture." He smiled toward her drawing pad. "Prettier than some."

Irma felt she'd used up her month's supply of blushes, and she wasn't the fainting type, so she did what came naturally to her, she grinned.

25

Winn noted two adorable dimples, said "Ah" again, and grinned himself.

"I really must be going, sir. This is highly irregular."

"But enchanting. Besides, no one can fault you for giving directions to a poor lost soul who has been wandering in circles for hours."

"Oh, are you lost then? Where is it you wish to go?"

There was no place on earth the viscount would rather be than here on this sunny hillside with this laughing girl, but he said, "I just need to know if this is the main road to Wallingford and the name of that structure across the way."

"Why yes, although Wallingford is still some miles away. The house you see is Bannister Grange. In fact, this is Lord Bannister's property."

"Then might I have the pleasure of addressing one of the legendary Bannister beauties?"

Irma looked down at her boots, which were smeared with dirt, of course, wishing more than ever she was more like her tall, blond, graceful sisters. Then she looked at the gentleman's boots. They were even more disreputable than hers. She flashed her dimples again and replied in perfect truth and some modesty: "I am one of Lord Bannister's daughters."

"Then, may I introduce myself, Miss Bannister? I am—"

"Oh no, Bannister is Papa's title. The family name is Snodgrass."

Lord Wingate blinked once but smoothly continued, "Miss Snodgrass, I—"

She interrupted again. "Only my sister Iselle gets to be Miss Snodgrass. She is the eldest, you see. I come after Inessa."

"Wait, let me guess." He cupped his chin in his

hands and pretended to study her. "Ivy? Inez? Imogene?"

That determined little chin of hers raised a notch. "Irmagard," she pronounced. "Miss Irmagard Snodgrass."

Not even all those months at the Vienna negotiations could keep Lord Wingate's lips from twitching, but the mainstay of the British diplomatic corps rose to the occasion: "No, I was right before. You are the Glory of Autumn, and so I shall call you."

Thrilled down to her dusty boots, Irma still had to say, "Mama would not approve."

"Nor of your being out here alone, I think. So I won't tell her if you won't, Glory. It suits you."

Laughing, she admitted, "My sisters used to call me Irm the Worm."

"And here I thought there was nothing more cruel than little boys. They used to call me Brig the Prig at school. That's short for Brigham."

"And were you? A prig, I mean."

"I suppose. I was studious and hadn't many friends. All I'd been taught till then was about duty and responsibilities."

Irma giggled to think of anyone calling him serious now, with his clothes in disorder and the breeze ruffling his hair. He looked more like a dashing hero from one of Maria Edgeworth's romances than any kind of scholar. She couldn't help wondering where he was going, and if he would be at any of the parties during the hunt week. Mostly she worried that he might ride away and she'd never see him again. To delay the parting, she asked if he had seen a carriage go by. "Actually, more like a caravan, I'd guess, with baggage carts and outriders and crested coaches."

"No, I came through the woods over that hill." He indicated the opposite direction from the road.

"I haven't seen anyone in an hour. Is that what you were doing up here with a pistol, Glory, waiting for some wealthy nob to waylay on the king's highway? And I thought you were painting."

She laughed again at his teasing, and felt so comfortable with him that she confessed, "I did mean to stop that stiff-rumped viscount before he reached the Grange, but only to put a flea in his ear, not lighten his purse."

Wingate couldn't think of too many other viscounts, stiff-rumped or otherwise, who might be on their way to Bannister Grange. The chit was full of surprises, even if this one did wipe the smile off his face. Stiff-rumped, indeed. The child should be back in the schoolroom till she learned some manners. "Might I ask why you needed to stop the fellow here, rather than greet him at the front door, or would that be too commonplace? I am only asking out of curiosity, you know." He pretended to wipe a speck of dust off his sleeve.

Irma took on a militant look, staring down at the roadway as if willing the carriage to arrive. "I am not ashamed of my motives. I need to speak to him before he sees my sister. Once he gets a glimpse of Iselle, it will be too late and he'll ask for her hand no matter what I say. They all do."

"And you don't want this, ah, well-breeched viscount to offer for your sister? That doesn't sound like any female of my ken."

"What I want doesn't matter. Iselle does not want Lord Wingate to offer because Papa will make her accept."

"Is she committed to another, then?"

"That is not for me to say. She does not wish the connection, and so I shall tell his toplofty lordship, if he has not gone by already."

Winn couldn't help probing. "And what if he is as toplofty as you say and cannot be dissuaded?"

"Then I shall tell him that insanity runs in the family. If he knows about Mama and the War Office, he won't doubt me for a minute."

His own mother hadn't mentioned anything about Lady Bannister and Whitehall, but that could wait. For now he had to find out what was so objectionable in his suit. "What has you and your sister so set against the poor chap, if there is no other suitor she prefers?"

"He's ancient and fusty and never smiles. He speaks eight languages and collects art. Why, Ellie cannot understand a London hackney driver, and she collects broken hearts! Old Iron-Breeches will only intimidate her and make her miserable."

Winn swallowed hard. "You are young. Perhaps your parents know what is best for your sister. She has remained unwed all these years, after all."

"She still may wish to marry a man of her own choice." Irma turned to him. "Are you wed?" she asked bluntly.

"Why, no."

"See?" At his blank look she tried to explain. "You have to understand, a man of your parts." She waved her hand around, unfortunately the one with the pistol she'd belatedly grasped. Wingate stepped back. "Sorry. But look, your expensive horse, your fancy tailoring, and your cultured accents." His raised eyebrows made her hurry on: "I am not trying to offer Spanish coin, I am just stating facts. You must have had lots of females thrown at your head . . . unless you are ineligible?" He shook his head, no, smiling again. "There, that proves my point. You have not married out of your own choice. Iselle should have the same right."

"Ah, but Glory, there are duties and responsibilities that go beyond one's own wishes." He almost reached out to tuck one of her reddish curls back off her forehead. Almost. "Speaking of which, I have stayed too long off the correct road, and I am sure you will be missed. Au revoir, Glory."

"Farewell, sir, uh, Lord . . . ?"

"Just call me Iron-Breeches, Glory. And that's six languages, not eight."

# 4

With so many houseguests at Bannister Grange that week, clandestine visits between bedchambers would not have been surprising. Lady Bannister's scratching on her husband's door, however, was enough to give that gentleman severe palpitations. He grabbed for his nightcap, then he grabbed for the decanter of brandy. Whatever Irene wanted in the middle of the night, in her curl papers and face creams, Isa was going to need fortification.

"Well," she said, "when are you going to do it?"

"It?" He tried to swallow past the lump in his throat.

"Bring Wingate up to scratch, you clunch. He's been here three days already, and nary a sign of an offer. Everyone knows that's why he came, so why the delay?"

"Fellow's been deuced slippery, I can tell you. Whenever I mention the gel's dowry or hint about all the young bucks coming to call, he changes the subject. Wingate's a born politico, that's for sure."

"I can't like it. Letting him spend too much time in Iselle's company might not be the best idea."

"You mean he might realize she's a beautiful bacon-brain." He took a swig and made a sour face. "Only fair to let the chap know what he's getting before stepping into parson's mousetrap."

Lady Bannister ignored both his grimace and what could only be aspersions on their own ar-

31

ranged marriage. "It's that wretched Irmagard. I ordered her to stay by Iselle's side, to carry along the conversations, you know. What does the impossible chit do? She turns scarlet the minute Wingate enters the room, then turns tail and hides among the dowagers. Thank goodness I did not take her to London, if this is how she acts at her first introduction to a highly placed peer."

Lord Bannister nodded. "I never thought I'd see that brazen chit turn craven. Lud knows she never minded her tongue before. Leastways she hasn't had a chance to lecture Wingate on the sins of fox hunting yet. She ain't been next or nigh him."

Lady Bannister dismissed her youngest child's vagaries; she'd given up on drumming the rudiments of decorum into the thick red head ages ago. She nervously rearranged the items on his lordship's dresser. "There's more. I cannot rest easy with a rake in the house."

Isa tried to smother a snicker. She couldn't be fearing for her own virtue, not in those five yards of flannel. "Don't see how anyone not up to snuff got on your invite list anyway."

"I didn't invite Sir Evan Farrell, you jackanapes. As if I ever would, when we are not even at home to him in London. Lord Rothingham got the gout, so the baronet escorted Lady Rothingham, of all the luck. She's his godmother, can you believe it? And still one of the highest sticklers in polite society. I couldn't do anything but ask him to stay, even if he is a womanizer and a gambler."

"Don't see what's got you in the boughs. The fellow's a man milliner. Barely sits a horse. Not even Iselle is ninnyhammer enough to take some coxcomb over a regular out-and-outer like Wingate. 'Sides, I ain't heard much talk about Farrell in the clubs recently, no duels, debts, or debauches. Nothing to his discredit except his taste in clothes." He snorted. "Farrell's naught but a caper merchant."

Now it was Irene's turn to sneer. "If you could see beyond your fat red nose, you'd know Sir Evan is also devilishly handsome, with every compliment to turn a girl's head on the tip of his silver tongue. I had to warn him off some years ago, but it was easier to divert Iselle's attention in London than here at our own house party. You'll just have to work a little harder on Wingate."

What Lord Bannister wanted most from the viscount was that steel gray stallion for stud. He also wanted a good night's sleep without his wife's prune face giving him nightmares, so he nodded and bowed and swore to have a private talk with Wingate on the morrow.

Most of the company was assembled in the drawing room before dinner when Lord Bannister strolled in with a smile on his face and his arm about Lord Wingate's shoulders. They'd come to terms about the stallion; somehow Iselle's name never entered the conversation. Isa's smile disappeared when he caught his wife's eager expression. He solemnly shook his head no, glad he was across the room.

Wingate also took note of the silent communication between his host and hostess, and grinned to himself. It was a near-run thing. As his eyes scanned the roomful of elegantly dressed lords and ladies, he observed how Glory was dressed this evening in shell pink sarcenet, which brought out the flames in her hair, even across the room. He saw she was quick to offer another glass of ratafia to Lady Rothingham as soon as he entered. The middle sister, Inessa, was doing her duty by quietly conversing with the local cleric, a likable young fellow named Allbright. That sister was a sweet, well-behaved miss, from all Wingate had observed, with the eldest's beauty but not the same allure. Inessa was more reserved, not a social butterfly like the stunning Miss Snodgrass.

His mother had been right: Iselle Snodgrass was one of the most beautiful creatures he'd seen, in the boudoirs and ballrooms of half the European capitals. She'd make a lovely duchess, if he wanted to spend the rest of his life doing the social rounds with a gorgeous goosecap. If ever there was a chit with more hair than wit, it was Miss Iselle Snodgrass. Why, she couldn't even be on time for dinner, he saw, watching Lady Bannister's anxious eyes keep flicking toward the door.

Wingate was listening idly to Lord Bannister crowing to his neighbor Frye about the mare he was going to breed, when he caught Lady Bannister crook her finger toward her youngest daughter. Glory bounced over to her mother's seat—Lud, the chit never seemed to move at anything but a hurry; her curls were already escaping their pins—and stooped to hear Lady Bannister's whisper.

"Of course I'll go find Iselle," she said aloud, loudly enough for others to hear. "But she cannot be so late, Lord Farrell is not down yet either." Then she clapped a hand over her mouth. Lady Bannister rolled her eyes. There were a few twitters from various corners.

Wingate stepped into the breech, thinking again how very young his Glory was, how unready for polite drawing rooms. "I saw Farrell's man hurrying with another batch of fresh neck cloths when we passed in the hall. I'm sure he'll be here momentarily to dazzle us with another new creation."

Lord Bannister muttered something about dashed popinjays, and conversations resumed. Irma flew from the room, likely in search of the truant sister.

Wingate waited a moment, then slipped out after her.

The hallway was empty, as was the grand stairwell spiraling to the upper reaches. "Now where the deuce has that baggage—"

"Ssh," he heard, from behind an enormous arrangement of chrysanthemums on a hall table. Winn stepped closer. The youngest daughter of the house was flat against the wall, out of sight of the drawing room and the stairs. If ever there was a minx up to some devilment, he decided, this grinning, green-eyed sprite was it. "What the devil are—"

"Hush, you'll ruin everything." And she boldly reached out and took his hand, pulling his dignified lordship into the shadows beside her, wedged between a grandfather clock and a flowerpot. He really ought to demand an explanation; he definitely ought to release her warm hand. He did neither.

The grandfather clock started to chime the hour, uncomfortably close to Wingate's ear. Irma squeezed his hand, peering up the stairs. He followed her gaze and was finally rewarded with the sight of Iselle gliding down the upper hallway toward the landing. She was gowned in ivory silk, with a blue net overdress that flowed about her willowy figure from ribbons that tied just beneath the minute bodice. Her gold hair was piled on top of her head like a crown, with one long tress falling over her shoulder to rest along the expanse of creamy flesh left exposed by the plunging décolletage. The viscount took a deep, loud breath, and found his hand cast into the flowers.

Before the clock had finished striking, Sir Evan strode down the opposite hallway. The London tulip was as exquisite in his dress as Iselle. Whereas Viscount Wingate was precise in his black satin knee-smalls and tailcoat, with immaculate white linen and stockings, Farrell was a peacock in aqua velvet, with saffron-silk stripes on his waistcoat, an enormous amber pin in his intricate neck cloth, and enough ribbons and chains crossing his chest to anchor a coal barge. Now it was Wingate's turn to bristle when Glory sighed in appreciation.

Farrell and Iselle met at the upper landing. The baronet bowed and offered Miss Snodgrass his arm. Iselle inclined her golden head and lightly placed her gloved hand on his velvet sleeve. They proceeded down the stairs. When the pair was halfway down, Irma stepped out from the shadows. She didn't leap out or spring out or hop out, she merely took one step away from the wall and whispered, "Boo."

Wingate looked at her in amazement. Glory had not been pitching gammon after all: insanity must truly run in the family.

Somehow, while he was staring at Irma, Iselle had lost her footing on the stairs. Iselle, who never put a foot wrong, who was the most graceful dancer in all of London, tripped. Iselle screamed. Irma screamed. The viscount made to dash for the bottom of the stairs, but found himself held back by two small fists clutching his coattails. No matter, Farrell had caught the girl. Wingate's stomach settled back where it belonged. He would have gone to the pair, collapsed now on the stairs, but the back of his coat was still in Glory's hands.

Farrell was seated, holding Miss Snodgrass as she trembled. In the fall and subsequent rescue, one of his fobs had become tangled in Iselle's hair. He struggled to release the curl, but managed to pull the whole topknot down around her shoulders. Iselle tried to catch the falling hairpins, and succeeded in dislodging the dandy's elaborate neck cloth. When the baronet reached to save his miraculous creation, somehow the crested button on his coat sleeve snagged on the fabric at Iselle's plunging neckline, with even more plunging results. Iselle screamed again and jumped up, trying to hold the scraps of fabric together, but Farrell's silver-buckled evening pump was firmly atop the net overskirt of her gown, which pulled away, leaving opened seams in the ivory silk.

My God, Wingate thought in horror, the chit is half naked! The death grip on his coat had been relaxed, so he started to shrug out of the tight-fitting garment, to throw it over the now-hysterical female on the stairs. Instead, he felt a decidedly unladylike kick to his shin. "Ouch!" he yelped, and looked down to see a dark blot from Irma's kid slipper smeared across his silk stocking. "Hell and tarnation!"

But she was screaming by now, and so was the sister on the stairs, despite Farrell's feeble attempts at comfort. The deuce, they'd have the whole house party out here in a flash. Wingate clamped his hand over Irma's mouth—and her pearly little teeth chomped down on his flesh. And she winked! The bedlamite actually winked at him as he sucked his finger, before she set up another howl.

The Bannisters, their servants, and their guests were all pouring into the hall by now. Only Inessa's sobs could be heard for a moment while every stricken gaze focused on the couple on the stairs. Then Lady Bannister shrieked before fainting dead away. Lady Rothingham gasped, two of the younger ladies yelled for their vinaigrettes, some of the gentlemen nobly turned their backs, and Lord Bannister turned as red as a baboon's behind.

"She fell, Papa," Irma explained, as three footmen carried Lady Bannister away and levelheaded Inessa snatched up the hall rug, threw it over her sister, and led the still-weeping Iselle back up the stairs.

Evan Farrell stood, tried to straighten his clothes, ran shaking hands through his hair. He staggered down the stairs. "I ... I am terribly sorry, Lord Bannister, and I take complete blame for the unfortunate accident. Clumsy, don't you know. New shoes." He swallowed audibly. "I am"—another swallow—"prepared to do the honorable thing to relieve the lady's embarrassment."

The servants and guests alike exhaled. Dobbs, the butler, started herding them back to their appointed places. He signaled for another round of drinks to be poured in the drawing room, and sent a message to Cook that dinner might be a tad delayed.

Lord Bannister was mopping his brow. "Gentlemanly of you, I'm sure," he complimented Farrell. "No one's fault and all. Still, don't look right." He turned to Wingate, who had stayed on in the hall with Irma. The baron was obviously hoping for another solution, one with a higher title and bigger fortune. The viscount didn't need Irma's pinch to stay mum.

Farrell squared his shoulders. "If you are worried about my reputation, I have sown all my wild oats. I haven't been in debt or haunted the gaming dens in ages. I hadn't thought to wed, but my affairs are in order so I can keep your daughter in prime style, my lord, if that's a concern." He made an attempt at a laugh. "I suppose a wife shall complete my reform, what? Had to marry someday, I suppose."

Lord Bannister nodded. "You'll do. Better than I expected of a popinjay like you, in fact. Not what her mother wanted for the gel, I have to admit, only a baronet, but you'll do. Tell you what, give you a year to get used to the idea of leg-shackles. Bride clothes and all, don't you know."

Irma pulled on her father's sleeve. "Papa, I don't think it should wait so long."

"What's that? Think the coxcomb will lose his nerve?"

"No, I just don't think Iselle will be comfortable until she's wed. You know how the countryside can gossip, and what with the house party still going on and all . . ."

"Miss Irmagard is right, my lord," Farrell said. "I wouldn't wish Miss Snodgrass to be the subject of scandalbroth. With your permission, I shall take her to London, with Lady Rothingham along of course, and obtain a special license. We can be wed and return for the hunt ball to quiet any talk there might be."

"That's a big sacrifice, my boy. I appreciate your doing this for my girl."

Farrell took a deep breath. "It's the right thing to do, my lord."

The baron patted Sir Evan on the back. "Good man. I'll have her meet you in the library in an hour. There's a decanter in there, if you need the courage."

An hour later, after a visit from her father and a lecture from her mother, a trembling, white-faced Iselle dragged herself to the library.

In the adjoining room, the breakfast parlor, Irma stood with her ear to the connecting door. That's where the viscount found her, after changing his disordered apparel and having supper on a tray.

"Your behavior needs explaining, young lady," he began, only to be hushed again. He shrugged and put his own ear to the door.

"Miss Snodgrass," they heard, "your father has given me permission to pay my addresses. Would you do me the great honor—"

Then they heard Iselle's joyous shout: "It worked!

39

It worked! Just like the Worm said it would! Oh, Evan!"

Irma took Lord Wingate's hand and led him out of the room, grinning.

# 5

"It was a conspiracy! The whole thing was a brilliant conspiracy! And here I thought I merely had to avoid being alone with Miss Snodgrass to foil the plan to see us wed. What, did you think I was too fusty to take part in your scheme?"

Irma blushed. "Not fusty at all, my lord. I think your reputation must be a hum. I saw you looking through that keyhole into the library!" They were back in the drawing room, ostensibly listening to Inessa at the pianoforte. Wingate had not taken Lady Bannister's pointed suggestion that he turn the pages for Inessa, claiming to be much too unmusical. The Reverend Mr. Allbright, invited to make up the numbers for dinner, volunteered for the job so Wingate was free to take a seat in the far corner, next to Miss Irmagard. Glory was looking like a cat in the cream pot.

"Well, I had to see the outcome of your plot, since I was dragooned into participating, or not participating as it were. I mean, what with having my clothing mangled, my leg battered, and my fingers nibbled on, I felt I deserved some reward."

Irma giggled, which his lordship felt was almost reward enough. "You were trying so hard to be noble!"

"And you were acting like the most empty-headed skitterwit in creation. I congratulate you, Miss Glory. I only wish Wellington had your help planning strategy for the Peninsular campaign. The war would have been ended much sooner."

Irma studied her gloved hands in her lap. "Thank you for the compliment, and for not ruining Iselle's chance at happiness. And, although I should have said so much sooner, thank you for not crying rope on me for that meeting on the hillside, especially after the awful things I said about you, Lord Wingate."

"My friends call me Winn."

"Oh, but I couldn't—"

"We are friends, though, aren't we?" He didn't wait for an answer. "And as a friend, I demand to be considered a fellow conspirator in the next skirmish."

Irma flashed her dimples. "To save Nessie from your evil clutches?"

He grimaced. "Exactly. Your father called on me while I was changing, to make sure my hopes weren't dashed by losing Iselle and to reacquaint me with Miss Inessa's beauty and goodness."

Pride and just a smidgen of envy colored Irma's tones as she told him, "Nessie *is* good. She is kind and caring, besides being beautiful and talented. She would make any man a fine wife." Irma paused so he could listen to her sister's sweet voice raised in a tender ballad, then she started twisting the strings on her reticule. "You, um, aren't by chance considering her, are you?"

Winn pretended to consider the outrageously forward question, studying the angelic vision at the instrument. "Hm. Perhaps I should."

"You mustn't!" came back promptly, bringing a smile to his lips.

"I thought not. I suppose I had better be seen paying my addresses to another young lady."

"No, that would only raise hopes in some poor

female's heart. You might even be forced to marry the girl."

"What if I pretend to fix my interest with you, then, so your estimable parents won't thrust Miss Inessa at me? Just a pretend flirtation, you understand."

Irma laughed out loud, then bit her lip when several frowning heads turned in their direction. "Whoever would believe a paragon like you would choose a sad romp like me over Inessa?"

Winn could think of any number of gentlemen who would prefer a spirited, loyal, and intelligent dazzler to a milk-and-water beauty. Some men favored diamonds; he for one fancied rubies. He held his peace, watching the sparkle in Glory's eyes as she continued.

"Besides, if you don't drop the handkerchief, Mama means to attach Mr. Frye."

That brought Winn back to the drawing room with a start. He looked around and spotted the man she mentioned, sprawled in a side chair, staring at the girl at the pianoforte like a dog that's missed dinner for two days. "That middle-aged mushroom? For Inessa?"

"He's wealthy, and raises champion racehorses."

" 'Pon rep, you wouldn't let—No, of course you wouldn't. I demand a part in the maneuvers. What's your strategy to be this time, General?" He gestured toward the pianoforte, where young Allbright had joined his baritone voice to Inessa's soprano. "Somehow I doubt another compromising situation will arise."

"No, I have a much better plan." She fumbled with her reticule, whose strings were now in knots. "I merely need a sample of Mr. Frye's handwriting. Well, not his actual handwriting. I was hoping to stay down after the musicale and offer him a few more brandies, then ask him to write out the recipe

43

for a poultice for my mare. That was the best I could think of. But you can do much better, if you really want to help. Do you?" His nod answered her eager question. "You can stay with him till he's truly foxed, then get him to scribble something truly terrible."

"Like what?" Winn took the purse away from her and unwound the strings. "A seditious statement against the government? A blackmail threat?"

Irma took back the reticule, fumbled inside, and pulled out a pointed quill. "It doesn't matter what, as long as he's so disguised he doesn't notice the pen." She triumphantly presented the item to the viscount, who checked around to make sure they were unobserved, smiling to himself at the intrigue, before examining the quill more closely. He raised his eyebrows. "Tiny pinholes?"

"Mama cannot stand a messy hand. She says it denotes a flawed character."

"So the tampered pen and Demon Rum shall strike him from the lists?"

Irma bit her lip. "As far as Mama is concerned. It might be best if you got him to write something Papa wouldn't like, a love poem or such." She patted his hand in reassurance. "You'll know what to do; you can speak six languages."

So the pride of the Foreign Office was supposed to stay up half the night with a slimy cit he hardly knew, get the toadeater castaway enough to blot and bedaub an incriminating letter—and all for an engaging green-eyed, grinning chit who had such confidence in him, he could move a mountain.

He did better than move a mountain. He moved two.

Only the family was in the breakfast parlor the next morning, having seen Iselle and her new fiancé off to an early, private departure.

Irma was dressed in jonquil muslin when she took her place at the table. Before buttering her roll, she took a scrap of paper from her pocket. "Oh, Mama. I found this in the library when I returned a book this morning. You know how you wished for a sample of Mr. Frye's writing, since he responded to your invitation in person, recall? It seems to be a bill of sale to Lord Wingate, if I make it out correctly, so perhaps I should just see it returned. Dobbs mentioned that the two gentlemen were in the library late."

"Making inroads in my best brandy, too," Lord Bannister grumbled. "Bill of sale, you say? Let me see that, missy." He held the paper one way, then the other. "Blasted chicken scratches, if you ask me."

"You are simply too vain to wear your spectacles," his life's companion sniped from the opposite end of the table. "Hand it here."

" 'Bag filled by Sneeze or Crud?' What in tarnation? Blast! It must mean a bay filly by Breeze out of Crusader! By damn, that blighter's gone and sold Wingate the yearling I wanted!"

"Oh, pooh, Isa, what's another horse? Let me see the handwriting."

"What's another horse? You might as well ask what's another arm or leg, Irene! I wanted *this* horse, and that dastard knew it. Hang it, I can't make out the sale price. I offered the blackguard five hundred pounds, and he turned me down."

"Five hundred pounds for a horse?" Lady Bannister shrieked, jumping out of her seat.

"A thousand? Could that be a thousand?" The baron whistled. "Dash sight higher than I wanted to go. And instruction in fencing on Mars? What the blazes?"

Lady Bannister reached her husband's end of the table and snatched the paper out of his hands. "Let me see that, you blockhead. I'm the expert." She took the page over to the window. "Faugh, what a mess. Not even being in one's cups is an excuse for such a mishmash. Yes, one bay filly, um hm, for the sum of one thousand pounds, hm, and . . . and an introduction to Fancine O'Mara."

"Why, that dirty dog! The filly I wanted and the highest flyer in London town!"

"What's a high-flyer, Papa?" Irma asked, earning glares from both parents. Inessa had gone pale; now she started crying into her serviette. "You mean she's a . . . a courtesan?"

"Go to your room, Irma," Lady Bannister ordered. "You are too young for this conversation." Still intent on the blotted sheet, she never noticed that Irma stayed. Wild horses could not have dragged her away.

"Blast, the filly I wanted."

"Fancine O'Mara. Look at all these splotches and blots, a sure sign of a disordered temperament. Those lust-laden loops, the prurient penultimates, the prodigal pressure. And yes, the margins are definitely miserly. Why, the man is a cad!"

"He's never going to be welcome at one of my hunts, I can tell you that."

"And he's never going to be welcome in my house, and you better tell him that, too."

"Me tell him?"

"Well, you didn't think I was going to let an old reprobate like your friend come calling on my sweet Inessa, did you? My pure, unsullied darling? No, I'd rather see her lead apes in hell than be besmirched by one such as he, even if she spends the rest of her days helping the vicar with his charity work."

Just as Inessa wailed that she didn't want to die a spinster, Viscount Wingate walked into the room, dressed in riding clothes.

"Pardon," he said, "but I was up early, and your

butler said I might break my fast here. I can see you are having a family talk, though, so I'll just—"

Irma assured Winn that he was welcome, to help himself to the sideboard and take up a seat. Lady Bannister glared at her, recalling she'd been dismissed. Lord Bannister glared at the viscount, thinking how the bloke had all the blunt in the world, and entrée to all the best bordellos. Inessa whined that she loved babies.

Into the ensuing silence, Winn casually remarked, "I couldn't help overhearing your mention of the vicar. No one has aught to say of him but the highest praises. My uncle the duke has a living open at his seat, a large, wealthy parish up near Rutland. That's close to the Belvoir hunt, I believe. He asked me to keep an eye out for a likely young cleric. It would be a real step up for a good man. I was thinking of offering it to young Allbright, if you wouldn't mind my stealing him away."

"Why not?" Lord Bannister growled. "You've got everything else."

"We'll all miss him," Irma chimed in over her father's rudeness, "especially Nessie." Inessa whimpered about a house of her own, a little cottage would do. Irma hurried on as if her sister had not spoken, or sniveled. "But we'd never put a damper on his career, would we, Papa? Kelvin Allbright's such a fine, upstanding man, isn't he, Mama?"

Lady Bannister nodded, wondering how she would keep possession of the bill of sale for her files, marked *D* for depravity. "He comes from a good family, writes a neat hand. High-minded horizontals." She drifted out of the room with the vague excuse of preparations for the ball.

"That's very kind of you not to stand in the fellow's way," Lord Wingate said after accepting a cup of coffee and a wink from Irma. "Who knows how high a churchman can rise, with the right connections. Of course, he'd need the perfect helpmate. Someone who can serve the needy and entertain the bishop. Someone like your charming Miss Inessa, for instance, who is much too good for a frippery fellow like me."

"Belvoir, eh?"

"Oh, Papa, please."

"Tea with the bishop, what? That would please your mama; you could get his autograph."

"My Kelvin might even *be* the bishop someday, Papa."

"Your Kelvin, is it? Well, Irene said she wanted to see you all settled by the hunt ball. Send him to me, Nessie, we'll talk."

# 6

"You were magnificent, Lord Wingate!"

"Winn."

"That, too! Why, the horse, the high-flyer. I swear you couldn't have done better!"

"So we statesmen are not such stodgy, paltry fellows after all, eh, Glory?"

"I should say not. It's a wonder we lost the colonies. I daresay you must have poured buckets of brandy down Mr. Frye's throat to get that paper."

"No, the makebait was barely disguised. He merely drives a hard bargain. I must have been the one who was cupshot, paying a thousand pounds for a filly! Never in my life have I been so outrageously extravagant. And my poor head!"

"Oh dear, and it was all my fault!" Irma cried, clutching at his arm.

"Don't shout, sweetheart!" he moaned, but he squeezed her hand on his arm, and did not let Irma draw it back to her side.

They were walking in the woods, unsupervised since Lady Bannister was closeted in her sitting room with Vicar Allbright's latest sermon. Yes, the *i*'s were dotted with a dollop of devout dedication, but, ah, the *a*'s were awash with ambition. Poor Kelvin had ridden over to ask an opinion, and he was stumbling home with a new bride, a new position, and no Sunday sermon.

Lord Wingate, despite his throbbing head, was

meanwhile basking in the light of another crisp day, and Irma's grateful admiration. The companionable silence was broken only by the sound of their booted feet kicking up leaves, and the occasional bark of Bridey, the old hound bitch, who waddled along behind them. Winn was thinking what a relief it was not to have to make idle chitchat, and Irma was struck dumb, for once, at his endearment, and the fact that Viscount Wingate had actually sought out her company. She pretended to study the treetops so she wouldn't be caught staring at him in his fawn breeches and high-topped Hessians.

After the fresh air had cleared his head somewhat, Lord Wingate commented, "Well, now there is only one sister to be saved from sacrifice on the altar of marriage."

"You need not concern yourself, my lord."

He stopped walking. "I thought we were friends. Of course I am concerned."

A squirrel was suddenly found fascinating as Irma considered whether Winn was more concerned with her possible forced marriage—or his own. "Fustian, they'll never push me in your direction. Not even Mama is so buffleheaded."

"What, does she think I am too old for you?"

"What does old have to do with Mama's plans? Mr. Frye was ages older than Inessa. Besides, you're not too old. I am too young. Too unschooled and unpolished for a top-of-the-trees gentleman like you. Mama will be the first to tell you."

So she didn't think he was too old? The viscount's waistcoat buttons nearly popped, his chest swelled so. He started walking again, Glory's hand still in his. "But she must have noticed how we've become friends. Won't she hope for more?"

Irma sighed. "Not Mama. She'll realize that with Iselle gone and Inessa promised, we are thin of company. She'll thank you for being amused by her harum-scarum adolescent."

Winn was amazed again at Glory's lack of vanity. Hadn't anyone ever told her she was beautiful? And would she believe him if he said it? "In truth I am amused with your company, entertained by your charm and wit, and knocked cock-a-hoop by one of your smiles."

Which, of course, restored that glorious grin, dimples and all. "Flummery, sir, but I accept the compliments all the same. Nevertheless, Mama has made her choice for me. Algernon Thurkle. Squire's son." She took her hand back.

"What? That cawker? I could cut him out with my eyes closed. Shower you with flattery, strew flowers in your path, write sonnets to your dimples."

Irma laughed at the absurdity of the nonpareil at her side making such a cake of himself over a hobbledehoy female. "And leave me the bobbing-block of the neighborhood when you leave, with Squire Thurkle and Papa still dickering over how many acres make a proper dowry. No thank you."

"But I want to help. Or is there someone you prefer waiting in the wings?"

"No, but I can discourage Algie's suit in a snap. He's hunt-mad, just like most of the gentlemen in the neighborhood, and not half inclined to wed yet anyway. I only have to disrupt his sport again to make sure he cries off."

"Again?"

"You cannot think I approve of what they do to the poor fox?" Earnest green eyes looked beseechingly into his brown ones, and Viscount Wingate swore off fox hunting on the instant.

"Ah, what then? I mean, once you dispose of the unlamented Algernon, is there some totally ineligible beau you mean to spring on Lady Bannister when she is desperate? A highwayman, perhaps, or a hog butcher? I know, a lawyer."

"Silly, I don't have any beaux."

"Then you'll be coming to London to devastate the ranks of bachelors?" he asked hopefully. Not that he hoped she'd catch the eye of every Buck and Blood on the lookout for an incomparable, but that she'd get a chance to spread her wings out of her sisters' shadows. She should have the chance to know her mind, make her own choice, he thought. He also thought that was deuced noble of him.

Irma hadn't really considered what would happen after she rid herself of the Thurkle toad . . . or after his lordship left. "Mama swears she'll never go to London again, and positively not with me in tow. I suppose she'll ship me off to Nessie or Ellie, once they are settled, to be the doting aunt." She shrugged. "No matter. I do not intend to marry."

Winn chuckled in a superior manner. "You are young, Glory. You'll change your mind when you meet the man of your dreams."

There was hardly a chance of that happening, she thought despondently, not twice.

Baron Bannister's big day had arrived. He was strutting about the courtyard like a cockerel in his scarlet hunt jacket, greeting friends and neighbors, getting in the way of the grooms bringing the horses and the servants handing around stirrup cups. The day was overcast and blustery, but not too inhospitable for the hunt. Never that. Finally everyone was mounted, the horn was ready to be blown. Bannister ordered that the keeper be signaled to release the hounds.

Nothing. The horses grew restive and unruly. The baron sent another servant around to the kennels. Nothing. "Thunderation!" he bellowed, and kicked his horse onto the track leading behind the stables. Many of the assembled riders followed.

At the kennels, only two excited young pups bounded toward the horses, getting underfoot and causing at least one high-strung gelding to unseat its rider. Fat old Bridey heaved herself up and plodded out to greet the party.

"What the hell?" Bannister muttered as he dismounted by a ring of kennel men, grooms and two whippers-in who were nudging, coaxing, cajoling the rest of the hounds to get to their feet. His dogs, his prize black and gold hunting pack, were asleep! If not asleep, they were barely awake, tongues lolling out of the sides of their mouths, tails barely managing a thump or two. And they all had bloated bellies. Some rascal, everyone agreed, some spoilsport, fox-loving, bleeding-heart rascal had feasted the pack, with drugged meat. Most of the neighbors knew exactly which rascal it had to be, the same one who put pepper on the trails and unstopped the earths. They rode off, laughing, at Squire Thurkle's invitation to get up a good ride at his place. He could guarantee the dogs were eager for a run, Squire crowed, for he'd never let that minx of Bannister's next or nigh his hounds, his horses, or his sons.

Lord Bannister wasn't laughing. Red-faced, he made his way to the stables, followed by a few disappointed huntsmen and some smirking grooms who came to gather the mounts from the houseguests who decided not to follow the hunt so far a distance on such an inclement day. Lord Wingate dismounted and led Toledo after the others.

"Irmagard Snodgrass!" he could hear Lord Bannister bellow. "Get out here now."

Irma stepped from her mare's stall, straw on her skirt, her curls tumbled down her back, but her chin thrust upward as she faced her father across the stable aisle. "I am right here, Papa, you needn't shout."

Bannister was so angry, words stuck in his throat. "Did . . . did you . . . ?" He slapped his riding crop against his booted leg in frustration.

Irma's arms were crossed defiantly across her chest. "Did I feed the hounds and lace their meat with laudanum? You know I did. You needn't worry about the dogs; I was very careful with the dosages. I couldn't be sure with the puppies or old Bridey, so I just fed them, with no drugs."

"How in God's name could you do such a thing, miss?" he thundered. "Just tell me how?"

"How not?" she answered. "Fox hunting is barbaric, and so is this practice of handing your daughters over willy-nilly to the first available man. Or boy, like Algernon Thurkle. I got rid of him, didn't I?"

"Oh, that you did, missy. He'll never be back, nor half my friends and neighbors! And willy-nilly is it? I haven't seemed to hand my daughters over to anyone I want. First a rake, then a cleric. That's not who *I* chose for sons-in-law. And I begin to see your hand in all of this, you misbegotten brat. Why, if your mother wasn't such a coldhearted woman, I'd swear she played me false, to beget such an unnatural child!"

Irma noticed the grooms and others moving around the stable, not nearly out of hearing. "Papa," she began.

"Don't you try to turn me up sweet now, you impossible baggage. Hand you over to any man I want? Why, I'll hand you over to the first man who asks, with good riddance to you and good luck to him!"

"You cannot mean that, Papa. You are just angry at missing your hunt. Look, it's coming on to rain anyway."

Maybe Thurkle's dogs would lose the scent in the wet. That didn't calm the baron's fury a jot. Now they'd all sit around the fire over at the manor house, joking about Bannister's drugged dogs and devil-ridden daughter. A laughing-stock, that's what she'd made him. "Too late, missy, too late. I'll offer your hand to the first man who asks you to dance at your mother's ball. Aye, and I'll throw in that extra parcel of land I was going to add to Inessa's dowry, to sweeten the pot. She won't need it, and the poor bastard who gets you will. The first unmarried man, do you hear, missy? And you'll be there, Irmagard, or I'll drag you by your hair. And you'll dance, by Jupiter, for you sure as hell won't be sitting down."

"Papa, you wouldn't!"

He would.

The second time Lord Bannister's riding crop whistled through the air Winn knocked over a bucket in 'Ledo's stall, then cursed. Loudly. He kicked the wooden bucket noisily, just for insurance. The baron stormed past him, shouting at the grooms. The viscount waited for the stable hands to busy themselves with their chores, then he sought out the far, unused stall where a slim figure stood shaking.

He walked in and called "Glory?" She turned away, but he gathered her into his arms anyway, and held her as she sobbed against his chest. He tried to smooth back the damp tendrils of her hair, saying "Hush, Glory, hush, sweetheart." She kept crying. When he felt the moisture seep through his shirtfront to his skin, he cursed and gave her a shake. "Blast, why did you have to stand here and admit the whole thing? I swear you've got more bottom than brains!"

"And a sore bottom to prove it," she mumbled against his lapels before raising a tear-streaked face. "But I had to make sure Algie and his father got a disgust of me."

Winn took out his handkerchief and wiped at the dampness. "You succeeded then, in aces. You'd think they were made to miss their suppers for a month instead of one day's sport. You silly chit, though, why couldn't you just have told that chaw-bacon no? Or let me warn him off for you?"

"You would have done that for me?"

"Of course. We're friends."

She took his handkerchief and blew her nose, a loud, unladylike honk that made him smile. "Thank you," she said when she was finished. "I've never had such a friend." She looked away, shaking out her skirts. "I suppose I've made a rare mull of it now, haven't I? Every gull-groper and basket-scrambler will be scurrying to dance with Lord Bannister's hey-go-mad heiress." She waved her hand around the stable. "I'm sure the servants and guests will have spread the word to every fortune hunter for miles around that Papa will come down heavy for anyone taking me off his hands."

"Algie?"

"No, he wouldn't take me now if Papa threw in the home woods, three tenant farms, and his best sow. Algie does love his dogs. Oh, I'll die of morti-fication!"

"Perhaps your father will change his mind. He wasn't thinking clearly at the time," Winn understated.

"No, Mama won't let him. She'll have spasms for sure after this ruckus, afraid she'll have me on her hands forever. She'll be too embarrassed to take me about, and Ellie is going on her honeymoon, and Nessie's going to visit Kelvin's parents, so she can-not even ship me off to either of them!" Irma started weeping again.

Winn opened his arms and she stepped into his embrace, dampening the other side of his shirt-front. He held her close anyway, stroking her back. "Hush, little one, it will be all right. Trust me."

# 7

Lord and Lady Bannister opened the ball with the first dance, as was customary. As was also customary with the couple, they spent as little time as possible in each other's company. After a few bars of music, the baron signaled the hired orchestra to stop playing. He held up his hand and announced his daughter Inessa's betrothal to their own Kelvin Allbright, after which Nessie and her vicar took the floor. While the happy couple danced by themselves, servants circulated with glasses of champagne. Irma snared one off a passing tray, downed it, and reached for another. Lady Bannister slapped her hand away and dragged her out from behind the potted fern to stand with the family for the toasts.

Then they were mobbed with well-wishers, Lady Bannister's cronies, Nessie's friends, neighborhood churchgoers. Irma managed to toss down another glass of champagne during the congratulations, which lasted through two more sets. Nessie was swept off by one of her disappointed suitors, and Lord Bannister took Kelvin off to meet some of the London guests. Irma was left standing at her mother's side, in full view of the entire ballroom.

Mama was smiling and nodding to the guests, accepting compliments on the ball and on Inessa's good fortune. Irma was smiling—Mama pinched the flesh between her long white glove and her puffed white lutestring sleeve every time she didn't—and wishing she had another glass of champagne. Actually, she wished she had a glass of hemlock.

They all knew, of course. She could tell by the way the young women tittered and the older women avoided meeting her eyes. The men were worse, inspecting her as if she were on the block at Tattersall's. She could almost see them tabulating her dowry versus the trouble she was bound to cause. To the other side of the ballroom, Master Thurkle was waving his hands in her direction, most likely telling his chums about one hunt-hampering hobble after another. Bless you, Algie, she thought for the first time in her life, for telling them what an uncomfortable, prickly wife she'd make.

There were other knots of men standing around between dances, glancing at her and laughing with their friends. They were likely laying wagers on who'd be fool enough to ask her to stand up, or who needed her father's blunt that badly. That loose screw with the dingy neck cloth and the frayed sleeves couldn't be too particular. Nor could some of the fops headed for the library where card tables had been set up. Lose a fortune there, gain one back on the dance floor, what? Sooner or later one of the dirty dishes would approach her, even if it took a few more glasses of champagne for him to get up the nerve.

Maybe she could manage to tear a flounce. That would postpone her doom for a dance or two. Unfortunately, the white lutestring was in the simple Greek style, with nary a ruffle, flounce, or demi-train to get caught under her foot, no matter how hard she tried.

"Stop squirming, Irmagard. I don't mind them assuming your attics are to let; I shan't permit them to think you have body lice."

Then again, one more glass of champagne might

do the trick. Her head already felt thick and muzzy. Not even Mama could expect her to stay in the ballroom when she might cast up her accounts on the hapless soul who'd dragged his courage to the sticking point. Irma giggled at the thought.

"Well, I am glad to see you are no longer in the doldrums over this contretemps," a voice spoke into her ear while Lady Bannister greeted another well-wisher.

Irma turned and smiled. She couldn't help herself, Lord Wingate looked so superior. His coat was midnight blue trimmed with silver that made the silver in his hair look even more distinguished, and he had a diamond in his starched cravat. "Good evening, my lord. Actually, I think the champagne has more to do with restoring my humor than anything. Would you be so kind as to procure me another glass?"

Winn looked closer at the young woman and caught the hectic flush on her cheeks, the slight waver in her stance. Once again he cursed her parents. "Devil a bit, I think you've had enough already. What you need, my girl, is a walk in the fresh air. What do you think your father will do if I ask you for a stroll?"

"I think he'll have an apoplexy. Shall we go?" Irma tugged on her mother's sleeve and loudly whispered, "Lord Wingate has invited me for a *walk* on the balcony. If I am not back shortly, tell Papa I fell off."

Lady Bannister scowled, but she couldn't very well refuse the highest ranking gentleman at her ball. "You'll return at the end of this dance, Irmagard, or I shall come drag you back myself, broken legs and all."

The viscount fixed the shawl more securely on Irma's shoulders when they reached the balcony. He led her away from the other couples taking the cool night air and advantage of the dark corners. "I'm sorry you'll have to go back."

Irma leaned on the railing and stared up at the stars, trying to see them through the blur of tears. "Oh, it's not your fault. And thank you for this reprieve at least. You truly are the most chivalrous of gentlemen. I wish . . ."

"What do you wish, Glory?"

She wished with all her heart she was older, prettier, more refined—and not about to be affianced to some unknown, unloved, and unlikely shabster. What she said was "I wish this dance will never end."

Winn chuckled. "Usually it's some young mooncalf who utters that bit of fustian. Or at least a female who's been waltzed senseless. In your case, it's not quite the compliment a gentleman expects."

"Oh, do stop teasing. You of all people know how hopeless my situation is."

"I told you not to worry, didn't I?" He took her arm for the walk back toward the entrance of the ballroom.

"That's all very well and good, but no one is about to condemn *you* to a life sentence."

"The verdict isn't in yet, Glory," he whispered when they reached Lady Bannister's side. Then the viscount raised Irma's hand to his lips and kissed her fingertips. She knew what he was doing, trying to frighten other suitors off by making them think he had an interest in her. Such a ploy wouldn't fadge with Papa. He wanted an offer, not a bit of gallantry. Winn was just being chivalrous again. Still, her fingers tingled.

Happily, a commotion at the door drew everyone's eye before the music started for the next interval. Iselle and her new husband blew into the room amid laughter and exclamations and more congratulations. There was more champagne and more toasting, and no one paid any attention whatsoever to Irma, hidden at the edge of the family group. A few of her mother's friends did make snide references to *two* such joyous events, with cutting looks in the third daughter's direction, but the bachelors were busy chiding the latest benedict in their midst, or swigging more of the baron's wine.

When the orchestra struck up a quadrille, Evan Farrell escorted his new bride to the floor, and Irma's heart sank. Now she was exposed to the scrutiny of the assembly all over again. The young bucks were getting louder in their jests, bolder in their assessing looks, even with the viscount standing nearby. Papa's face was getting redder.

Then Kelvin, dear, sweet, affianced Kelvin Allbright asked her to stand up with him. She accepted with joy, then proceeded to step on Kelvin's toes, trip up the other couples, and purposely mangle the complicated figures of the dance. 'Twould take a brave man to dance with her after that exhibition, she figured, brave as well as pockets to let.

Her new brother-in-law asked her for the country-dance next forming, bless his dandified heart. Farrell did threaten to leave her to her fate if she scuffed his new satin evening pumps, but he smiled and offered to try talking sense into her father. Irma told him to save his breath, for Lord Bannister was barrelling around the ballroom, haranguing the knots of men on the sidelines. He was most likely raising her dowry even as she danced. She thanked Sir Evan as prettily as she could when he returned her to Lady Bannister, but her heart was sinking as low as her slippers. Not even Farrell's whispered promise to bribe his married friends into dancing with her could bring a smile to her lips.

The boulanger was next, then the Roger de Coverly. When no one asked her, Irma began to think the condemned man might even get his last supper.

Then a waltz was begun. Irma had never waltzed with anyone but her sisters, and now she never would, unless Papa'd finally found someone down at the heels and dicked in the nob. She kept her eyes on the floor so no one could see her struggle to keep from crying.

Then a pair of black satin evening pumps was in her view, and white stockings encasing well-muscled legs. "May I have the pleasure of this dance, Miss Glory?"

"No!" she snapped, before Lady Bannister pinched her arm. She rubbed the sore spot and hissed at him anyway: "Do go away, my lord. You know what Papa said."

"Yes."

"Well, you cannot want to marry me."

"Yes."

Winn took her hand and led her to the dance floor before Irma could interpret his response. Every eye in the room was on them, of course, and Papa's mouth was hanging open. Irma stood at rigid attention in front of the viscount. "My lord, Winn, please listen to me. I realize you are just being noble again, but Papa won't understand. He cannot force a gentleman like you to make me an offer, but he can subject you to a terribly embarrassing conversation for all of us. Please, perhaps if we just promenade around the room . . ."

In answer Winn took her in his arms and swirled her around the floor, keeping her spinning until she was laughing and out of breath. Dancing with her sisters was never like this!

"He'll offer you the Grange," she warned.

"It won't be enough. I have ten times more property than any man needs."

"He'll offer you his foxhounds, that's how desperate he is."

"I've given up hunting."

"Then he'll say you were trifling with me. He'll blacken your reputation."

"What? Brig the Prig? My name can stand a little scandal, I've been so good all these years. A touch of notoriety only adds to a fellow's consequence, anyway, don't you know? Look at Farrell. The man's an out-and-outer, yet he won himself a treasure in Iselle. Did you notice she is even more beautiful with a wedding ring?"

Irma did not want to talk about Iselle's beauty. "Papa will call you out."

He laughed out loud. "That's unlikely. I'm known to be a crack shot, and I doubt your father's been next or nigh a sword these ages."

"Then I suppose you'll be safe from his machinations." She sighed, almost regretfully.

"Safe?" He laughed again, brown eyes dancing with golden flecks as he twirled her around. "If I wanted to be safe, Miss Irmagard Snodgrass, I would have fled when I saw your watercolor painting, all vibrant and chaotic and full of life. I would have turned tail and run back to the intrigues of Vienna rather than take part in your skipbrain schemes."

Irma was about to protest that her tactics were not lackwit, they worked, for the most part, when she found herself back on the balcony in the chill air. Somehow she wasn't cold, for his arms were around her and he was whispering in her ear: "And if I wanted to be safe, Glory, I'd never kiss you like this, knowing I'll never be free of you again."

A few minutes—or a lifetime—later, he tipped her face up to stare into her eyes. "Say you care for me, just a little, Glory, and let me try to make you as happy as I know how. Otherwise, it's a life sentence for me, too, a whole eternity with an empty place in my heart."

Confounded by the dance, the kiss, the warm

breath on her cheek, she could only think to ask, "You mean, you really wanted to dance with me? You weren't just being kind and good because you felt sorry for me?"

"No, you little goose. I waited to make sure there was no young swain you smiled at to encourage. Of course, I might have had to call him out, but I waited to make sure." His hands were on the side of her face, stroking her cheeks with his thumbs. "And no, I didn't want to dance with you. I wanted to hold you in my arms again. I wanted—I want— to make love to you. I want to marry you. I love you, Glory. *J't'aime, te amo, ich du lieber . . .*"

"*You* love *me*?" She still couldn't believe it.

"With all my heart. I know it's been a short time, Glory, but do you think you can come to love me a little?"

"No, for I already love you so much I thought I would burst with it." This required another long kiss filled with promise, then a question. "Winn, do you believe in love at first sight?"

"How can I not? And I believe it will be love at the first sight of you each and every day of our lives. Now come, let us go make your father the second happiest of men." And he waltzed her back through the balcony doors to the dance floor. "What do you think would happen if I were to kiss you right here?" he murmured during one of the turns.

"I think Mama would swoon and Papa would halt the music to announce our betrothal. Please do."

He laughed and did, even though the music had been finished for ages.

Lord Bannister hosted the fall hunt, and Lady Bannister held the annual autumn ball. Both were memorable occasions in the neighborhood society, but never more than that year.

# "SWEET CHARLATAN"

by
Patricia Veryan

# 1

## Summer, 1812

"To the contrary, I have, I think, been more than patient." Sir Haughton Bridge took a pinch of snuff, sneezed, and flapped a snowy handkerchief at his peerlessly cut coat. A thin gentleman with a narrow secretive face, Sir Haughton was as small of soul as of stature. He was aware of the latter deficiency, and to compensate for it, had taken up a stance before the empty hearth of the charming withdrawing room, and thus was able to look down upon the two ladies condescendingly.

They sat side by side on the sofa that was as politely elegant as the rest of the furnishings in the politely elegant house in this politely elegant London square. Mrs. Hester Bridge, the elder of the two, was clad in dark grey, the sombre gown adding to the impression of crushed fragility that cloaked her. Her sad brown eyes were fixed upon her brother-in-law's face with silent but desperate appeal, and her thin hands were tightly gripped as she waited for him to continue. Miss Olivia Bridge watched her uncle in silence, but there was an irked flush on the delicate features that bore mute testimony to the beauty her mama had once been.

"It is a year since Bartholomew was killed," Sir Haughton resumed. "I could have required you to vacate directly I acceded to the title. Instead, I have allowed you to stay on here."

"Because you chanced to be in South America," put in Olivia daringly. "And it is more than a year since my brother fell. The Battle of Albuera was in May of last year, else I would not already have put off my blacks."

Bored, her uncle waved his snuffbox and said that was neither here nor there. "Though I am glad to see you have done so, Olivia. With your brown hair, you will not have looked well in black. Now that shade of peach," he lifted a quizzing glass to scan her dainty figure critically, "becomes you fairly well. I wonder, in fact, that you have reached nineteen years of age without your mama having been able to fire you off. I'd thought it pretty well settled you were to become Lady Quenington."

Mrs. Bridge cast a distressed glance at her eldest daughter and uttered a faint protest.

Olivia's voice was only slightly unsteady when she responded. "You are indeed out of touch, Uncle. Phillip was killed at Ciudad Rodrigo." She forestalled his anticipated remark by adding, "And if you mean to bring in Samuel Tilstone—"

"I am quite aware that young Tilstone fell at Badajoz. One might think you could have chose a civilian admirer after such a string of disasters."

For a painful moment Olivia's voice was suspended. She could picture so clearly her dashing brother and his two equally dashing friends. They had all grown up together, the boys admitting her to their games reluctantly when they were children, and Phillip and Sam vying for her hand in cheerful competition almost from the day she had left the schoolroom.

Mrs. Bridge caught a glimpse of anguish in her daughter's hazel eyes, and her heart swelled with rage. She said with rare ferocity, "You know that

Olivia was in blacks for nigh two years, Sir Haughton, and quite out of society. My dear husband died so suddenly, and then Bartholomew was killed—"

"Well, he'd not have been had he sold out at once," snapped Sir Haughton, irritated by this unseemly show of defiance. "Bartholomew was the head of his house and had no business buying a pair of colours in the first place."

Quick to defend her beloved brother, Olivia pointed out that Bartholomew had not been the head of his house when he joined up. "Papa's illness was very sudden and unexpected. And how could Bart sell out when he was in the thick of the fighting?" Her darkly lashed eyes flashing with resentment, she said, "Lord Wellington has need of all his officers, but Bart meant to apply for leave as soon as things mended a little."

"Instead of which he left my poor sister-in-law to fend for herself," said Sir Haughton, bristling. "Nor have you served her any better, for had you bestirred yourself to make a good match, you would have a husband to provide for your mama and your sisters."

Stung by this unjust criticism, Olivia's temper got the best of her. "I am indeed sorry," she said, "not to have found a gentleman to remove such a frightful burden from your shoulders, Uncle."

Sir Haughton's eyes narrowed. He had never cared for his brother's family. Especially, he had disliked young Bartholomew with his happy-go-lucky outlook on life and his revoltingly splendid physique. Well, much good his looks and his pretty hussar's uniform had done him. His cousins would soon be installed in this house he had taken for granted, and the uncle he had never treated with proper deference now had the title *and* the fortune! That gratifying knowledge alleviated Sir Haughton's anger, so that he did not shout as he had started to do, instead saying acidly, "It is to be regretted, Hester, that you have not instilled in your daughter a decent respect for her elders. It is clear to see why she was unable to win an acceptable offer, for surely, there is nothing more displeasing to a gentleman than a hurly-burly female who has not learned when to keep her tongue between her teeth. I am not here to scold you, however, but to tell you of your good fortune. I have decided to allow you to remove to my country house in Cambridgeshire!"

His grand gesture was wasted on Olivia. Horrified, she burst out, "What? That dreadful old ruin in the fens? You cannot mean it!"

Mrs. Bridge was no less horrified. "Oh, *no*, Haughton!" she wailed, a hand to her paling cheek. "I *could* not! It is so remote, and I cannot endure the damp! *Surely*, there must be somewhere else?"

"If that is not the outside of enough!" Sir Haughton's voice rose shrilly. "I am not obliged, I remind you, to provide for you at all!"

"I fancy the *ton* would be interested in that remark," muttered Olivia rebelliously.

He threw her a baleful glare. The wretched chit was in the right of it, however, for if word got out that he was refusing to meet his obligations, there would be the deuce to pay. "I could have put you into rooms somewhere, I remind you," he snapped. "But my nature is generous and despite my expenses, I decided you would be better served with a house of your own."

Distraught, Olivia cried, "But it is *not* a house! No, Mama! I will not be silent! You know very well that old ruin is too dilapidated to house *pigeons*! The paint is peeling; the windows are more board than glass; I doubt the chimneys have drawn this hundred years and—"

With a crashing stamp of his glossy boot, her uncle shouted, "One more word out of *you*, my girl, and I shall withdraw my generous offer! 'Pon my *soul* but you have my sympathy, Hester, to be saddled with such a virago!" Breathing hard, he fixed his niece with such a murderous glare that she was really frightened and said no more.

"Now," he went on, pointedly turning his back on Olivia, "I will tell you, Hester, that I have sent a man up to Cambridgeshire to be sure all is in—er, order. I trust you will be properly grateful when you see the house. Now, I must be off. I wish to be installed here by Christmas, so you will please be prepared to vacate by the first of November. I bid you good day, ma'am. It is not necessary that you show me out."

A muffled sob escaped Mrs. Bridge.

Torn between loathing and desperation, Olivia followed her uncle into the hall. Closing the door behind her, she held out her hand appealingly.

"Wait, sir! Please! I apologize for having been rude, but you know my mother's constitution is frail. I cannot think you would send her to a climate that can only undermine her health. Uncle, I *beg* of you, do—"

He had become scarlet, and now said explosively, "By God, but I can scarce credit what I am hearing! Out of the goodness of my heart, I have taken on the needless expense of having a perfectly sound house prettied so as to please my indigent relations! A fine house in the country, where Lucille and Imogene can grow up with space to breathe! And instead of a humble word of thanks, my generosity is fairly thrown back in my teeth by a chit of a girl with not the manners of a Westminster slum urchin! What your dear aunt will say when I tell her of your behavior, I quite dread to think!"

He turned on his heel, snatched his beaver hat

from the hovering parlormaid, and stalked out of the door the footman held open for him.

Looking after his jerkingly ungainly stride and the thin figure that not the finest tailoring could improve, Olivia hissed under her breath, "Your horrid wife might remind you, Sir Haughty, that my sister's name is *Isabel*. Not Imogene!"

She closed her eyes then, despair possessing her. That *awful* house! It would kill Mama!

She ran back into the withdrawing room, entering so precipitately that she caught her frail parent wiping away tears.

"Dearest Mama," she cried, hurrying to gather her mother into her arms. "Do not! Oh, do not! We'll come about!"

"There is nothing we can do, my love!" gulped poor Mrs. Bridge, clinging to her. "Your uncle has the l-law on his side. He is—is the head of his house. We have no choice." She tried to smile. "How silly I am being. At least, we will have a roof over our heads, and—and—" Her voice shredded and the brave attempt faded away. "Oh, Livvy!" she said brokenly. "I do so *loathe* that lonely old ruin!"

Olivia hugged her. "I know, dearest. But you will never have to live there. I'll find a way. Somehow . . ."

"How . . . my love? *How*?"

Olivia stood and began to wander about, racking her brains for an answer. Absently, she tidied the pile of books that Mama was always "going to read next" and extricated part of a newspaper that had been trapped among them. She stared at it blindly, then recoiled as she saw that it was folded to the casualty lists from the Battle of Badajoz. It must have been hidden among the books since April, then. Sam Tilstone's name seemed to leap out at her. Dear Sam. This wicked war had taken everything from them. Her darling brother, the boys who had loved her, and from whom she would have chosen her mate, even this house and the fortune that Papa had not thought to dispose among them legally, being so young and hearty a man. She glanced down the sad list. So many names ... so many fine young men who would never come home to marry and have homes and families ... How wicked a waste.

She frowned suddenly, as the germ of an idea was born.

Uncle Haughton had said they had until the first of November. Four months. Not much time, but perhaps it would serve ...

Mrs. Bridge sighed. "If only there were someone ... someone besides your uncle, to help us."

"Perhaps," said Olivia thoughtfully, "there is."

# 2

All too aware of her abigail's disapproval, Olivia avoided Sarah's eyes and looked fixedly out of the carriage window. The drive path wound through an extensive park, and woodland spread like a dark robe over surrounding hills, but Maiden's Court was neither as large nor as imposing as Pam had described it. Of course, she *was* somewhat given to exaggeration. But Pamela Hatfield had been Olivia's closest friend and confidante since nursery days, and had grown from a roly-poly, giggling child into a plump and much admired young damsel with a sympathetic nature and an incredibly retentive memory for gossip. She had been of invaluable aid in Olivia's search and, although initially dismayed by what she had declared to be "Prodigiously shocking and not to be thought of" had soon been eagerly contributing what she could to this daring venture. It had been Pamela who had sent the letter to Gloucestershire, and Pamela who had persuaded Mrs. Bridge to allow Olivia to visit her "wealthy friend from school days." "Only think, ma'am," Pam had urged, "Sylvia Whitland married Lord Medhurst when she was but seventeen. She is widowed now, and so very well connected. Who knows what might come of even a short stay?"

Who knew indeed, thought Olivia uneasily. This scheme was beyond doubting both wicked and immoral. But rack her brains how she might, she'd

74

been unable to think of anything else that might be accomplished in so short a time. The memory of her mother's white stricken face stiffened her resolve. Dear Mama was still not recovered from the shock and grief of losing her husband and her son within a year of each other, and had, besides, never done well in damp weather. Her last illness had been terrifying, and the doctor had stressed that she must be pampered during the winter months. Uncle Haughton's lonely old ruin, with the chill wind whipping from the North Sea to drive rain-laden gusts against rotting walls, and whistle through every crack around warped doors and casements, would be the very antithesis of pampering. It would instead be a veritable death sentence!

Olivia set her dimpled chin resolutely. She might be committing a wicked sin, and heaven forfend she should bring grief to anyone else, but the well-being of Mama and her sisters must now be her first concern. If this plan failed, and she was called to account, she would have to face the consequences. The prospect was so terrifying that she began to tremble, and had to tell herself firmly that she must do whatever was—

"Here you are, then."

Olivia started and glanced at her handmaiden's stern face. Sarah Tolling, tall and gaunt, her rigid moral standards currently at war with her devotion to her young mistress, nodded to the open carriage door and the steps a footman was lowering.

They had arrived! Taking a deep breath, Olivia accepted the footman's hand and alighted.

The afternoon air smelled of freshly scythed grass and blossoms, and the June sunshine was warm. But Olivia noticed neither sunshine nor fragrance, and was so cold she had to restrain herself from shivering.

The butler, short, neat, and dignified, was waiting on the steps of the three-storey house. Olivia wondered inconsequently why Maiden's Court was not constructed of Bath's famous golden stone. One did not expect a gentleman's country house to be built of red brick in such variation from a traditional Gothic design. Stupid! she thought impatiently. What does it matter?

The butler was appraising her with a steady stare. Perhaps she only imagined it to be condemning. Certainly, he glanced to the carriage in faint surprise.

"Mrs.—ah, Bridge?"

"I am Miss Bridge. My mama is ill and could not come."

His eyebrows twitched upward.

Sarah stamped up the steps and glared at him militantly, and he bowed and ushered them inside.

Olivia had a brief impression of a wide graceful hall, wainscoted walls, and luxurious red and white furnishings. Then came the swish of draperies and a stout lady, on the light side of fifty, hurried to them. Her black gown and cap proclaimed her loss, and her round comely face was pale and bore the marks of grief. She stretched out a hand as Olivia curtsied, and said in a high-pitched voice, "I heard what you said to Curtis, Miss Bridge. I am Mrs. Whitland. What a pity your mama is unwell. Come, my dear. Your woman can be unpacking your bags while you take tea with me."

Obedient to the butler's nod, a footman conducted Sarah up the stairs. The butler walked ahead of the ladies to throw open a door revealing a room that seemed all blue and gold and sunlight.

"Our morning room," said Mrs. Whitland, leading the way to a blue velvet sofa. "Do sit beside me. Are you very tired? I suppose I should keep the curtains drawn, but Alexis—" She paused, and blinked, then went on resolutely, "Alexis would not have wished an elaborate display of grief, for that was not his way. But you will know that, perhaps? I do trust your mama is not seriously indisposed. It was most kind of her to write me. It means so much to meet someone who—who knew him . . . before . . ." The flood of words trailed off. Suddenly, the deep blue eyes looked bewildered and anguished.

Repressing a pang of guilt, Olivia said, "My mother is not very strong, ma'am, and has become much more frail since my dear brother's death. When she learned that Captain Whitland had fallen, she thought— Well, since we had met him in Lisbon . . ." She paused.

"So your mama wrote. How very kind that you would come to tell me of it. You were able to see him long after—we did." With an obvious effort, the large lady summoned a smile and said in a lighter tone, "I do hope you will be able to stay?"

At this point the butler returned, followed by a maid carrying a laden tray. Olivia was glad of the hot tea and the jam tart, but accepting the cup and saucer, her hands shook.

Her hostess was quick to notice, and when the servants had gone, she said kindly, "Poor child. You have had your share of sorrow, I collect. Your brother fell last year—no?"

"Yes, ma'am. At Albuera."

Curiosity crept into Mrs. Whitland's eyes. "That was in April, as I recall. Fourteen months since. Forgive my remarking it, but I see you are still in deep mourning. I trust you have not suffered another loss?"

Lord, but guilt was a horrid thing! Feeling her cheeks become heated, Olivia looked down, and had no need to feign a nervous stammer. "I—I have suffered a . . . a very personal loss, ma'am. I was to have been married, you see."

77

"Oh, my! I am so very sorry. Was he a military man also?"

Olivia nodded and said in a thread of a voice, "That is why Mama thought— But you will be wishful to hear of your son, ma'am."

"Yes—but will it be painful for you to speak of military gentlemen, my dear?"

"How kind you are. And it is so wonderful to meet you after everything Alex—Captain Whitland told us. He spoke of you with such affection."

Mrs. Whitland was obliged to put down her cup and saucer, and press a handkerchief to her eyes. "You cannot know . . . how much it means to me. To hear those words. We all loved him so. Everybody who knew him thought . . . so highly of him." She blew her nose loudly, then regarded Olivia with a tremulous smile. "I expect you will have heard that he was—well, naughty at times. It was because of the duel with that wretched viscount that my dear husband bought him a pair of colours and packed him off into the cavalry. Not that we ever believed all that business about Alexis and the viscountess," she added hurriedly. "And the colonel, my late husband, never dreamed the war would take such a turn. Still, my son seemed to like the military life." She searched Olivia's face. "Did—did you receive that impression, Miss Bridge?"

Olivia gathered her rather scattered wits. "I think the captain liked army life very well. His was an adventurous spirit. He told me once that he was not cut out to be a country squire."

This would seem to equate with the nature of a man who dueled viscounts and seduced their wives, and she was relieved when Mrs. Whitland uttered a shaky laugh and said it was "like the rascal" to have made such a remark. "May I ask how long you knew him? He never wrote of Lisbon. I suppose

78

he was on leave there after that horrid fever he suffered?"

"Yes. My uncle had taken me to Spain to make arrangements for Bartholomew to be—returned to us." Olivia bowed her head, reminded painfully of her beloved brother and knowing how he would hate this imposture. "Captain Whitland chanced to counter us," she went on. "And when he saw we were in blacks, at once approached us."

"Ah. Then you had a prior acquaintanceship?"

"Well— I— Yes, ma'am. My brother knew the captain well, and we had met—er, several times. He—your son, was very kind, and of great assistance to my uncle."

This disjointed speech brought a keener look to Mrs. Whitland's eyes. "I am glad to hear it. Though, I do not recall that Alexis ever mentioned anyone named Bridge."

Olivia smiled sadly. "He used to say he was no great hand at writing letters. In fact, it surprised me that he—" She broke off, contriving to appear confused. "But you will have questions, I am very sure."

Mrs. Whitland was finding more questions than she would have dreamed, but she said kindly that her visitor would doubtless be glad to rest and change her dress before dinner. "I have put you into a suite that has an adjacent room for your woman," she said, as they walked into the hall. "Alexis is—was particularly fond of that suite. You will understand why, if you knew him well, and— William! *Do* take care!"

Olivia was staggered as a large and shaggy dog galloped from an adjacent room hotly pursued by a small boy. Both collided with her. Mrs. Whitland scolded, the dog put his tail between his legs and fled, and the boy flushed scarlet and muttered an awkward apology.

Olivia said gently that there was no harm done.

"Even so, it was not mannerly, child," said Mrs. Whitland. "And you know very well that I do not like Digger in the house when we entertain guests. This is my youngest son, Miss Bridge. Now make your bow politely, William. Miss Bridge knew your dear brother, and has been so kind as to come and— and talk to us about him."

A rebellious look came into the boy's green eyes. He made a stiff bow and announced that he would be seven next year. "Alexis never writ about someone called Bridge. I'd remember. Did you really know my brother?"

"Did I not say so?" Sighing, his mother shook her head. "I am sure I don't know what Miss Bridge must think of you."

William's lower lip became more prominent.

Olivia said, "We met your brother in Lisbon. That's in Portugal."

"I know it is," he said scornfully. "Alexis never went there. He'd of told me so. He writ me long letters 'bout *everything*," he added, fixing the guest with a challenging stare.

Olivia's pulse quickened. "He must have forgotten to mention it."

"Very likely," said Mrs. Whitland, forestalling her son's attempted response. "Miss Bridge met your brother on several occasions. Her own brother knew Alexis well."

"If he knew him," began the boy, "why didn't—"

"You will like to see the portrait of Alexis," interrupted his mother, her voice somewhat shrill. "It hangs here, as you undoubtedly noticed."

Olivia turned to the large portrait on the wall opposite the front door. Save for the state of her nerves, she would have noticed it before. She wandered closer. The gentleman was tall and well built, his hair worn rather longer than was now fashionable. Impressive in full regimental evening dress, his jutting chin was held high, and there was a fierce light in the piercing green eyes.

William uttered a hoot. "That's my *father*!"

Dismayed, Olivia jerked her head to another portrait. This man, also depicted in hussar uniform, was younger, with a lean face, a faintly sardonic smile, curling light brown hair, and his mother's deep blue eyes.

Mrs. Whitland and the boy were watching her.

There was only one thing to be done. With a little moan, she crumpled.

Sarah carried a tray into the spacious bedchamber and deposited it on the dressing table. Eyeing her employer's reflection worriedly, she said, "I still think it's a mistake for you to go downstairs, Miss Olivia. You'd do better to keep to your bed. It'd look more natural."

"No." Olivia adjusted a delicately tiered pearl earring, and pursed her lips. "Too much?"

Sarah poured a glass of ratafia. "Depends how much of a Tragedy Jill you want to look like." She saw the flash in Olivia's fine eyes and added quickly, "Best take some of this if you will insist on going down."

"I think not. It might make me flushed. But I'll take some of the cakes. I mustn't appear to have a healthy appetite for dinner—which I have, more's the pity. What have you discovered of Captain Alexis? His mama thinks I will know why he was particularly fond of this suite." She scanned the warm blue of the walls, the fine prints and paintings, the graceful furnishings, and shook her head. "It is charming, but for the life of me, I cannot guess which feature especially pleased him. What do you think?"

"Lord only knows, miss. I don't. I had a chat with

one of the kitchen maids. Proper dreamy-eyed about the captain, she was. He liked to sketch, she said. And he was a bruising rider, which is likely why he went into the hussars."

"Hmm. There is but one picture of a horse in here." Olivia stood and went to inspect a fine oil painting. "This is signed by someone called ... Constable."

"An omen!" declared Sarah bodingly.

Olivia flushed. "We must hope not." She sat on the bed. "Now, pray tell me about the man who carried me upstairs. When I felt him catch me, I vow I almost *did* swoon! Why do you grin, wretched creature?"

"I was sure you'd risked peeping at him, ma'am."

"And I wonder why I countenance your insolence!" But the twinkle in Olivia's eyes took the sting out of the words, and she added, "Of course I peeped. Such a handsome gentleman. But I suppose you have discovered he is wed and the father of several hopeful children."

Sarah lowered her voice and offered with barely suppressed excitement, "He is Sir Gerald Lainey and was Captain Whitland's bosom bow. Five and twenty. A bachelor. Very well to pass, and—"

"How well?" interrupted Olivia.

"Cook—a proper gossip she is!—said at least twelve thousand pounds a year! And one of the footmen told me his estate is in Warwickshire and a real showplace."

Olivia gave a little squeal and hugged herself.

"Which ain't to say he's got no lady fixed in his eye," added Sarah. "With looks like that, *and* a great fortune, he likely has the matchmaking mamas after him in full cry."

"Don't be crude," said Olivia, and went on crudely. "Besides, so long as he's not yet betrothed, there is hope. What luck! I may not have to persuade Mrs. Whitland to take us in, after all!"

Belatedly, Sarah remembered her aversion to this masquerade and crossed to take a black velvet evening gown from the press. She frowned at the design of seed pearls that edged the very décolleté neckline. "I suppose as you'll be wanting to wear this naughty thing?"

Olivia rested one fingertip on her rosy lower lip, and considered. "Is Sir Gerald to stay for dinner?"

"No. I think Mrs. Whitland wants to keep you all to herself for a day or so."

"Then we will save the velvet for a time when he does stay."

"And what if he don't, ma'am?

"*Do* try not to be such a gloom merchant, Sarah! Alexis Whitland was obviously a man of many friends. Likely, all of respectable fortune. I'd not thought of that till now, but one of them *must* prove suitable!"


"I sent Henry and George to their grandpapa for the summer." Mrs. Whitland nodded to the butler. "Yes, I will take just a teensy helping of the potatoes, Curtis. I had wanted William to go, as well," she went on, "but he begged to be allowed to stay at home." She sighed. "I wish my family had not been so spread out. Sylvia, my daughter, arrived two years after Alexis. She married and was widowed very young, poor dear. Then came Henry, and there's only one year between him and George, who is fourteen now. It makes it so lonely for William. You will understand that, Miss Bridge."

Olivia refused the potatoes and said she understood very well. "My brother and I were very close, for we are—were the two eldest. But I love my little sisters dearly. As I'm sure your older boys care for William."

"Well, they do, and are kind to him. But despite the gap in their ages, he was happiest when he was with Alexis. He fairly worshiped him. To lose him has been a devastating blow to us all, but especially to William."

"Poor little boy. I had guessed by the way Captain Whitland spoke of his youngest brother that he held him in deep affection." She gazed at the cruet, and sighed.

Mrs. Whitland watched her uneasily, but not until they were alone in the withdrawing room did she venture on a subject she dreaded. "I am not a clever woman, Miss Bridge, and have puzzled over a letter Alexis must have written just before that dreadful battle. It was a brief note." She gave a rueful shrug. "They always were. He said he meant to make a change in his way of life. I took it to mean he was hopeful of coming home, but now—I cannot but wonder ... Oh, *pray* do not be distressed!"

With a hand over her eyes, Olivia mumbled an apology.

Her disquieting suspicions increasing by the minute, Mrs. Whitland went on, "When you fainted at the sight of his portrait ... and from little remarks you have made, I have begun to think—Oh, my dear child, was there an—er, *understanding* of some kind between you and my son?"

Olivia dried her perfectly dry eyes, clasped her hands before her, paused, then forced herself to meet the troubled gaze of her hostess. Shocked, she thought, Great heavens! The poor lady thinks I have come to tell her I carry her grandchild! She said hesitantly, "Oh, ma'am, I do not know how to break it to you, but ..."

"Oh! My God!" gasped Mrs. Whitland.

"Had Alexis not been loath to tell you by letter, you would have—have heard of it long ago. I knew it must be judged very bad, and I will go away at once if you are—are outraged."

Longing for her vinaigrette, Mrs. Whitland said faintly, "Pray tell me the whole."

"Alexis made me an offer. And—I *know* I should not have done, but—I accepted. We were betrothed, ma'am. We hoped to be married as soon as he could come home to speak to you, and ask permission of my mama."

Mrs. Whitland gave a gasp of relief. "Oh, thank goodness! I thought—My dearest child, how very *glad* I am!" She surged out of her chair, and as Olivia at once rose, wrapped her in a strong embrace and said brokenly, "You cannot know what it means . . . to have the lady my beloved son had chose, here with me! *Dear* Olivia, you must tell me all about it. And promise me—*promise* you will stay a long, long while."

Returning that warm embrace, Olivia was scourged by guilt. This was even more dreadful than she had anticipated, but for the sake of her loved ones, she must keep on deceiving this kind-hearted lady. I will do all in my power to make her happy, she thought. I swear I will not take without giving in return. And with luck and Sir Gerald Lainey, you will *not* be trapped in that horrid, desolate old house, dearest Mama!

# 3

Mrs. Whitland, who enjoyed her comforts, was disinclined to rise before noon, and the following morning being bright and sunny, Olivia wandered alone through the gardens that spread from the rear terrace to the wide lawns, beyond which were neatly fenced paddocks.

Flagged pathways wound among flower beds that were ablaze with color. Tree-shaded benches offered rest or contemplation. Two gardeners toiled among the neat yew trees that lined the rear drive path, and a third was engaged in the task of scything the lawns.

The sun rose higher and the air grew warmer. Olivia discovered a cluster of lily of the valley. She was fond of the dainty little blossoms, and bent lower to enjoy their fragrance.

"My brother does not like people to pick his flowers."

"Then I certainly will not do so," said Olivia, straightening and meeting William's dark scowl with a smile. "Do you mean Henry?"

"*Henry!* Much *he* knows about flowers!" His eyes challenged her, and when she was silent, he declared, "This house belongs to *Alexis*. And the flowers, too. Flowers," he went on, as she regarded him in grave silence, "was—*is* his favorite things, which you'd know if you was going to marry with him."

She could all but feel the anguish behind the hostility. "I'm afraid I had not time to learn as much about him as I would have wished," she said gently. "I had thought his great passion was his horses."

He looked startled, then sneered, "I s'pose Mama told you that Alexis used to have that suite you're in. I s'pose she told you he liked to look out at the paddock, and that's how you knew."

"No. Your mama did not tell me that. If he liked the suite, why did he not keep it?"

With a pitying look he answered, " 'Cause he's the head of our house now and will have the room all the Whitland men have when they're the heads."

"I see. Thank you for talking to me about him, William. I used to have a brother to talk to, but he was a soldier, and—"

"He's not—what they say," he interrupted fiercely. "I don't believe 'em! *Any* of 'em! It's all rotten lies! Alexis would never go off and—and do that!"

"I'm sure he didn't mean to. Any more than my—"

"Your brother's *dead*!" he snarled, with the unrefined cruelty of childhood. Tears shone on his long lashes, and he dashed them away. "Mine isn't! He *isn't*!" He started to run off, then turned and shouted, "And he *wasn't* going to marry with you! He promised he'd tell me first when he picked his lady. He told me *everything*! He'd of told me if he was going to get killed, too! You tell raspers! I don't like you! I *don't*!"

Olivia's eyes blurred as she watched his galloping retreat. With a feeling of helplessness, she lowered the hand she had reached out to him.

"I apologize for William," said a quiet voice behind her.

The gentleman who had carried her up the stairs yesterday stood nearby with a curly brimmed hat in one hand, and anxiety in his grey eyes. His straight hair was thick and black, and his complexion, although clear, was inclined to be sallow. It was his only flaw, for he was even taller than she had thought, and his features were unusually fine; his chin firm beneath a shapely mouth, his nose straight, and his voice deep and well modulated.

"Oh," said Olivia, dabbing a handkerchief at her eyes.

"Permit me to introduce myself. I am Gerald Lainey. I had the good fortune to catch you when you swooned yesterday."

"It was most kind of you, Sir Gerald. And pray do not fancy I have taken offense because of what William said. Poor little boy. He is grieving terribly."

"How good you are to make allowances for him. May I walk with you, ma'am?" As though fearing she might refuse, he added a reinforcing, "I was one of Alexis' closest friends. But perhaps he mentioned me?"

"He did, of course." Olivia managed a smile. "And I welcome your company."

They walked on together. He said nothing for a minute or two, then remarked somewhat hesitantly that he was very glad Miss Bridge had come to Maiden's Court. "Your presence here will mean so much to Mrs. Lillian. Alexis was the apple of her eye, and she is quite distracted. It was always her hope—er, well, like all mothers of grown sons, she longed for—" He flushed, and broke off.

Amused, Olivia said, "You mean that Mrs. Whitland wanted grandchildren, naturally enough. My own dear mama cherished the same hope."

He pressed her hand briefly and sympathetically. "I heard of your loss. I am truly sorry, ma'am. I fancy that having known such sorrow inspires you with the desire to do all you may to alleviate poor Mrs. Lillian's distress."

Olivia could have sunk. Sure that her face was scarlet, she hid her guilty blushes behind her fan, mumbled a comment on the heat of the day, and took refuge on a shady bench. "I doubt I can be of much help, Sir Gerald."

He stood looking down at her with his grave, kind smile. "And I am clumsy, and should have realized it would be painful for you to speak of your affianced. Have I your permission to be seated, Miss Bridge?"

She gave her permission, thinking, What charming manners, and trying to picture her darling Bart waiting to be invited to sit beside a lady he admired. *If* Sir Gerald admired her . . . And to judge by the rapt gaze now fixed upon her, he did. Lowering her eyes demurely, she lied, "The thing is that because of his military duties, I was seldom able to meet Captain Whitland. And when I could see him, I was never without a chaperon."

"But of course. Though, I wonder he did not—" He stopped, as if he'd said more than he intended.

"Circumvent them?" She chuckled. "He tried, you may be very sure." According to Pamela, Captain Whitland was rumored to have been something of a rake so she thought that was a fairly safe remark, but glancing at Lainey from under her lashes, she surprised a shocked expression. "But I think he was only teasing," she appended hurriedly, "for he was never less than a perfect gentleman. He spoke often of Maiden's Court, and his devotion to his family was unwavering. I had rather hoped he might have written to his mama, but he wanted to tell her in person of our betrothal. Had he perhaps mentioned it when corresponding with you, Sir Gerald?"

"I believe I had two letters from him since he left

England. And I doubt either contained over ten lines. Would it be impertinent of me to ask if yours was a long-standing attachment?"

Olivia answered carefully, "Captain Whitland was acquainted with my brother, and we had met a time or two in London. He said nothing at that time of any plans to join up, but I believe there was . . . some scandal."

"Ah. You knew him before the duel, then. He likely took pains to shield you from all the gossip. Perfectly understandable. Any man with half a brain would wish to protect so lovely a lady."

His eyes were most definitely admiring.

Olivia lowered her own. "You are very kind, Sir Gerald. I think I must go back now. Mrs. Whitland will be looking for me."

He stood at once and assisted her to rise as though the effort might tax her strength. En route back to the house, he was all consideration. When Olivia prepared to put up her parasol against the bright rays of the sun, he at once took it and opened it for her. Approaching the terrace, his hand was under her elbow, guiding her up the steps. Her liking for him increased. Clearly, his was a kind and protective nature, and that he was also rich and very good-looking did nothing to detract from his appeal. Poor man, she thought, and wondered how many hopeful females had leveled their guns in his direction. He was undoubtedly accustomed to the tactics of hopeful spinsters and matchmaking mamas. He was attracted to her, she was very sure. But she knew men and had sensed almost at once that if she was to snare him, she would have to proceed with great care. Despite his youth, Sir Gerald was of a sober and somewhat pedantic disposition, whereas she had grown up with a loving but rather careless brother who had ignored the restraints most gentlemen employed when conversing with young ladies. She must guard her tongue. She must also be very sure of Sir Gerald before she revealed the fact that he would be expected to provide for her family. There was nothing more certain to put off a suitor.

Walking beside him into the cool dimness of the house, she was touched by shame and also by sadness. She had sunk to the level of a fortune hunter—a role she had always deplored. And also, she thought wistfully, this calculated campaign had not a trace of the romance she always had yearned for; the unutterable joy of being pursued by a man she loved with all her heart.

Sir Gerald threw open the door to the withdrawing room.

"Gerald!" A strikingly lovely young woman, her pale clear complexion and glowing red hair dramatically set off by a black gown, rose from a chair beside the empty hearth. "Thank heaven you are come! The most awful thing! I fear Mama has been quite taken in ... by ..." She stopped speaking, the distress in her green eyes changing to hauteur as Olivia came forward.

Jumping up from the sofa, William cried shrilly, "That's *her*, Sylvia! That's the wicked—"

Sir Gerald interposed, his voice sharp, "I think that will do, William!"

The boy scowled but was silent.

"Miss Bridge," said Sir Gerald, "allow me to make you known to Lady Medhurst. Miss Bridge, as you will know, Sylvia, was betrothed to your brother."

"She *wasn't*!" shouted William. "It's all fibs! She's—"

"Be quiet, sir!" snapped Sir Gerald.

Lady Medhurst dropped a hand onto the boy's shoulder. "You had better go away now, dear." Her cold eyes did not leave Olivia. "We'll chat later."

Olivia's heart sank. Clearly, this young beauty was in sympathy with William's doubts. There would be more questions, and she dare not make more mistakes. If she survived this day, it would be a miracle.

She was put to the test at luncheon. Sir Gerald was obviously a frequent and most welcome visitor, and that he would join them at table was taken for granted. Sylvia Medhurst treated him with the affection of an old friend, but once or twice Olivia glimpsed a look in her eyes that spoke of a deeper emotion. If the lovely young widow had set her cap for him, it was not surprising that she regarded her late brother's "fiancée" with such hostility. There was little evidence of that hostility while her mother was present. At every opportunity, however, she inserted a question about her late brother, and it took all Olivia's ingenuity not to betray herself. Luckily, she'd had the foresight to memorize many details relating to Lord Wellington's Peninsular campaign, and when Lady Medhurst asked point-blank exactly where in Lisbon Miss Bridge had met Alexis, she was able to reply that it was at a party hosted by Sir Charles Stuart. "Captain Whitland had been given leave after the Battle of Albuera. He said that the party was given to try and keep people's spirits up, because of the terrible losses we suffered."

"I can well imagine how distressed Alexis must have been," said Sylvia. "He was not a great admirer of Lord Wellington's methods. But I fancy you have heard his discourses on the subject, Miss Bridge?"

Sensing a possible trap, Olivia hesitated.

Mrs. Whitland said kindly, "No doubt your presence alone was sufficient to lift his spirits, my dear."

"There was not the need, ma'am," she replied,

praying this was not a misstep. "Your son was never indifferent to suffering, but neither was he crushed by our losses. If he felt despair, he certainly did not show it and was, in fact, impatient with those he held to be gloom merchants."

"You will be meaning Ned Willoughby," said Sylvia with a little frown. "Alexis never could abide the creature."

Sir Gerald's look of surprise warned Olivia. She said thoughtfully that she did not recall Alexis saying anything to the gentleman's detriment.

Sir Gerald said with his slow smile, "Ned Willoughby is no gentleman, Miss Bridge. He is a proper rascal, which is, I suspect, why Alexis liked him so well. You must, I think, have confused him with another fellow, Sylvia."

The widow shrugged, and changed the subject. Directly the meal ended, she commandeered Sir Gerald, and went with him to the paddocks. Mrs. Whitland conducted Olivia on a tour of the house. Hers was a sunny nature, and she was able to put grief aside and chatter brightly with her young guest. She sobered, however, when they came to the second floor. "I know you will like to see his room, my dear," she murmured.

The master bedchamber was enormous, and masculine from the great four-poster bed with its royal blue velvet curtains, to the prints and sketches hung on the walls. Mrs. Whitland said proudly that many of these had been drawn by her son. Most were of horses, but there were also likenesses of his family. The degree of skill was considerable, but rather stark, the strokes firm, and with no concession having been made to flattery.

"I replaced the sketches that were in your bedchamber, Miss Bridge. I was afraid they might make you sad."

Olivia hugged her impulsively. "You are so

thoughtful, ma'am. It is enough that I can look out upon what he used to see, and enjoy the view of the horses and paddocks, just as he must have done."

That she had scored was very obvious, and she congratulated herself on having said the right thing this time. She had no need to feign enthusiasm when Mrs. Whitland took her to see some of the dolls she enjoyed to dress. It was a charming collection, each doll being clad in the fashions of a different period, and authentic to the tiniest detail. Impressed, Olivia asked, "Did you make all the garments yourself, ma'am? What a remarkable seamstress you must be."

Her hostess glowed with pleasure. "A labor of love, my dear. I always longed for daughters, but Sylvia was something of a tomboy and never played with dolls after she was five years old. I had so hoped— I mean— Are you fond of children? Alexis used to say he wanted a large family."

"Yes, indeed," said Olivia, smiling into the wistful eyes. "Three of each, he said."

A mocking laugh sounded. Coming to join them, Sylvia said, "Now how can this be? My brother could not abide children. Pestiferous brats, he used to name them. It was Mama who wanted the large family for him—not Alexis."

Mrs. Whitland sighed, and admitted that was true.

Vexed to see her disconsolate expression, Olivia said, "But do you not think, ma'am, that what a gentleman tells his brothers and sisters, and what he says to his betrothed, are very different things?"

Before her mother could respond, Sylvia said sardonically, "So different as to be nigh unbelievable, I declare."

It was this exchange that prompted Olivia to beg to be excused from joining the family at dinner. Mrs. Whitland was all concern, and a dinner tray was sent up to her room, but her anxieties about the desperate course she now meant to undertake, had banished Olivia's appetite. After Sarah left her, she sat up and tried to read to pass the time. By midnight, the house had been quiet for almost an hour, and she donned dressing gown and slippers, took candle in hand, and eased the door open.

Not a sound disturbed the stillness. Holding her breath, she crept along the hall. Thanks to the afternoon tour, she knew the way, and at last came to the distant corridor where was the master suite. She paused, ears straining to detect the faintest sound. There was none—until she opened the door. It emitted a creak that seemed earsplitting. With a scared whimper she darted into Captain Whitland's parlour and leaned weakly against the wall, her heart pounding madly.

The taut seconds crawled past, but there came no sign of alarm or investigation, and with a sigh of relief, she at last crossed to set her candlestick on the big desk before the windows. The long central drawer was cluttered, and she began to sort quickly through the contents. There were letters from friends, fellow officers, and members of his family. She skimmed over reports from his man of business having to do with the estate, and several bills of sale from Tattersall's. In a separate pile were letters written on dainty paper that still held a faint fragrance. Feeling very wicked indeed, she opened one, and a moment later, her face burning, whispered, "Oh! My goodness!" and replaced the letter on its little pile. Captain Alexis Whitland had, it would seem, been skilled in the art of *l'amour*!

In a side drawer she found something of far greater use: a journal. Delighted by this piece of luck, she settled into the chair and began to read. The earliest entries were dated in May 1808, and were not easy to decipher, for the captain's hand, although bold, was far from neat, so that many words eluded her. Some notations were very brief: Meet Franklin at White's for luncheon ... Borrowed a pony from Granger—*Don't forget!* Others were more detailed. June 9th's entry read: Met Sam (unintelligible) at Tatt's. He tried to break my shins for another monkey. Confounded gall! Claims his wife is ill again. Stuff! June 11: Dropped a pony on Wonder Why. Blasted nag didn't even place! <u>Wonder why</u> I paid heed to Monty!! June 12: Danielle's cough much worse. Must send her to Italy, poor sweet. Her (unintelligible) husband was heard remarking she's become "a bore." Will attend to the muckworm. After she sails. July 5: Sam cornered me in White's and made a cake of himself and of me, blast him! Be damned if I ever lend a man a helping hand again! Thought the (unintelligible) fellow was going to kiss me! Lord help his wife if he had—she'd have been an early widow!

Olivia laughed softly.

"What are you doing in here?"

The voice, sharp with suspicion, came from behind her, and Olivia's blood ran cold with fright.

# 4

William looked angelic in a long white night-shirt, brown curls tumbled, and cheeks flushed, but with antagonism glaring from the green eyes that were so like his sister's. "You're reading my brother's secret book," he accused. "You got no right! No one's got the right to open that drawer!"

"It wasn't locked," said Olivia. But glancing down instinctively, she saw now that the wood around the lock looked splintered. "And it helps me," she went on with oblique truthfulness, "to read about what he did every day."

The boy gave a mocking snort, but gazed at the book longingly.

Olivia offered a bribe. "Would you like me to read it to you?"

His head swung up. "I already read it. *All!*"

She nodded, and returned her attention to the page.

"You better go," he warned, edging nearer. "Else I'll tell Mama 'bout you."

"I shall tell her at all events, William. You see, someone has forced the drawer open. A thief, I'm afraid."

"No it were not! I mean—no one *took* nothing." He bit his lip, then said with an air of desperation. "I'spect *you* did it!"

"But, I couldn't have. You said you had already

read the book, so this drawer must have been broken into before I came here."

He scowled at her, but he was pale and his lower lip trembled.

In her kindest voice, Olivia said, "I want so much to learn all I can about him, William. Won't you forgive me for reading his journal? Not that I can read much. His writing is rather difficult to—"

"He writ good! Alexis did *everything* good!" Blinking through slow-gathering tears, his voice shredded. "I miss him . . . so much!" he gulped, and without warning hurled himself into her arms.

Olivia hugged him close, her head bowing over him. He was just a very little boy, trying to deal with a child's bewilderment at the finality of death, and to cope with his crushing grief. Sobs wracked his small body, and tears of sympathy stung Olivia's eyes. She said shakily, "Only look at us! Alexis would have laughed at me and said I was a watering pot." She gave him her handkerchief. "Do you know what I think, William? I think he would not want us to be sad. He'd want us to remember him as he was. To think of when he was kind, and happy. When *we* were happy, just being with him."

A pathetic face emerged from the handkerchief, and red-rimmed eyes blinked up at her. He said, "You got tears, too. I s'pose that means you did love him a bit."

Olivia wiped her eyes quickly, and evaded, "There. Is that better? Now, it's very late, but just for a little while, we'll read his book together. Perhaps you can help me with the words I don't know."

And so it was that he perched on her knee, and she read—with many hurried revisions—while he corrected or added words that she thought sufficiently obvious for him to provide. She made him giggle when they came to a notation she pretended to interpret as having to do with a hog that had "with malice aforethought dug up Mama's prize roses."

"Dog!" chortled William. "Not hog!"

"Oh yes. We met, I remember. Is it the same dog? I forget his name."

"Alexis called him Digger, 'cause that's the only thing he does right. He's not let in the house, 'cause he chewed a chair leg, and old Lady Grantley sat on it, and it fell down." He hugged his sides gleefully. "She's bigger'n three monks, Alexis used to say. And she got all red in the face, and puffed like a-a—"

"Grampus?"

He nodded, screwing his head around to look at her. "What are they? I asked Sir Gerald, but he didn't know. He said he'd tell me, but he forgot. He doesn't know much."

"Don't you like him?"

"Alexis likes him," he said, as if that was sufficient recommendation. "Don't you know either?"

Olivia suggested dubiously, "I think it's a fish."

"How can it be a fish? They don't breathe, so how could they blow?"

"That's a very sensible argument, and I'm afraid I don't have a sensible answer. We'll go into the library tomorrow and look it up. But just now, I am an elderly lady who needs her sleep. Will you be so good as to escort me to my chamber, kind sir?"

He was amused, the journal was replaced, the drawer tenderly closed, and, hand in hand, the conspirators tiptoed along the darkened hall.

Next morning the library yielded the information that a grampus was indeed a type of fish, and when it was found that whales were such creatures, William's enthusiasm demanded that he at once rush to share this choice discovery with his mama. Olivia had now become something of a cause célèbre with the boy, and sensing that she could find no surer path to the mother's heart than by lifting the spirits of her child, she exerted herself to entertain him. In the days that followed they played games, took Digger for long walks, rode, and chattered comfortably together.

Mrs. Whitland told Sir Gerald that she blessed the day Miss Bridge had come to them, and declared she did not know how she would go on without her. Sir Gerald, increasingly in agreement with these sentiments, took to paying morning calls while Mrs. Whitland was yet in her bedchamber and William was at his lessons.

Sylvia Medhurst was a frequent visitor. Her manner toward Olivia was unchanged, and it was clear that she was irked to find Sir Gerald so often in her company. At every opportunity she detached him from Olivia's side, and then engaged him in low-voiced converse. These tactics worried Olivia and she was sure that Sir Gerald would avoid her company. Instead, he became even more attentive, seeming genuinely interested in her family and engaging her in reminiscences about Alexis. Having twice caught herself on the brink of an error, it dawned on Olivia that Sylvia was behind these less than subtle interrogations and had browbeaten the handsome baronet into setting traps for her. She was on her guard after that, but because Mrs. Whitland and William never tired of talking about the man they both had loved so deeply, and with the additional help of Alexis' journal, Olivia was able to avoid disaster. The widow was hoist by her own petard. Not only did Sir Gerald fail to entrap her rival, but because they were so often in each others' company, his admiration of Olivia increased. As the lazy summer days drifted past, this fact became ever more obvious, a development as gratifying to Olivia as it was infuriating to Sylvia.

Sir Gerald, however, was a careful gentleman, and not once did he even hint to Olivia that he had anything more than friendship in mind. The time was growing short, and the letters from home were becoming more insistent that she must come home and help prepare for their unhappy move. Olivia had still not dared confide in her mother, partly from fear that she might fail, and partly because dear Mama would have been horrified by this deception.

Alone in her room on an oppressively hot afternoon in late July, Olivia had determined to advise her parent of the true state of affairs. The words were hard to find, for she was torn between fear of waiting too long for Sir Gerald to declare himself, and a reluctance to ask Mrs. Whitland for the help she was sure would be willingly offered.

Her introspection was cut short when William scratched on her door. He had been invited to join his two older brothers at their maternal grandfather's summer home on the Isle of Wight. Olivia's heart was wrung when he said gruffly that he had told his mama he couldn't go because, "Alexis wouldn't like Miss 'Livia to be left 'thout a gentleman."

Kissing him, Olivia knew it was no use. She had come to love the little boy and his gentle mama, and simply could not impose further upon them.

Soon afterward, Sir Gerald came riding up from the rear drive path. She watched him speculatively. He had a splendid seat, and carried his dark head proudly. He was very kind, rich, and handsome. And if he did not always see the humor in a situation; if he was inclined to be ponderously grave, and to consider with infuriating care before offering an opinion (which was usually noncommittal), surely these were small faults. She must concentrate on finding a way to—as Bart would have said—

bring him up to scratch. He glanced at her window, and she waved. His face lit up and his smile flashed at once. Smiling also, she walked to the door. It was a difficult world, and one had to fight to survive. If he—*when* he offered, she would be a good wife. And she would put aside the foolish dreams of youth.

Half an hour later, walking beside Sir Gerald among the flower gardens, she declared with rank insincerity that she had no thought of marriage.

He looked shocked. "Dare one ask the obvious? Surely, so lovely and charming a lady does not mean to take the veil?"

Olivia could picture Bart's reaction to that remark, and it was all she could do to restrain a hearty laugh, which would be fatal. She managed, instead, to look downcast. "If it would solve my problems, I might do so. But I have obligations I could no more foist off upon a convent than upon any gentleman who might be willing to offer for me."

He said solemnly, "I can think of no obligation that should deter a gentleman, were his affections deeply engaged."

She shook her head and sighed, and when he begged that she would consider him sufficient of a friend to confide in, she hesitated before saying with apparent reluctance that it would indeed be a great comfort to have the benefit of his wisdom. "For truly, I am at my wit's end."

To recite the unhappy story brought home to her the really terrifying possibility that she still might fail. Her voice trembled when she finished, "And now, my dear mama and my two little sisters and I are . . . are about to be dispossessed."

"Dispossessed? Good God! You never mean your uncle means to put you out in the street? He must be an utter cad! I wonder he is not pilloried for such despicable behavior!"

He looked quite fierce, and her heart warmed with gratitude. "Not put in the street, sir. But he means to pack us off to a dreadful old ruin of a house in East Anglia. It is remote and damp and draughty. My mama is frail, and has become more so since my brother's death. It is—it is my fear that she would not long survive in such a dreary place."

A strong hand was placed over hers. His voice husky with ardour, he said, "Your filial loyalty is to be commended, dear ma'am. You are the most brave and loyal lady I ever have met. No, pray do not be distressed. I know I must not speak while you yet mourn poor Alexis. However—" Olivia held her breath, but he broke off abruptly, exclaiming, "Jove! I wonder who this may be?"

Whomever they might be, Olivia could have strangled the occupants of the curricle that raced up the drive at reckless speed. It came to a halt at the foot of the steps, and two gentlemen alighted, tossing the leathers to a stable boy as they hurried to the front door.

His romantic mood broken, Sir Gerald was apprehensive as they returned to the house. They walked into chaos. Mrs. Whitland's abigail rushed past holding a pan that reeked of burnt feathers; Curtis crossed from the withdrawing room to the morning room looking shaken and carrying a tray of glasses and a decanter; two maids clutched each other, weeping copiously; William sat huddled at the foot of the stairs.

Dismayed, Olivia ran to put her arm around him. "Oh, my dear—whatever is it?"

He clung to her, and lifted a white, bewildered face. It's—it's Alexis," he whispered. "They've found him. He's not dead after all. They're bringing him home!"

* * *

Captain Whitland, they now discovered, had been severely wounded during the terrible third storming of Badajoz; his clothing burned, his hair scorched off, and his face so blackened by a mine blast that he had been unrecognizable. Mistaken for an enemy officer and in a deep coma, he'd been left with other French wounded and eventually returned to their forces. His recovery was slow, and his memory impaired. He spoke French fluently, and when he gradually came to know who he was, he said nothing, knowing he would assuredly be judged a spy if he was discovered. For two months he had lain in the hospital, but as soon as he gained sufficient strength, he'd made a daring escape. His long and desperate journey back to the British lines had almost ended in disaster when some Spanish peasants, thinking him to be one of the hated French, had shot him down again. A compassionate Scots dragoon sergeant had put a stop to their plans to burn him alive, and upon learning his identity, had conveyed him to the allied forces, by this time on the march to Madrid. His long ordeal had wrought havoc with his health, and as soon as the army doctors had judged him able to survive the journey, he had been brought home.

Olivia's fears of immediate unmasking proved unfounded. When the gallant captain was borne tenderly into the house two days later, she looked down on an emaciated wreck, a man barely able to take the hand his mother reached out to him. Mrs. Whitland fought sobs to gulp emotionally, "Only l-look, my darling boy. Here is—is your own dear lady to stay at your side."

The sunken blue eyes turned to Olivia, but they held nothing more than a dull interest.

Grateful that she had not been immediately denounced as an impostor, Olivia decided that her best course was to creep away under cover of darkness, and pray that she would not be sought out and prosecuted. This plan was foiled when William came to her bedchamber just as she was preparing to depart, and begged her to help him pray that his brother's life be spared. The child was shivering with terror, convinced by his adored Alexis' changed appearance that he had been brought home to die. Olivia could not abandon him in such a state, and was obliged to stay for at least one more day.

It became very clear that she was expected not only to be ecstatic with joy, but to wish to be constantly at her fiancé's side. She undertook the role at first with reluctance and trepidation, but as the days passed, her feelings underwent a change. The captain was an admirable patient. He never complained, and managed to summon a smile even when his blue eyes were clouded with pain and speech was beyond him. Olivia had always admired courage, and her nature was kind. She spared no effort to make him more comfortable, smoothing his pillow when it became rumpled, bathing his face with cool lavender water when the summer afternoons became very warm, reading the newspapers to him when he murmured a request for news. Often, on those hot, quiet afternoons, her head would nod, and she would awaken to find his eyes fixed upon her with a puzzled expression, as though he tried to reclaim some memory that eluded him. She was sure that at any minute he would remember and demand an explanation, but invariably his grateful smile would banish the look of bewilderment, and she would think, One more day. Just one more day.

But one more day drifted into another . . . and another . . . The captain had become the center of all their thoughts and efforts. William hung about the door of the sickroom, yet was afraid to go inside, peeping in at the gaunt stranger who was his brother, and murmuring anxious requests for information from whoever emerged. The servants were elated, and tiptoed about, chattering in excited whispers. When the nurses sent Olivia away so that she could rest, Mrs. Whitland took her place. Her temperament was optimistic, and she was soon declaring radiantly that Alexis was improving. Did Olivia not think he was less often in pain? Had she noticed that his eyes were not quite so sunken, and that he looked more alert? Olivia had indeed noticed these things. And because she had also noticed some disturbing emotions of her own, she was torn between fear and delight, and could not bring herself to be sensible and go away.

On a sultry afternoon two weeks after the captain's return, she was sitting by the bedside, sewing. He had been chatting with her, betraying a humorous embarrassment about his "terribly erratic memory," then had not spoken for some time and, glancing up, she saw that he had dropped off to sleep again. She tiptoed across the room to close the curtains, then returned to her chair. Almost at once, he had insisted that he be shaved each morning, and although his cheekbones were still too prominent, there could be little doubt that he was less skin and bones than when he had first come home. He lacked Sir Gerald's perfect features, but even in his present condition she could readily understand why ladies would be attracted to him. The light brown hair that tumbled untidily over his forehead had a tendency to curl, which she thought charming. There was often a hint of mischief in his blue eyes, and if his nose was not quite straight and his chin too square, there was strength of character there, and humor in the firm lips.

Watching him, she found that she was smiling, and she sat straighter, embarrassed as the door burst open. Sylvia Medhurst rushed into the quiet bedchamber in her customary impetuous fashion, to sink to her knees beside her brother with tears pouring down her cheeks.

"Thank God!" she cried brokenly. "Oh, thank God! My mama-in-law insisted we must go up to Scotland, else I would have been here days ago!"

Olivia stood, irritated because Sylvia had awoken him, but intending to leave them alone.

A thin hand moved with remarkable speed to clasp her wrist. She was the recipient of a smile that so weakened her knees, she sat down again of necessity.

Sylvia asked in a choked voice, "Darling Alexis. Do you remember me?"

The tousled head turned to her. He grinned, and said fondly, "Of course I do, Mrs. Widgeon." But as she swooped to kiss him, his eyes lifted to Olivia. "But I don't seem to remember . . . everything," he added.

"You will, dearest," said Sylvia. "Won't he, Miss Bridge?"

The hostility was gone from the tearful green eyes. Olivia heard herself declaring that the important thing was that Captain Whitland was safely home, surrounded by those who loved him.

Still gazing at her, the captain asked, "Do *you* love me?"

With a slightly hysterical laugh, Sylvia said, "Of course she does, you great silly! Miss Bridge is going to be your wife, isn't she?"

Olivia's heart seemed to stop.

The captain sighed and closed his eyes. "Olivia . . ." he murmured.

Sylvia bent and kissed him again, then crept out, handkerchief pressed to her lips.

When Olivia attempted to follow, his grip tightened. She said softly, "I will let you sleep, sir."

His eyes did not open. "No."

She sat still. Once again, she had been reprieved. Did he really believe they were betrothed? She had heard tales of men who had lost all knowledge of their former lives after being wounded. Was there a possibility that he might be similarly afflicted? If that were so, and she stayed, she might just be able to brazen it through. He was still far from well, of course. Perhaps he would never be completely well again, poor soul. But to be the wife of an invalid would not be so terrible. Her cheeks burned as came an afterthought, Especially *this* invalid.

# 5

Olivia was now able to put off her blacks, and a footman was despatched to London with a carefully worded letter advising Mrs. Bridge that her daughter had met a charming and *very* eligible gentleman while visiting her "schoolfriend," and desiring that a box of her gowns be sent to Maiden's Court.

When Alexis saw her wearing the prettiest of these, an arrested expression came into his eyes, but he only said in his whimsical fashion, "Well, it's time and enough for my lovely lady to be done with mourning me." He then threw his "lovely lady" into considerable trepidation by adding thoughtfully, "Though I must say, ma'am, that demure pink sarsenet is a far cry from the colours you sported in Spain."

It was increasingly evident that he had been involved with someone while on the Peninsula, and that his impaired memory had confused Olivia with that lady and decided they were one and the same. It could have been worse, Olivia told herself, but it was unsettling, none the less.

She was not the only one to have changed her gown. Outside, the air was growing cooler, chrysanthemums and dahlias had augmented the thinning blooms of the roses, and some trees were already beginning to wear golden leaves amid the green. September was here. *September!* And Uncle Haughton had given them until the first of November to remove to East Anglia . . .

Now that Alexis was well on the road to recovery, the two middle sons of the family were allowed to come home. They were fresh-faced, well-bred boys with charming manners, but Olivia could well understand why Mrs. Whitland had arranged for them to spend the summer with her papa. With the best will in the world not to tire the invalid, their elation at his return could not be suppressed, nor would Alexis admit they exhausted him. After several days of their exuberance, Olivia and their mama conferred, and the two healthy young male animals went cheerfully off to the Isle of Wight once more.

Soon, Alexis was up and about, although he required assistance to negotiate the stairs. He was overjoyed when he was at length permitted to venture into the gardens. Olivia was seldom far from his side, her patience and devotion winning the admiration of the household. William spent every possible moment with his brother, and had taken to referring to Olivia as "Aunty 'Livia." Alexis did not question this designation, nor had he ever questioned the matter of his betrothal, but as he improved, his questions about his affianced's family and background became more searching.

They were sitting on the rear terrace one crisp morning, the captain settled into a cushioned garden chair, watching Olivia leaf through the pages of the *Morning Herald*. It was one of those especially magical days that autumn brings: the air spiced with wood smoke, the sky intensely blue, the bright sunlight waking the golds, russets, and scarlets of the trees to a brilliant clarity.

Olivia shook her head over the account of a tragic duel that had been fought by two young scions of the nobility. "How wicked," she murmured. "To ruin their precious lives only because of a foolish disagreement."

"Mmm," said Alexis lazily. "I fought a duel, so Mama tells me. I expect you know all the scandalous details and will have judged me a very frippery fellow." Before she could comment, he went on, "But you must admit, I've since gained some wisdom. I won you. Didn't I, Mistress Olivia?"

His lips smiled, but his eyes were keen. Unable to meet them, she took refuge in the newspaper once more, and replied that she could never have accepted anyone she believed to be a frippery fellow.

He chuckled. "Well done. And what does your mother think of me? I'm ashamed to admit, m'dear, that I have no least recollection of your family."

Her heart skipped a beat. "You met Mama in Lisbon. And you knew my brother for some years. But you have not met my sisters."

"Are they as beautiful as you?"

With a smile she said archly, "Then you still find me beautiful?"

"In a lover's eyes, his lady is always beautiful. Though, I'll own you are not so demonstrative as you were."

Alarmed, she stammered, "In wh-what way?"

He moved very fast and pulled her to him. "In this way . . ."

She'd not dreamed there was so much strength in his arms, and before she could resist she was being soundly kissed. Her heart thundered, her head spun, and jerking away she gasped, "Al-lexis! You must not!"

He sank back against the pillows. "Right as usual, beloved. I must not overtax myself."

She scanned his closed eyes and drooping lips suspiciously. "That is not what I meant."

"Eh? Do you not like to be called 'beloved'?" He

111

looked up at her, his eyes glinting with laughter. "But you did not object in Spain."

Flustered, Olivia thought that this Spanish relationship must have been a warm one. Was it possible they had been betrothed? Or even *married*? Good heavens! If that were so, the lady might present herself on the doorstep at any moment! Oh, how dreadful was the business of deception! And now he was eyeing her in the puzzled way that was so disconcerting. She struggled to regain some common sense, and said unsteadily, "And what if your dear Mama—or William—had seen what you just did?"

"Oh, Mama is, to an extent, broad-minded. And we *are* betrothed, after all. But—Egad! You're never put about because I gave you just a little buss?"

"Just a *little* . . . !"

He sighed. "Yes, I know. My apologies, love. But I am not a well man, and you shall have to be patient if I seem feeble."

"Oh! I did not mean *that*, either!"

"I think," he said with an aggrieved air, "that you are become hard to please, Olivia. Which is strange, now that I recall . . ."

In a near yelp she demanded, "Recall—what?"

"Only that I do not seem to think of you as 'Olivia.'" He wrinkled his brow. "Why have I a vague recollection of a more—ah, voluptuous sort of name? Like—Bellissima, or Aphrodite . . . Was I used to call you so?"

"Not—in public," she managed.

"You are being kind." He looked downcast, and said wistfully, "I suspect the truth is that my mind still plays me tricks."

Yes, but for how long? wondered Olivia in despair. But even if his memory was improving daily, even if the future held only heartbreak and disgrace, she knew that she would not leave Maiden's

Court unless she was revealed for the unscrupulous fraud she admitted to having become.

The next day, Sir Gerald Lainey, who had been in London, sought them out in the book room. Alexis was pleased to see his old friend again, and Olivia was both flattered and moved by the sadness in Sir Gerald's eyes as he bowed to her. He chatted gaily enough, but his conversation seemed forced, his laugh too hearty, and she was relieved that he stayed for only a short while before going off in search of William, saying he'd brought a small gift for the boy.

She watched his graceful, erect stride, and hoped earnestly that he would find his happiness; preferably, with Sylvia. Stifling a remorseful sigh, she asked, "Do you wish me to read to you?"

"No, thank you, Miss Bridge. I wish instead to talk to you."

She folded her hands and waited. He was silent for what seemed a very long time, as if what he had to say was difficult. Once again, Olivia feared that her moment of truth had arrived, and she nerved herself to endure a scathing denunciation.

"Have I done you a disservice by turning up again?" asked Alexis quietly.

She gave a gasp. "What a dreadful thing to say!"

"Is it? Yet of late, you draw away from me do I dare to so much as touch your hand."

This was quite true, but only because his slightest touch made her tremble so.

When she did not speak, he leaned forward, watching her intently. "Is it truth that you were in a fair way to becoming Lady Gerald Lainey?"

"Why—why no! He never really— That is, he did not offer. He was very kind but in a friendly way only, I promise you."

"I doubt Gerald viewed his—kindness—in such a light," he said dryly.

Olivia looked down at the hands now tightly gripped in her lap, and was silent.

"My dear," he said in a very gentle voice, "what is it that so troubles you? Is it Bart's death? Or is it perhaps that you wish me to step aside?"

"No!" Her heart wrung, she met his eyes and found there a look of such compassion that the need to confess, to have done with all this misery overwhelmed her. "It is—" she began.

"Here you are, Aunty 'Livia!" All knees, elbows, and exuberant grin, William galloped into the room, tumbled over Digger, who pranced happily around and upon him, and almost overturned his brother's chair.

Olivia flew up. "Oh, pray have a care!" She bent over Alexis, and scanned his face. "Are you all right?"

" 'Course he's all right," declared William, struggling to free himself from Digger's affection. "He's home and not dead. And he doesn't like to be maudled over, Aunty. Do you, Alexis?"

Alexis smiled into Olivia's anxious eyes. "It depends upon who does the maudling. Aaah! Not *you*, stupid brute! Digger! Get *down*, sir!"

Digger jumped off this ungrateful human's lap, grinned unrepentantly, flung himself down, and fixed a thoughtful gaze on the cane propped nearby.

"Mama said I must let you talk," said William, sitting cross-legged at his brother's feet. "But you're done talking after all this time. So now Aunty 'Livia can tell me the rest of the story about the dragon. You don't mind, do you, Alexis?"

Dismissing some uncharitable thoughts, the captain leaned back against his cushions. "Not in the least. I find stories most—ah, diverting."

Olivia slanted a quick glance at his guileless smile. "I am sure you would prefer to be left in peace," she said. "William and I can go—"

114

"Oh, no you can't! I am very partial to dragons, am I not, Will?"

The boy nodded. "Yes, he is, Aunty 'Livia. We used to have one in the Home Wood, you know. Alexis and me. It lived in a tree, with its pet."

Intrigued, she said, "Your dragon had a pet?"

"Why not?" said Alexis. "Everyone needs a pet. Especially dragons, who tend to be ostracized. He had a pet goose. Who also told stories. Never look so uneasy, m'dear, they were not at all of the—er, barracks' room variety. Only one day the goose told the dragon such a funny story that the dragon roared with laughter and accidentally cooked the goose." He added with a bland smile, "That's where the expression originated, actually."

The qualm of unease that had again afflicted Olivia was forgotten. She restrained a laugh and said severely, "Well, I think it's a very sad tale."

"No, do you? We liked it. But perhaps you're right. I suppose one really should be careful when making up stories. For children, at least."

It was guilty conscience, Olivia told herself, that caused her to keep reading double entendres into his remarks. He was in one of his whimsical moods, that was all.

"Anyway," said William, "Aunty 'Livia's dragon is different. He lives inside a great big wind that turns round and round all the time. Sometimes, he hops out and commands the people to do what he wants. Yesterday he told the king to take the most beautiful princess up on a mountain, and—"

Alexis lifted a hand. "Why?"

"Wait and see. Go on, Aunty 'Livia. What happened then?"

"Well," Olivia lowered her voice dramatically, "it was a dark and stormy evening, and the poor princess was terribly afraid."

"Probably had a fear of heights," suggested Alexis. "I know a fellow who—"

Olivia overrode with determination, "She had a fear of the dragon. But she knew she was the only one who could save her father's kingdom, so—"

Alexis raised his hand again, and inquired meekly, "How?"

"By going up the mountain, 'course," explained William. "*Everyone* knows dragons always want beautiful princesses."

"Whatever for?" asked Alexis, patently astonished. "I mean, it's not as if she was a lady dragon, or that they could have—"

"Captain!"

"Have much to chat about," he went on, blinking at her.

"He didn't want to *talk* to her," said William.

"I wouldn't have thought he would. Knowing dragons. But I don't quite see how he could expect to do much—"

"He wanted to eat her," said Olivia, fixing him with a stern stare.

"Oh, well then, he really was a slowtop. Beautiful princesses are always slender, and I doubt she'd have even filled up his back tooth. He'd have done much better to seek out the fattest female in the kingdom, and—"

William shrieked, and rolled about on the floor.

Olivia choked back a giggle. "And I think that will be quite enough from you, Captain Whitland! Come, William. We will walk in the garden and finish our story in peace."

Still chortling, William jumped up and took her hand.

Alexis stood and peered about for his cane, but it was nowhere to be seen. Nor was Digger. "Very well," he sighed. "Abandon me. But I do think," he appended as Olivia opened the door to the rear terrace, "that you will have to come up with a more believable story next time, Miss Bridge."

Those ominous words haunted Olivia throughout the rest of the day, and long after she had retired she paced the floor of her bedchamber, unable to be still. She saw again his lean face, set in that unfamiliar and grim expression; heard again the words he had uttered in that harsh voice she scarcely recognized. He had not come down to dinner, for which she could only be grateful. Her fears had been justified; his innocently whimsical insinuations had been far from innocent. He had remembered. And, guessing why she had come here, he was enjoying a game of cat and mouse before denouncing her.

Who could blame him? However justified her motives had seemed to her, *he* could only judge them despicable. She had deceived his mother and abused her hospitality by means of an outright lie. When he had so unexpectedly returned from the grave, she had brazenly continued with her masquerade and tried to trap him into wedding a "fiancée" he had never before laid eyes on.

Common sense urged that she leave at once to avoid a terrible confrontation. But she had become so fond of them all. Dear Mrs. Whitland, with her merry optimism and unfailing kindness; William, who had clung to her in his grief and given her his love and trust; and even Sylvia, who had loathed her at first, but now looked at her with gratitude because she believed, as did they all, that her devoted care had helped win Alexis back to health. Alexis. Most of all, that gallant gentleman who had won, first, her respect and admiration, and then, her whole heart.

Through the long dark hours she alternated between weaving impossible plots and surrendering to heartbreak, her misery intensified because she had failed her beloved mama and her sisters. At dawn, huddled in a chair before her parlour fireplace, she gave in at last. She must pack now and be gone before the family awoke. And wondering how to break it to Mama that they were after all doomed to the horrid house in the fens, she fell asleep.

She awoke to find Sarah smiling down at her, and warm sunlight streaming in at the windows. "Oh, my!" she exclaimed, pushing back the covers. "Whatever o'clock is it?"

"Eleven, Miss Olivia, and so soon as you've washed, I've your breakfast ready."

When Olivia climbed back into bed, Sarah set the tray across her lap, and said with a twinkle brightening her gaunt face, "I fancy you'll be wishful to hurry, miss. The master's back, and sends his compliments and can he come up at once?"

Olivia spluttered over a mouthful of tea, and replaced the cup hurriedly. "Back? Did he go out this morning?"

"Aye. And all day yesterday. Slept the clock round you have, ma'am. You must've had a very bad night, for you looked so wrung out, we hadn't the heart to wake you." Again, the furtive amusement lit Sarah's features. "Most impatient to see you, is the captain."

"W-well, he cannot see me now! I'm not dressed." How could she have been so stupid as to fall asleep just when she should have been creeping away? "Good gracious!" she exclaimed. "Who put me to bed?"

"Mr. Curtis carried you to your bed, Miss Olivia. I was here, and it was all quite decent and proper. And you, sleeping like a babe through it all. Why do you not eat your egg? You look fairly starved, and—"

But Olivia's appetite had fled. Denying hunger, she dressed in a whirlwind of speed, choosing the blue muslin gown the captain admired. The day was warm, and she took up her fan with a hand that trembled and hurried to the parlour door. Even as she reached for the handle there came a soft knock, and Alexis stood there, facing her. He looked dashing in a dark blue coat that had certainly been tailored by Scott, pearl gray pantaloons, and gleaming Hessian boots. Town attire, she thought, retreating numbly.

Alexis held the door open and asked that Sarah leave them. When she had scuttled out, he limped to Olivia, leaning on his cane. "I trust you are feeling more the thing today, Miss Bridge?"

His trust was misplaced; she was shaking, and her mouth felt dry as dust. "Much better, I thank you," she lied.

"Good." He took her icy hand and led her to the window. "I've a surprise for you. At least," he murmured, opening the casement wide, "I think it will be a surprise."

Following his gaze, Olivia saw a carriage drawn up on the drive path. Servants were unloading a small mountain of luggage, and William was attempting to restrain Digger from knocking down two dark-haired maidens.

"Isabel!" she gasped. "And—Lucy!"

He bowed. "Your mama is in the morning room. With my mama."

"Oh!" Instinctively, she started to the door. "I must go to—"

He caught her wrist. "No, madam. First, you and I must reach an understanding."

The icy look in his eyes made her shrink. She babbled nervously, "It is very good of you, sir, to have brought them here, but I had not—"

"Asked me? No. But I guessed that was your plan. That they stay here, I mean. Rather than go to Cambridgeshire."

She felt the blood drain from her face and closed her eyes for an instant. "I—suppose Mama told you."

His smile was faint and mirthless. "You forget, ma'am. You told me. In Lisbon."

"You know I . . . did not. Who did?"

"Lainey." He limped away and stood before the empty hearth, watching her steely-eyed. "I could wish you had seen fit to confide in me."

A lump rose in her throat. She bit her lip and mumbled, "I tried, b-but—"

"I gave you every chance. But you would have none of it. I can only conclude that my homecoming put you into an even more, er—difficult position than the web you'd already spun for yourself."

She stood with her head bowed, feeling cheap and wretched, and half whispered, "Sir Gerald knows nothing of that. When did you guess the truth?"

"I didn't have to guess. I may have been knocked sideways for a while, but I hadn't lost my wits altogether, and I knew blasted well that the barque of frailty— I mean that my, er—friend in Spain had not in the slightest resembled Miss Olivia Bridge."

She looked up at that. "Do you say that you knew? From the beginning?"

"From the beginning."

"But why did you let me go on? Why did you not put a stop to it?"

"Why should I? It was most diverting to watch your"—his lip curled unpleasantly—"your devotion. I wondered for how long you could sustain your little masquerade. And I also began to think that Lainey had a colossal gall to appropriate my—er, fiancée. So I decided to give him a run for his money. I must admit, however, it never occurred to me that you might have really fallen in love."

Anguished, she thought, Oh, but I have! I have!

He said, "He is waiting for you in the book room.

Whatever your motives, you were kind when I was ill, and out of gratitude for that, I've told him only that your affections changed during my absence. So do not be in a fret that this will come as a great surprise to him." He limped over to open the door for the girl who stood in white-faced silence, and added airily, "Oh, by the way, Lainey is perfectly willing to provide for your family. And perfectly able. Very plump in the pockets, and a splendid-looking fellow, as I'm sure you noticed. Besides which, there is the title, of course."

The sardonic words seemed to flay her. Blinded with tears, she arrived somehow at the book room. She paused briefly, to compose herself, then went inside.

Sir Gerald turned from the window and hurried to her, both hands outstretched, but his expression faintly aghast. Whatever his inner qualms, he was ever the gentleman, and said warmly, "My dear Miss Bridge."

Smiling, she took his hands . . .

When Alexis limped into the quiet room half an hour later, she was still standing gazing out of the window. He watched her for a long moment, with a look on his face that would have astounded her. Then he enquired, "Will it be proper for me to congratulate Sir Gerald, ma'am?"

Olivia drew a steadying breath, and turned to him. "Most decidedly, Captain."

"Ah. Then your stay with us was not a complete loss, was it?"

She had never dreamed that his endearing smile could also hold such utter contempt. Nor that to find it leveled at her could be so incredibly hurtful. Words failed her, and she fought to keep her countenance.

Leaning heavily on his cane, chin haughtily upraised, eyelids drooping over disdainful eyes, Alexis was every inch the proud aristocrat.

For one minute.

In his agitation, he had failed to notice that his cane had not been improved by Digger's attentions. The splintered malacca snapped abruptly.

With a shocked cry, Alexis sprawled on the floor.

Olivia shrieked with terror and flew to kneel beside him. Sobbing out pleas that he open his (hastily) closed eyes, she chafed his hand and slapped frantically at his pale face.

"Gently! Gently!" he protested.

"Oh, my darling! My darling! Thank God!" gasped Olivia, and burst into tears.

How it came about that she was in his arms while he dabbed his handkerchief tenderly at her wet cheeks, she could never afterward recall. She knew only that she was babbling out her confession even as she clutched and wrung at his neck cloth. "I would *never* have done so wicked a thing," she gulped, "had I not been so . . . desperate."

He managed to loosen her stranglehold, and croaked, "No, but—"

"It would have k-killed Mama, do you see?" she explained, blinking pathetically into his face.

"Yes, but I—"

"If you did but . . . but *know* how frightful it was! To tell such *raspers*, when your dear mama and William were . . . so kind."

"But why—"

"And now—that you should be so—so generous, so noble—"

"I always am."

Thrown off stride, she finished rather uncertainly, "—As to bring my family here, when I have been so wicked."

"*Very* wicked." He tightened his hold on her. "What are you doing now?"

"G-getting up. We cannot sit here on . . . on the floor like—"

"How you do talk," he complained, and silenced her with admirable proficiency.

Dazed, Olivia leaned back in his arms and smiled up at him.

"That," he said, rather breathlessly, "is a great improvement, but it does not solve my problem. I require to be enlightened regarding the character of Olivia Bridge. Is she by way of being an adventuress?"

Her dreamy look faded. "Certainly not!"

"Ah. Would you judge her rather, an incurable wanton?"

"Oh! If you imagine—"

"I am known to be deficient in imagination. Be still, woman! Now, since you hold that Miss Bridge is neither an adventuress nor a wanton—"

"If you are trying to shame me, I'll own I deserve it, but—"

"You deserve everything you will get. Later. However, despite all your outrageous sins and shams, to say nothing of your naughty dragon stories, Olivia—*why* did you confide in poor Lainey, and not in me?"

His eyes held so yearning a look that she had no recourse but to stroke his cheek and murmur lovingly, "Why do you name him—poor?"

"Because he likely thinks he has won you, and I must disillusion him."

"I—er, think you need not," she said, a dimple peeping.

"What? Why you rascal! You let me think—"

"Yes, but—well, he is a very dear man, but I rather doubt he *really* loved me. In fact, I suspect he was secretly relieved to be rejected. And besides, when you came, dearest, you were so very ill and

123

had so much to bear. I just couldn't bring myself to add my burdens to your shoulders."

The light in her eyes banished his last fear. He crushed her close against his heart, and after a little while, murmured between well-spent interruptions, "My sweet charlatan ... Most beloved amateur adventuress ... It is my dearest hope that you will spend the rest of your life allowing me to shoulder— God—*bless* it! Get that confounded hound off!"

William hauled Digger away, and they both joined the group.

"Why do we sit on the floor? Are you telling him a story, Aunty 'Livia?"

"She just finished it," said Alexis, not taking his arm from about his lady, nor his eyes from her blushing radiance.

"Oh! That is too bad of you, when I wasn't here! How did it end, Alexis?"

"Why—the beautiful princess lived happily ever after, of course."

"With the dragon," put in Olivia pertly.

Alexis threw back his head, and laughed. "Most definitely with the dragon," he said.

# MY LORD'S LADY

## by
## Leslie Lynn

# 1

All was as it should be. The stately, hallowed halls of the British Museum were cool and hushed, and vacant—precisely the way he enjoyed it.

*"Laurentian Wilburforce Cranston!"*

The shouted name echoed around him, bouncing off the gilt-framed portraits of England's former monarchs, who suddenly appeared to glare with disapproval at such a disturbance in their august midst.

The mere shock of hearing his given name, which he never allowed spoken, brought him to an abrupt halt. It had been years since anyone had dared to speak it, much less shout it out in this vulgar way. The nine syllables, enunciated just so, reminded him of Eton, where he'd bloodied more than a few noses over just such a taunt.

Both Leticia and Lawrence looked up at him wonderingly. He gave each nearly identical face a reassuring nod before turning to confront the source of such an outrage.

Seated on a stone bench directly under a life-size portrait of Queen Elizabeth was a stiff-backed, silver-haired woman swathed in stark black.

His face muscles shifted from the set-down he'd had every intention of delivering to quiver into a semblance of pleasure.

"Tildie?" He breathed his former governess's name, disbelief holding him immobile.

"Come here to me. At once!" she commanded.

No one commanded the nonesuch, Lord Vane, but then very few would have known his full name or how to use it to such advantage. For just an instant, time fell away. He did as he was bid, crossing the marble floor with the twins dutifully following in his wake.

Tildie's dark eyes were as full of intelligence as they had been twenty years earlier. Only silver hair and the fine lines fanning across her pale cheeks proclaimed the passage of so long a span. Then suddenly he recalled the most astonishing change of all.

"Your Grace, what a pleasant surprise." He bowed over her outstretched hand smoothly. "May I present my children, Lawrence and Leticia."

His son's very proper bow and Leticia's perfect curtsy curled pleasure and pride through his chest. They were children to be proud of.

"Very nice," she snapped at him, while curving her mouth into a peculiarly sweet smile for each child. "However, why are they spending the day in this dreadfully dull place? They should be at Vane Park playing in the woods or riding through the fields. You, of all people, should know that, Laurentian!"

Very properly, his son stared straight ahead as if oblivious to Tildie's words, but his daughter gazed up at him with wide cornflower blue eyes. Her delicate face was a study in awed disbelief. He assumed, and rightly so, that she had never heard him spoken to in just such a tone.

His old governess's leveler didn't faze him, for he expected nothing but her straightforward honesty. Time could never dull the memory of this woman who had descended upon Vane Park and opened up the world for the first time, beyond his mother's stuffy sickroom and his father's somber library.

"The children have just arrived from the country, Your Grace." He returned with just the right touch of composure. "The Little Season is the perfect time to bring the children, as it fits into the course of study I've laid out for them."

"Never did cure you of your obsessive need for orderliness, did I?" she sniffed. "More's the pity. Although I still hold out hope it can be accomplished one day."

Even Lawrence could no longer maintain his proper stoic facade. His set mouth quivered as he slid his father an entranced glance from the corner of his eyes.

A man used to control by a flick of his head, Vane did so now. "Children, there are very fine examples of Flemish art at the end of the hall. Your tutor will be questioning you later."

He watched until they were safely settled beneath three enormous canvases. Only then did he confront Tildie, once a governess, now the Dowager Duchess of Worthington.

"Your Grace, I wasn't aware you were in town yet or I would have been the first to call."

"You will be!" Her normal clipped tone might have put a lesser man off. "I shall expect you for tea this very afternoon. No one else knows we've taken up residence. We only arrived last night, but this morning Georgina insisted she couldn't wait another instant to view the Elgin Marbles. The chit's been keeping me waiting for nearly an hour while she admires them. Just like her!"

A punctual man, Vane lifted his brows in disbelief that a girl straight out of the schoolroom would keep the dowager duchess cooling her heels.

Suddenly feminine laughter drifted around them, the sound sparkling the air like soft notes of favorite music. Vane turned to watch two women hurrying toward them. The taller woman was the younger with a lithe body and the smooth characterless face of inexperience. The older woman barely reached her shoulder. She had luxuriant dark hair framing a perfect, serene, oval face. Large brown eyes and uptilted noses, too short for real beauty, proclaimed the two, mother and daughter.

"I'm surprised the mother doesn't keep Georgina in line," Vane drawled, noticing the elder's features in repose fell into slightly stern lines.

"Good God, Vane, Georgina *is* the mother!"

Vane was mildly surprised. But Tildie's life, since she'd left Vane Park, was a mystery, beyond the fact that four years ago the old Duke of Worthington had suddenly married her. After three years, he'd unexpectedly turned up his toes.

"There you two are at last!" Her Grace's scold was punctuated by an indulgent smile. "Look who I've found while you kept me waiting. Vane, meet my stepdaughter, Lady Georgina Sherbourne and my step-granddaughter, Sabrina."

Lady Georgina Sherbourne's serene countenance split into a wide smile that banished utterly any remnant of sternness; sherry washed through her eyes, and her mouth, which had appeared thin and straight, curled into a lush smile.

"At last we meet!" She stretched her hand out in an all-too-friendly manner.

Her fingers curled strongly around his own as he bent over her hand. She was much too coming. His interest disappeared as quickly as it had come.

"I am delighted we shall have the opportunity to become better acquainted, my lord." That light musical laugh, airy and free, was hers.

Her easy manner contrasted sharply with her daughter's blushing cheeks and demure curtsy. The Lady Sabrina seemed a pattern-card of propriety, an unusual trait to find considering the impropriety of her mother.

He'd received a missive from the dowager duchess about a fortnight ago. It had been as surprising as it was vague. Now, dismay coiled through his chest. His eyes narrowed with a suspicious glance and focused on his former mentor.

She met his stare with the same clear eyes he remembered so well. They had examined him from head to toe that first day as he'd stood dutifully beside his mother's sickbed. He suppressed a shudder; she'd changed his life irrevocably that day—and although it had been for the better, he was perfectly content as he was and needed no managing female to interfere for him now. Not even if that female was Tildie.

"Georgina, take Sabrina and fetch Vane's children from contemplation of those insipid paintings!" The duchess never merely asked, she commanded.

"Of course, Tildie." With another easy smile the lady was gone, hand in hand with her daughter.

"I recognize that suspicious visage, Laurentian. You have nothing to fear from me."

He cocked his right eyebrow and slid his mouth into its habitual sneer. "I'm no longer nine years old, needing direction. Neither am I hanging out for a wife—even one chosen by you, Tildie. As unexceptional as your step-granddaughter appears, schoolgirls are not in my line."

Laughter shook her until her fingers trembled around the silver handle of the ebony cane she held before her.

"Goodness, Vane, you may rest easy!" Her bark of genuine mirth reassured him somewhat. "I have absolutely no intention of making a match between you and Sabrina. I give you my word! Come to tea, my boy. Then I'll tell you what I'm about."

"Lord Vane's phaeton is pulled by the most magnificent grays I've ever seen." Georgina allowed the green velvet drape to fall into place and turned to confront Tildie, who sat stiffly upright upon the settee, smiling beatifically. "Is that why you have me peering out the window like the veriest green goose? To impress me with his horseflesh? What game are you playing?"

"I'm greeting our first guest." Tildie turned her head to the door, evading any further questioning. "Ah, my boy, right on time, as always."

He loomed large in the narrow doorway of the town house, his shoulders so broad they nearly brushed the wood as he stepped into the parlor.

Georgina had heard many stories about the nonesuch over the years, and not all of them from Tildie. But the storytellers had neglected to mention how his deep auburn hair brushed back from a wide forehead, or how his cornflower blue eyes were set in a face that was at once masculine and beautiful. He was an Adonis who should have taken her breath away, even at her advanced thirty-five years. But, he engendered quite another feeling—annoyance. Those magnificent eyes should be lit with dancing lights to match their beauty. And that mouth shouldn't be so rigidly set, making his square jaw unnaturally stern. A man of his reputation held the world in his palm, and should be full of the joy of living. The fact that he was not sent little pinpricks of uneasiness along her flesh.

Georgina resolutely shook her head, smiled brightly, and slid down next to Tildie on the cream brocade settee. "My lord, your grays are quite magnificent." She felt sure an appreciation of his horseflesh would fetch a pleasurable reaction.

Instead, cool blue searched her face. "Thank you, Lady Georgina. They are the best stock to come out of Tattersall's in the last ten years." His deep voice was as chilly as his eyes.

"I'm certain you made a thorough study before you purchased them, Laurentian," Tildie nodded knowingly.

He flicked her a sardonic glance. "Of course, Your Grace."

Those little pinpricks suddenly gained strength. Surely, something, someone, could elicit a response from this infuriatingly superior man. "You seem to know a great deal about horses, my lord," she said sweetly, for she did not give up easily.

"Laurentian is a master at all he endeavors. And you will find he is considered a nonpareil of the first order."

The man didn't even have the good grace to demure at Tildie's fulsome praise! She felt a flush sear her own skin at his calm acceptance—as if it was only his due.

"Of course," she muttered into her teacup, hiding her disgust.

"Which is precisely why Vane will be of such valuable assistance to dear Sabrina."

That pronouncement certainly attracted her attention, but Tildie took no notice of her stunned reaction, continuing relentlessly.

"Laurentian, the reason I wrote and asked you to call upon me is because I require your help. As you can see, Sabrina is not joining us for tea. She is resting. Those dreadful measles that plague the countryside afflicted her this past spring, and she is still not robust. In addition, she is much too shy to gracefully withstand the pressures of a full Season. So we have come now to ease the dear child into town ways." She paused expectantly. "And who better to help us do so than the nonesuch himself?"

Although Georgina recognized the truth, she couldn't, for the life of her, understand why the dowager duchess was laying it so bluntly at this unyielding man's door!

"Darling Tildie, I'm afraid Lord Vane is much too busy to take the time for our slight difficulties."

Tildie frowned at her, and Vane spoke as if he hadn't heard her protest. "For you, Tildie, I would be delighted to assist in any way I can."

That took the wind from her sails. Yet, he persisted in withholding any emotion. If he was annoyed at her thinly veiled sarcasm or bored by the thought of escorting a schoolgirl about town, all was hidden well beneath his calm exterior. Oddly, that made her distinctly uneasy. Never one to hide her own feelings, Georgina set down her teacup and glared at him.

"Splendid, my boy!" Tildie declared stoutly, ignoring Georgina's sudden lack of good manners. "Since Sabrina is not yet out, we can have nothing but small gatherings with family and friends. Yet perhaps you might drive us through the park and just generally make your approval known. Let's say tomorrow, midmorning?"

He never smiled his agreement, but in one fluid movement bent over Tildie's hand, nodding. Georgina had to admit he was remarkably graceful for such a large man.

"Until the morrow then, Your Grace." He executed a perfect leg, first to Tildie and then to herself.

She barely controlled her tongue until he was free of the parlor. She leaped to her feet and paced the faded Oriental carpet in a most agitated manner. "Tildie, are you absolutely sure this is necessary?"

"Georgina, we discussed from the outset the advantage Vane presented. I only wrote him after we had thoroughly agreed on our course of action." Her deceptively innocent tone was not lost on Georgina.

"However, you neglected to mention Lord Vane

134

was so . . . so overbearing and full of his own consequence. Surely that will not serve to put Sabrina at ease. I should think she will be terrified of him!"

"And you, my dear?"

Georgina met Tildie's amused smile and thrust her chin to the ceiling. "I find him annoying. Does the man never smile? He should. His countenance is made for merriment."

Tildie regarded her for a moment before she related, "My fondest memory of Laurentian is the moment he sat his first horse. He took to riding as naturally as breathing. Just as he did to every other physical pursuit once he was released from keeping vigil at his mother's sickbed. But, of course, he continued his studies relentlessly, never ceasing to worship at his father's scholarly altar."

Understanding spilled through her, and her annoyance evaporated away. "I should have realized what you are about." Georgina jumped up, crossed to her chair and knelt, taking one veined hand in her own. "Darling Tildie, you feel your job with Vane is not yet completed, correct?"

The duchess's snapping eyes softened as she stroked Georgina's hair. "Wise child. I should have known you would see through my ploy. I left Vane Park to go to your dear mama because Laurentian's father thought he should have a tutor to ready him for Eton. It is one of the regrets of my career. Now I believe we can all benefit from some time together. There is much to admire in Laurentian. Eventually, Georgina, both you and Sabrina will see that."

Tilting her head up, Georgina cupped Tildie's palm to her cheek. Unaccustomed to seeing a trace of sorrow in her normally bright eyes, Georgina reached for a lighter tone and found her sense of the ridiculous. "Just so long as you are not playing matchmaker for Sabrina. Don't be angry, Tildie, but your Laurentian and I would not deal well together as mother and son-in-law."

Tildie's laughter rolled through the parlor, filling the room with vibrance. "I agree with you, Georgina," she gasped, wiping a tear of laughter from the edge of her eye. "Vane is definitely not Sabrina's match!"

# 2

Lady Georgina waited for him alone, sitting a large powerful-looking roan that pawed restlessly at the cobblestones in front of the Worthington town house. The dashing hat cocked over her left eye and the form-fitting habit of dark blue velvet stood in sharp contrast to the serene countenance she turned up to him.

"Lord Vane." She acknowledged him coolly and correctly, then spoiled the pretty picture she made by rushing on enthusiastically, "Your message arrived, and I couldn't wait another moment to be in the saddle." Light musical laughter filled the quiet seclusion of St. James Square and a brilliant smile transformed her from a proper lady to something of a minx.

For some odd reason that disturbed him. Lady Sherbourne was a jarring note in the otherwise pleasant reunion with his old governess. He would be most happy to assist Tildie in launching her step-granddaughter, but he wasn't completely comfortable with her step-daughter.

Unaccustomed to allowing anyone or anything to disturb his well-organized life, Vane flicked her a sardonic glance, wishing to put her safely in her place.

"You don't ride in the barouche with the others, Lady Sherbourne? I would think you would wish to keep your daughter company on her first visit to Rotten Row."

"Rest assured, my lord, I shall stay at her side every moment!" She met his sarcasm with her own, glaring at him from dark eyes. "And, from this vantage point, I can be on guard for any potential problem."

Her pert answer grated. Why couldn't she voice the banter polite ladies of the *ton* practiced? She *should* be like the other mothers who launched their hopeful daughters, full of charming, insincere flattery calculated to elicit his interest.

But she wasn't.

He took a huge breath of acrid city air as he realized she had succeeded where legions of others had failed: his interest *was* caught, even if, he told himself, it was simply annoyance he felt.

The barouche rounded the corner from the mews just as Tildie and Sabrina descended the front steps, breaking the cord of tension that vibrated between the two, who danced their mounts so carefully around each other. Sabrina was just as she should be, clothed in a demure powder blue pelisse and poke bonnet trimmed with morning glories. Once again, he marveled at the difference between mother and daughter, then turned his horse in a tight circle to the side of the barouche.

"Good day, Your Grace . . . , Lady Sabrina." He made sure they were comfortably settled in the coach.

"Ah, my boy, I see you and Georgina have had time for a comfortable coze. What think you of her mount? Does it meet your high standards?"

With deliberate slowness he allowed his gaze to wander over the horse's lines, then couldn't resist continuing up Georgina's body, to rest, finally, on her indignant face.

"I think he looks a killer. Not a lady's mount at

all," he drawled. "I fear he may be too much for Lady Sherbourne to handle."

"At last, my lord, a subject about which you obviously know nothing!" she snapped. "Shall we go?"

Sabrina looked anxiously from her mother to him, but Tildie controlled the moment immediately. "By all means, let us set out forthwith." The barouche rattled forward, lumbering heavily over the cobblestones.

His gut tightened in anger. He gripped the reins with iron fingers, urging his horse to follow. He had allowed himself to be provoked, something that had not occurred since those first hellish months at Eton. Curling his mouth in disdain at this uncharacteristic lapse, he began a polite conversation with Tildie, completely ignoring the source of his discomfort.

But as they moved through the hustle of the city streets, his gaze slid often to Georgina ... Lady Sherbourne. True to her word she remained at her daughter's side, pointing out all the sights of the city: hawkers selling everything from a dusty mountain of potatoes heaped on the pavement, to cups of fresh "country" milk, to hothouse flowers. They passed a small girl offering large red apples from a basket. She took each out and shined it individually, holding it up hopefully to the passersby.

Lady Sherbourne reined her mount as if trying to decide, then she tilted her head, smiled and waved to the child, before hurrying to catch up with the coach. She bent to say something, very softly, to her daughter.

For the first time he saw Sabrina's gentle smile, and a light flush rose to give healthy color to her translucent skin. From his vantage point, he could see pleasure transform Georgina's face. Obviously she'd succeeded in distracting her daughter. The obvious love and respect the two shared was quite apparent.

Suddenly Georgina glanced up and caught him watching her, but she looked away quickly. From then on, they were both careful not to meet the other's eyes.

Bloody hell! He was acting like a green 'un. Surely he was long past such nonsense!

Resolutely he withdrew into the icy aloof bower that had always served him well.

Fortunately, Rotten Row was well traveled this day. Dashing riders and an assortment of carriages thronged the way and proved a good distraction. He nodded to a few acquaintances and managed a brief salute to a racing rival. Then dutifully, he paused to greet the Countess Lieven and introduced his party.

She lifted her brows slightly in surprise, but otherwise greeted Tildie with her usual charm. The tale of the old Duke of Worthington marrying his deceased invalid wife's companion had been a nine-days wonder four seasons ago, and the countess had an unusually good memory. Vane pulled away from the carriage to allow the women to converse easily across the cart path.

"Vane! Hello!"

Glancing a few paces behind, he spied Peter Amesley. The slight breeze ruffled his classically curled brown hair, but otherwise the boy's appearance was a credit to him.

With a flick of his head, Vane beckoned him forward. When the countess's carriage pulled away, he urged the young man up to the side of the barouche.

"Your Grace, may I present Peter, Lord Amesley, and one of my dear friends." He gestured appropriately, "The Dowager Duchess of Worthington, Lady

Georgina Sherbourne, and her daughter, Lady Sabrina."

Peter studied Tildie curiously for a moment, then his eyes lit in a smile that had caused many a heart to flutter in the *ton*.

"Your Grace, may I be so bold as to tell you how delighted I am to meet the estimable 'Tildie.' " He winked broadly in Vane's direction. "You see, I was Vane's fag at Eton, so was privy to his praise of you."

"Of his years at school I know little, young man. We must talk. And soon." Tildie's voice brooked no protest.

But Vane felt he was on safe ground; Peter had been four years behind him, so had escaped knowing the worst. And, after all, this was what he had promised. He looked to Her Grace and the almost imperceptible movement of her head settled the manner.

"I'm having a small dinner party tomorrow evening, Peter. Very much *en famille.* Her Grace and I have much to catch up on. Join us."

Peter was as smart as a whip and as wild as the north wind, but at heart as pleasant a friend as Vane could wish for. After a brief glance at Sabrina's blushing countenance and a more lingering regard of Georgina, astride her roan, he nodded.

"I look forward to it. And I promise to reveal all sorts of tales about Vane for you." With a grin he was off, mingling among the riders now choking the way.

"Well, Laurentian, I'm sure we'll all look forward to a cozy dinner with Lord Amesley and to hearing about your school days," Tildie declared firmly, settling a shawl over her shoulders.

"An evening discussing my boyish exploits is not my idea of entertainment," he drawled, his words for Her Grace, but his eyes remaining sardonically on Georgina's face.

"On the contrary, my lord, I'm sure the evening will be memorable." Georgina's mouth curled in a peculiarly roguish smile.

"Yes!" A soft voice intruded on their conversation. "Particularly, my lord, if your children will be joining us."

Everyone stared in surprise at the suddenly animated Sabrina.

Noting their surprise, she glanced quickly from her mother to him. "You did say *en famille*, didn't you, my lord?"

"Of course he did! I, too, look forward to seeing Lawrence and Leticia again!" Tildie, never one to beat around the bush, added her opinion. "It shall be quite the thing for all of us. Now I believe I've had enough excitement for one day and would like to return home."

The return trip to St. James Square went slowly, the streets now clogged with the bustling life of the city. The roan was frisky among the carriages and horses milling past, but Georgina kept him under control. Admiration for her horsemanship grudgingly pushed its way into the other emotions she inspired in Vane, none of which he wanted to examine too closely.

Why a woman, albeit a lovely one, who was every bit of his thirty-five years, and who had a bold and sassy demeanor, which he'd always deplored, should stir such deep feelings was beyond his comprehension.

Lost in thought, he nearly missed a look of horror widening her eyes.

Some lout had tipped the apple girl's basket, and was tormenting her by rolling all the apples into the street. She frantically chased first one and then another across the cobblestones, disregarding the danger.

Before Georgina could rein her mount, he dug his heels into his horse's flanks and galloped into the fracas. Leaning over, he plucked the child from beneath the wheels of an on-coming phaeton and swung her effortlessly up before him.

He stared straight at her tormentor. "Gather up every apple," he commanded.

Trembling in fear, the lout did what he was bid. The gathering crowd applauded wildly, nearly drowning out Georgina's gasp of relief beside him. He set the girl, wide-eyed, on the sidewalk, and walked his mount to and fro making certain all the fruit was returned.

Georgina slid from her roan to kneel in front of the grubby child, taking her own handkerchief to wipe the little girl's tear-streaked cheeks.

"Are you all right, child?"

"Thanks to his fine lordship," she nodded. Suddenly she thrust two gleaming apples into Georgina's gloved hands. "For him and you, his lady."

Clutching the fruit basket to her skinny chest, she disappeared with flying dirt-streaked skirts into the crowd.

Sunshine shone full upon Georgina's face, setting off golden lights in the dark hair waving against her forehead beneath her ridiculous hat. Sherry washed into her brown eyes as she gazed up at him. For the first time, he noticed that they were neither stern, nor bold, but soft.

"You saved that child's life, Vane," she breathed with a little catch in her voice.

He shrugged. "These street urchins are a resourceful breed. The child would have saved herself if we hadn't been passing."

Georgina held his gaze unabashedly. Then her lush mouth bent into a slow smile.

* * *

The thoughts Vane inspired as he stood in the foyer, biding them a correct farewell, were confusing. For the first time Georgina noticed his impeccable riding clothes—the superbly tailored black riding jacket showing off the width of his shoulders and the buckskin breeches that molded to him. His Hessians were polished to a mirror sheen, even the exertions of their ride had not dimmed their luster. He presented a magnificent picture.

But it was his demeanor that seemed so jarringly out of place. It was that feeling of distance between himself and the rest of the world that disturbed her so. It wasn't an armor of pomposity at his own much-vaunted importance as she'd first thought. Such a man would not have taken the time nor wasted the energy on the apple girl today.

His beautiful blue eyes were cold, instead of sparkling with life under Tildie's fulsome praise. Even Sabrina's softer words of admiration washed over him, his disciplined features revealing nothing.

"I will send my carriage for you tomorrow at seven," Vane murmured, clearly eager to quit their presence.

She closely watched the well-formed lines of his lips, wondering again how deeply they might curl if he ever smiled. She stared after him as the front door clicked shut.

"An odd gentleman, is he not, Mama?"

At her daughter's gentle inquiry, she removed her riding gloves and hugged Sabrina warmly. "Yes, an odd gentleman, indeed. However, his children seem delightful. Perhaps tomorrow evening we can solicit our stern lord to allow us to play games after dinner."

Sabrina's bright catch of laughter struck a cord deep inside Georgina, and tears pricked behind her eyes. Anxiously scanning her daughter's face, she saw with relief that the last lingering red spots had faded from beneath her pale skin, and her eyes were less shadowed from her illness.

"If anyone can convince him to unbend, Mama, it will be you," Sabrina giggled.

If the man did nothing else for them, at least he had brought her darling back to life.

"I agree, child. Now rest before luncheon," Tildie ordered, but with a slight softening of her usual crisp tones.

Blowing kisses, Sabrina traipsed lightly up the stairs.

"She is better," Tildie declared. "It was the right decision to come here."

Wrapping her arms about her shoulders, Georgina paced restlessly across the black and white marble squares. "So it seems. But I think you hoped to find Lord Vane more approachable."

"What I *hoped* for, was to have my two dearest charges meet at last and become friends. It is an event I am devotedly determined to see happen."

Georgina stopped and stared at her beloved Tildie, feeling the hard beat of her heart against her ribs. This woman had been the bulwark of her life for as long as she could remember. She could no more lie to her than she could fly to the moon.

"Darling Tildie, I'm sorry this isn't turning out as you wished," she said simply, reaching out to clasp her stepmama's hands. "Vane and I ..." struggling for words, she swallowed down a knot of pain that she should have to disappoint Tildie so. "Vane and I do not rub together well for some reason. I wish for your sake it was otherwise."

Tildie's gaze deepened in intensity, her shrewd eyes oddly noncommittal. "Don't fret, dear child. I can wait to see what tomorrow brings."

# 3

On the morrow, a misting rain settled a heavy fog over the city. The day seemed to crawl by until, at last, the carriage conveyed the women to Vane's town house, looming in the vaporous gray, its many windows glowing in the night like monstrous eyes.

Sabrina giggled nervously. Tildie, as usual, swept up to the front steps as if she were the queen herself. In the wide oak-paneled foyer, they were greeted by an imposing butler, who was every bit as stern-faced as one might expect.

Georgina wasn't quite sure what she was feeling. She was happy that at last Sabrina seemed to be enjoying herself. Yet a vague apprehension haunted her. A footman whisked away their wraps before the butler ushered them into a spacious, yet inviting drawing room, its walls hung with a soft rose silk.

That definitely surprised her—somehow rose silk and the formidable Laurentian Wilburforce Cranston didn't seem to go together. The butler indicated a cushioned bench with scrolled wooden sides in front of the enormous black marble fireplace, where a comfortable fire blazed. Both Tildie and Sabrina sank down, but Georgina preferred to stand, warming her hands against she knew not what.

"I shall inform Lord Vane of your arrival."

"That won't be necessary, Foweley."

The commanding tone attracted all eyes to the doorway where Laurentian—Drat the man! Why couldn't he have a normal, pronounceable name? And what did his friends call him?—stood, dressed rather formally for an evening at home, in stark black and white. A large diamond winked blue flames within the folds of his cravat.

He crossed to Tildie, taking her hand for a kiss. Sabrina blushed madly when he performed the same over her fingers. Was it Georgina's imagination that he hesitated ever so slightly before raising her own hand to his lips?

No doubt that odd uneasiness she always experienced in Vane's presence must have caused a little skip in her heartbeat.

"Will Lawrence and Leticia be joining us soon?" she asked politely, eager to break the lengthening silence.

"They will be brought down for dinner. Lord Amesley is a favorite of theirs," he drawled coolly, withdrawing from her side to a spirit decanter set out on a sideboard across the room.

"After dinner, my lord, we would so enjoy spending time with the children," she plunged ahead. "Perhaps a game of blindman's buff?" She met the mocking curling mouth with a defiant smile. "Have you *never* played games, my lord?"

"Of course he has!" Tildie replied with spirit. "Remember when I taught you jackstraws, Laurentian?"

"It is one of my fondest memories, Tildie." His voice was sweetened with kindness. "But I fear Lady Georgina is correct."

His cool gaze made her feel warm, as if she was blushing.

"I've forgotten how to play games. Even jackstraws."

"Jackstraws! By gad, what a novel idea!" Lord

147

Amesley strolled into the room, laughing. "Brings back fond memories of my childhood." He stopped in front of Sabrina and smiled down at her. "Shall we show them how it is done properly, Lady Sabrina?"

Sabrina sent his a fleeting glance, nodded quickly, and then stared fixedly at the tips of her kid slippers.

Amesley's boyish charm cracked the air of tension that seemed to spring up, unbidden, every time Georgina was near Vane. She sighed in relief. Really, this wasn't quite how she had envisioned London—these odd feelings that had jarred her usually jovial nature so dramatically off course.

By the time she had seated herself, out of Vane's line of sight, Amesley was describing his school days.

"I was a bit of a portly lad," he exclaimed with every evidence of good humor.

At this admission even Sabrina glanced up in surprise. Truth to tell it was difficult to believe there had ever been a bit of spare flesh on the tall, lean young man.

"Got teased unmercifully from the other boys when I first arrived at Eton." A deep chuckle banished any notion that he harbored a lingering sense of injustice. "Used to stash food in my pockets to devour later. One day Delacorte found me eating a scone. Snatched it away, knocked me down, and took my store of sweets. By then a group had gathered to watch me trying to wrest them back."

He smiled at Vane standing with one shoulder propped against the mantelpiece. "Suddenly Forry was there. Never spoken to me before; but, there he was, calmly walking into the midst of that circle of taunting boys. Never moved a muscle. Just dissected Delacorte with words. By the time he'd finished, the crowd was on my side. Delacorte was forced to return my food. He never bothered me again. Nor did anyone else." Amesley gave one satisfied sigh and tipped a glass of brandy down his throat. "Never have known quite how Forry accomplished it."

"Quite simple," Vane drawled, flicking an invisible speck of lint from his impeccable coat. "Delacorte was a bore. Still is. No one liked him. Still don't. You, on the other hand, were extremely likable. When presented with such a choice, there was only one logical course of action to embrace."

Only because she'd been watching so intently did Georgina catch a faint shadow in Vane's—Forry's—eyes. Forry. What an unusual name. She'd never heard anyone use it with Vane before. Somehow it made him seem more human.

Truly, who was the man? His nature was a mysterious contradiction; he seemed remote from the world, yet she had seen evidence of his kindness.

"Dinner is served." Foweley stood in the doorway.

Vane appeared anxious to quit the room; he presented his arm to Tildie and swept her out. She followed with Sabrina, each of them taking one of Amesley's gallantly presented arms.

As promised Lawrence and Leticia were waiting, standing behind their places. Vane's son was dressed in a scaled-down replica of his dark formal wear, and Leticia was in a pink frock, which made her cheeks glow like ripe apples.

In fact, to a mother's keen eye, both children appeared flushed. It was a trifle warm in this small dining parlor, and she felt she mustn't overstep her bounds again.

The highly polished table was sized so she and Lawrence were seated on one side, and across, Amesley was flanked by Sabrina and Leticia. Vane sat at one end with Tildie in the place of honor at the other.

Georgina smiled into the little boy's stern face and resisted the urge to brush back an errant curl of red-brown from his forehead. He was so like his father. How she'd love to see him run and play.

"Are you feeling well, Lawrence?" she asked softly.

Immediately he stiffened his shoulders and sat up even straighter in his chair. He looked at her with his father's blue eyes, and blinked. "Yes, I am quite well. Thank you, Lady Sherbourne."

His children possessed beautiful manners, she conceded that to Vane. But, as course followed course, she noticed that both the children merely picked at their food. Even Letitia, the livelier twin, became progressively quieter. And this was supposed to be a treat!

What had the man done to make his children so unhappy in company? Once again, she had to fight to keep from saying something totally out of place. She determined to stop worrying as Lawrence dutifully held her chair when they were finished. Impulsively she reached out to reassure the young man that his manners had been perfection. She touched his hand, then lifted her hand to his forehead.

"Goodness child, you're burning up!" she exclaimed.

"I beg your pardon, my lady," Vane remarked with what Georgina regarded as maddening calm. "Is there a problem?"

"I should say so! Your son is burning with fever!"

Vane crossed the room in two strides and peered down at the boy. "Are you unwell, Lawrence?"

Responding to his father's commanding voice, Lawrence again stiffened his spine.

"I am fine, sir."

"No he's not, Father! And neither am I!" Leticia's high voice caught on a sob. "We both felt ever so sick, but didn't want to miss the party."

Sabrina rushed to the little girl's side and knelt to press a hand to her forehead. "Oh, Mama, Leticia also has a fever."

"A physician must be called at once, Laurentian!" Tildie ordered.

With a flick of his head, Vane sent Foweley hurrying from the room to do just that.

"And these children must be tucked snugly in their beds," Tildie continued with authority.

Instinctively Georgina moved to help, but Vane's cool stare stopped her in her tracks.

"I will attend to that chore myself," he stated simply. Reaching out he clasped his son's hand and calmly retrieved his weepy daughter from Sabrina's arms. "Amesley will escort you into the parlor. I will join you there as soon as I am able."

Feeling rather like a schoolgirl put in her place, Georgina obeyed his dictate as obediently as Foweley had. She sat quietly in the parlor, lost in thought, and sipped the tea hastily brought by a maid. Sabrina and Tildie conversed in low tones in the window embrasure.

The clink of crystal as Amesley poured himself a brandy finally broke the long silence. "Poor little tykes," he murmured, staring down into the amber liquid. "I hope it isn't serious."

"I have my suspicions," Tildie sniffed, turning from the window. "But we must simply await the doctor's verdict. In the meantime, while I have you to myself, I wish more answers about Vane! What really happened to the boy at Eton that he is taking such great pains to hide from me?"

Accustomed to Tildie's straightforward nature, Georgina hid a smile as Amesley's mouth dropped open in shock. Curious to hear the answer herself, she leaned forward as he paced in front of the fireplace.

"Madam, you are just as Vane stated!" Amesley shook his head, a charming smile curling his mouth. "I can't tell you much. By the time I arrived, Vane was well on his way to being the nonesuch he is today."

The quality of Tildie's disappointment vibrated through the room as she stared at the young man fixedly.

Lord Amesley blinked several times before narrowing his eyes. "There was one rumor I recall," he offered in consolation. "It was about Vane coming to fisticuffs. But I never had the nerve to ask him. Still don't," he declared, pinking slightly.

His embarrassment brought a smile of understanding from Sabrina.

"Ah!" Tildie sighed as if his vague recollection had clicked everything neatly into place in her mind.

The parlor doors swung open. Immediately Georgina's eyes flew to Vane's face. It was as implacable as ever, though his skin did seem tauter across his high cheekbones. After Vane came a short rotund gentleman, who could only be the physician.

"It's measles," the doctor proclaimed without preamble. "I've quarantined the house. Sorry for it, but must stop this deuced epidemic! Beg pardon, ladies." He nodded at Vane's stoic countenance. "I shall return tomorrow when the spots will be at their peak."

Georgina could only wonder at Vane's calm acceptance. What was behind his cool eyes as he studied them all? Did he truly feel only detachment, even for his children's plight?

"It seems our little gathering will be of longer duration," he drawled, flicking a glance to Amesley. "I apologize for any inconvenience it may cause you."

"Rubbish, Vane!" Amesley declared, clasping his friend's rigid shoulder. "I've needed a repairing lease. Couldn't have chosen better companions than my godchildren and these delightful ladies."

"Nicely spoken, Lord Amesley," Tildie beamed at him in approval. "In truth, the circumstances could hardly be better. Georgina and I have just seen Sabrina through just such a bout. I'm sure between all of us, your dear children couldn't be in more capable hands!"

"Gracious as ever, Tildie." He walked over to the sideboard and poured himself a generous glass, then set it down, apparently forgotten, and crossed to the fireplace.

To Georgina's searching eyes, he did appear to relax slightly.

"For now, I believe we should retire," his naturally deep voice resonated with confidence. "I've sent messages to your servants. As soon as your belongings arrive, they will be brought to your rooms. Foweley will show you upstairs to the rooms I've selected."

Ever vigilant, Foweley appeared to usher them out.

"Lady Sherbourne, may I speak to you alone for a moment?" His words stopped her on the threshold.

Quickly she stole a glance at Tildie, whose pleased countenance disquieted her. She twirled abruptly to walk back to where Vane had taken a wide, almost defiant, stance before the black marble fireplace.

She thrust up her chin and glared challengingly back at him. "Yes, my lord?"

There was a flicker of curiosity in his eyes. That fact pleased her for some odd reason.

"I wished to thank you, but it seems I can't even do that without irritating both of us," he drawled. "Why do you suppose we can't rub along, Lady Georgina?"

The sound of her name on his lips spun tension between them, making her feel uncomfortably vulnerable.

"I'm not sure," she answered slowly, "but that's of no importance now." The words tumbled over each other with her nervousness. "The important thing now is the children. Tonight could be difficult, I know from experience. I'll sit up with them if you'll allow me."

He shook his head, his gaze locked on her face. "No, I will perform that duty myself. I want to be near my children if they need me."

Not detachment after all. Perhaps there might be a basis for friendship in their odd relationship, after all. Eager to settle her thoughts in private, she nodded once and turned abruptly away.

Foweley was waiting to lead her up the staircase and down a carpeted hallway.

"This is your room, my lady. Your daughter is next to you, and Her Grace is across the hall."

She paused just inside the pretty cream and white bedroom, deciding whether to go to Sabrina or Tildie first. Curiosity won out. Why had Tildie worn such a self-satisfied smile when Vane called Georgina back to him?

She tapped lightly at Tildie's door, then entered without waiting. Tildie was buried in the deep chair that faced the blazing fire. She did not glance around, even when Georgina clicked the door shut.

As Georgina drew closer, she heard Tildie's pleased humming and caught that same look of pleasure curling her mouth.

"Tildie!"

She glanced up dreamily. "Ah, child, how was your comfortable coze with Vane! Pleasant I trust."

Georgina gasped, her hands flying to her throat in shock. It finally all clicked into place in her own mind! Reaction caused her to collapse on the low stool near the fire. "You *are* matchmaking! But not for Sabrina—for me!"

# 4

Tildie eyed Georgina with mild reproach. "*I* am doing nothing. You and Laurentian are handling it quite well yourselves."

Caught in the grip of disbelief, she stared into her stepmama's calm face, for once speechless.

"Darling Tildie, we don't even *like* one another," she finally replied.

"Ah, but is that really true?" Tildie's lips twitched into a conspiratorial smile. "Or are you instead fighting your attraction to one another?"

Stunned by Tildie's unabashed, and hitherto unknown romantic nature, Georgina could only shake her head in disbelief. "I am thirty-five years old—long past the age for such romantic notions. I am too old to fall in love," she declared firmly.

"What utter nonsense!" Tildie's eyes snapped in the firelight. "If that were true, I would never have married your father at the advanced age of fifty and six! Do you know why I did so?"

Was it the chaotic emotions Vane inspired, or the fact she was nearly overcome with glimpsing this side of her beloved Tildie, whom she thought she knew as well as herself, that closed her throat with tears?

"I shall tell you," Tildie exclaimed, leaning forward in the chair. "It was springtime four years ago. We were having our usual game of whist in the parlor, and naturally I was beating your father all to flinders. And as usual he was grumbling." In the dim light Tildie's face softened with remembrance. "Then he looked at me and said, 'Matilda, you are the best cardplayer I've ever met, I don't want to lose you. My daughter and Sabrina don't need you as a companion as much as I need you for a wife."

Her rosebud mouth deepened at the corners. "I looked at him glaring at me so fiercely from beneath his shaggy gray brows, while he absently rubbed at the gouty foot propped before him, and I suddenly realized I loved that man. I had loved Laurentian, and I loved you and Sabrina as I think a mother does her children. But what I felt for your father was quite different. So I accepted his offer. And that is the only reason I did so."

Tildie slid back into the depths of the chair, her face concealed in shadow. "So there you have it! I'm sorry if I shocked you, Georgina. But strong emotion is not bounded by years, and so you should know!"

The tears that had closed her throat now spilled from her eyes. Licking them from her lips, Georgina knelt down to lay her cheek against the soft wool of Tildie's black skirt.

"I'm so glad it was a love-match," she whispered. Against her closed eyelids danced images of her father in his last years, and in each remembered scene he was smiling. "You made him very happy."

Tildie touched her chin with the curve of her fingers, and Georgina raised her tear-streaked face.

"Darling Tildie, I know you love me. I know you wish for my happiness. But I have been a widow for nearly fourteen years." She laughed lightly and caught Tildie's hand. "I may not be too old to fall in love. But I am sorely out of practice."

"I am positive you have the means to regain the ability." The firm voice was the remembered one from the schoolroom.

"Even with a relentlessly stern man who never smiles?" she asked with equal seriousness.

"Answer me this, Georgina. Have you ever wondered what Vane's mouth would look like if curled in laughter?"

It was as if Tildie was privy to her thoughts. Stunned, she didn't answer.

"And would you not like to be the one to bring about such a change," she continued evenly.

At these final words, Georgina rose slowly to her feet. In these strange circumstances, trapped in Vane's home surrounded by his belongings, his children, and ever conscious of his disturbing presence, she was at a loss to answer. In truth, she was afraid to give voice to the vivid, not entirely unpleasant, exhilaration curling through her veins.

"Darling Tildie, I'm not prepared to answer at this precise moment," she said sweetly. "Let us see what tomorrow reveals."

Vane stood in the hall outside Lawrence and Leticia's rooms, gazing through the pane window into the darkness. Dawn was coming weakly, fighting its way through the mist of rain and gray fog, which hung like a pall over the city.

A sound waffling through the open door of Leticia's room sent him immediately to her side. Even in the dim light cast by the bedside candle he could see the shadow of dozens of spots across her rounded cheeks and forehead.

"Father," her whisper was little more than a breath.

"I am here." With one finger he touched the tip of her nose. "All is well, Leticia."

"Are Lady Sabrina and her mother still here?" she asked slowly. Her eyes were heavy with sleep and kept drifting closed.

"Yes, they are here." Wanting to comfort her, he

continued to rub the tip of his finger over her tiny nose. "They shall be here until you and Lawrence are well."

"Good," she sighed, and allowed her lids to shut. "Lady Sabrina is so pretty . . . and her mama . . . has smiling eyes. . . ."

He stayed until the even rise and fall of her small chest beneath the cover told him she slept peacefully. Then he stooped and tucked the cover more tightly around her. He crossed the hall to follow the same ritual with his sleeping son.

He stood again by the hallway window, but this time he didn't lift his eyes to the outside world. Instead, he fought a battle within, against his helplessness in the face of his children's suffering. But he managed to quell the rage with his iron will, just as he had learned to conquer all strong emotion so long ago.

A few hours later the doctor found him still standing in the hallway keeping watch over his children. After examining each child, he cautioned:

"The fever is down. It should vanish once all the spots have appeared. But you must keep them quiet for as long as possible." He gave Vane a sympathetic smile. "It will be difficult to keep active youngsters abed once they are more the thing."

Vane raised his brows in disdain. "*I* shall see to it."

"Of course, my lord!" the doctor blustered. "In any case, I will return at the end of the week, unless you need me before."

Vane, now reassured about his children's safety, bethought himself of his guests. He found them all gathered in the breakfast room.

"You look dreadful, Laurentian! You should seek your bed at once!" Tildie declared frankly. "But first, tell us what says the doctor."

"The fever should break by tonight. But you need not be concerned. I have the situation in hand."

He was strangely touched by the worried faces turned toward him; yet, he had been self-sufficient for so long, it was impossible to let the barriers down. His gaze paused at Georgina's slightly stern countenance. Now her eyes were not smiling—as Leticia had observed—they were wide with a deep crease of concern between them. The expression was appropriate, but he marveled that he missed the sassy wit and bold self-confidence that filled the atmosphere around her with life.

"Is there anything you *will* allow us to do to help?" Her voice was polite, but her choice of words did not escape him.

"Yes, Vane! Can't let Lawrence and Leticia languish in the sickroom without a bit of fun." Amesley flicked him a smile. "Lady Sabrina and I are all set for that game of jackstraws when they are well enough."

Lady Sabrina flushed, but instead of staring down at her toes, managed to give Amesley a smile that indeed made her pretty. Extremely pretty, Vane noted, although she lacked her mother's animation.

"Thank you for your concern, but I shall look after the children myself." Years of control could not be so easily abandoned. Expecting opposition, he glanced quickly toward Georgina, but she remained uncharacteristically silent. He unbent enough to grab a piece of toast from the sideboard. "I shall join you all at dinner and inform you of the children's progress."

It was a promise he had every intention of keeping, but as the hours ticked by, even his iron will wasn't proof against exhaustion. He'd brought a chair and propped it against the wall between the children's rooms so he'd be within earshot. After the doctor's visit and their breakfast, strangely enough, both had fallen back to sleep. After the third time he caught himself nodding off, he sought his own chamber.

He carefully removed his whipcord chocolate jacket and unwound his neck cloth to place it carefully into his valet's waiting hand. Then to Marlowe's horror, he flung himself half-clothed across the bed. Too well-trained to do more than cluck with disapproval, the valet left Vane in peace, closing the door quietly behind him.

Vane stretched and sighed, conscious of the responsibilities facing him. He would close his eyes for a few moments, no more.

As exhaustion overtook his willpower, he found himself in the grips of a powerful dream: He wandered through a cold stone building, alone. Taunts and jibes echoed off the walls, which closed in around him, trapping him. There at the end of the hall stood a group of laughing, shouting boys. He was back at Eton, very small, very frightened, very much out of his element.

The boys surrounded him suddenly, and they pulled his too-long flaming red curls, teasing him. In that circle of hostile faces, there wasn't one spark of sympathy. He had no one to defend him, but himself. This was not the first time they had attacked him, or the tenth, or the fifteenth. But, of a sudden, he determined it would be the last!

The feel of his fist against the first boy's jaw sent a shock quivering through him. The crunch as his hand smashed into the second's nose was terrifying. And a sense of power grew within as he successfully fought them off.

They all ran then, and he ran, too, his breath gasping through his tight hot throat. He ran back through the hallways to his room, latched the door, and grabbed a glass to examine the bruises forming on his face. Badges of honor. He grabbed up a scissors, determined to cut off the hateful curls—but instead, he ran a comb through them, taming them somewhat and only trimmed them slightly.

He shivered with cold and lifted his lids to blink into utter darkness. Taking a deep breath, he remembered where he was, *who* he was. What he had *dreamed.* That day, so long ago, he learned the truth of power— he never gave up his individuality. It was then he made his decision to be the best in everything so no one dare taunt him again. And he buried deep within the powerful emotions that had surged through him when taking revenge against his attackers.

Painstakingly over the years, he had built an icy wall of aloofness. It had served him well. He shook his head to clear it. It still did.

The connecting door to his dressing room creaked open. Marlowe stood in his night robe holding a lighted candle before him. "My lord, you are awake."

"Good God, Marlowe, what is the time?"

"Midnight, my lord."

"Midnight! Why didn't you wake me?" His roar of outrage sent his valet scurrying around the chamber, lighting a candelabra on the mantel and poking up the fire.

"I would have done so, my lord, but the Duchess of Worthington forbade me."

Knowing just how forceful Tildie could be, Vane was somewhat mollified. He nodded coolly at his quivering manservant. "It's done, Marlowe. I suppose Her Grace has also been attending the children."

His valet's relief at the return of Vane's habitual calmness was so enormous, he forgot himself and actually laughed. "Oh, I should say, my lord. The ladies have taken over the sickroom."

He should have seen through their demure acquiescence at breakfast, especially Georgina's uncharacteristic silence. Now, he had no recourse but to accept their help with as much grace as possible.

"Since the ladies have surely retired, I shall be in charge once again. Carry on as usual, Marlowe."

"Oh, but, my lord . . ."

"That will be all!" Vane stalked from the room, still in dishabille.

As they had last night, both children's doors stood open to the dimly lit hall. Lawrence was sleeping peacefully, his skin cooler to Vane's touch. He tiptoed into his daughter's bedchamber and stopped as if he'd walked into an invisible wall.

Georgina, her rich brown hair tumbling about her shoulders, was curled up in the rocking chair next to the bed. Her eyes were closed, the long dark lashes outlined against the cream of her cheek. He stood for a moment regarding her. Then he realized there was a slight chill in the room, as the fire had burned down to embers.

The chair rocked her gently toward him as he tucked a quilted coverlet around her. She stirred, the coverlet slipping down to reveal her night robe had parted. The rules of his world dictated that he not awaken her. In truth, he should remove himself at once. But good manners and a sense of gratitude for her care of his children commanded he not allow her to sprawl uncovered in the chair.

He tried again, kneeling before the chair. As he tucked the coverlet behind her, covering her transparent night rail, his face brushed her soft hair and he felt her sweet breath against his throat.

His grip was all steel lined with velvet as he eased her back into the depths of the chair, away from his warmth. In sleep, her lips were slightly parted and full. He wondered how they would taste against his own.

As he watched, her eyes fluttered open and her gaze met his.

"Forry . . ." She said his name on a sigh.

Desire burned hot coals low in his abdomen. Suddenly her sherry-washed eyes were full of awareness, and he knew she too felt the desire pulsing

163

between them. She shivered, and shook her head slowly in denial.

"Georgina." Unwisely, he reached out to pull her into his arms, to taste those forbidden lips.

"Mama, I . . . Oh!" Sabrina's soft shriek brought them both to their senses.

Georgina, holding his eyes, withdrew into the protection of her coverlet. He couldn't seem to look away either. He jumped to his feet and backed across the room.

Women had their place in his life, he had just moved his latest mistress out of the snug house in Bishop's Woods; but, he had no intention, now or at any time in the future, of disrupting his ordered existence with falling in love.

Gruffly he ordered Sabrina, "I am here now, so take your mother off to bed."

Pulling on the thick plait hanging over one shoulder, she glanced nervously in her mother's direction, but still didn't move from the doorway.

"Lord Vane is right, Sabrina. Come, we shall return to our chambers." She rose from the chair, her heavy hair curved across her cheek, hiding her face.

In the dim light, he couldn't make out the expression in her eyes. Without speaking, she gathered her daughter to her side and defiantly walked down the long hall away from him.

He forced his breathing into its natural rhythm. A lifetime of control would not be lost in one moment of weakness, he decided as he paced the corridor outside his children's rooms. He would conquer these feelings, whatever they were, just as he ordered everything else in his life, of that he had no doubts!

# 5

The effort he took to stay out of Georgina's way for the next three days was the distraction that caused him restless nights, he decided. His preoccupation was so great that he lost to Amesley at cards, something he rarely, if ever, did. Naturally, he blamed this on his excessive concern for his children.

He had limited his contact with all the ladies to the most transitory, so as to not single out Georgina. It seemed to be inordinately easy to accomplish. At one dinner Georgina begged to be excused due to a headache, and the next evening he had urgent business to attend to.

Certainly he was not experiencing any difficulty dealing with his feelings. In fact, if they were all not forced to remain together in his house, he felt sure he would have already conquered—whatever it was that bothered him.

It didn't seem fair that the mere glimpse of her in Leticia's room could conjure up the urge to taste the forbidden fruit of her mouth. But after the debacle of losing to Amesley, he seemed to be unable to focus on anything but these feelings she inspired.

Usually he took what he wanted with cool detachment. In this case, that course of action was not possible. Although Georgina was a mature woman of his world, and he knew from personal experience her counterparts enjoyed liaisons wherever and with whomever they pleased, he sensed that she, for all her bold manner, was not of that ilk. In addition, she was Tildie's beloved stepdaughter.

But even more frightening to him was the loss of his carefully cultivated control. He even went so far, one night in his study, to list the difficulties a misalliance with her would create. For a few hours that exercise reassured him. But on his next glimpse of her, the list, the reasons, all went out of his head. He had not been this emotional since that fateful day at Eton when the cowardly Laurentian Wilburforce was re-created into the aloof Vane.

Vane decided to generate another excuse to miss dinner this evening after the night before when the company dined practically in silence. It was so marked that even Sabrina attempted to break the tension by initiating a topic—the Elgin Marbles—which failed miserably when the others noticed a look that flashed between Georgina and himself. Just as he was about to declare insanity, he was interrupted in his library by Amesley.

Amesley strolled in, without knocking, casually cupping two brandy snifters in his long fingers, attempting to control a monumental grin. "I'm to be the brave one who dares confront the lion in his den," he quipped.

Really this was too much! Lifting his brows, Vane forced his mouth into its habitual mockery and took the amber-filled crystal between two fingers. "What are you blathering on about?"

"Vane, it's as plain as the nose on your face that you and Georgina are avoiding one another. The intriguing question is why." He settled his lean frame in the chair on the other side of the hearth as blithely as you please.

"Don't be absurd, Peter! It does you no credit." Vane tossed the brandy down. Its burn was a refreshing reminder that the world still had some normalcy. He met his friend's eyes. "I assure you it's all in your imagination."

"Mine. And Tildie's. And the little Sabrina's as well." He let that sink in while he fetched the decanter and poured another glass for Vane. "In any case, I know for a fact Georgina's avoiding you. Told me so herself," he declared with aplomb.

Irrationally, that rankled. "How peculiar," Vane returned more tersely than he'd intended. "I hadn't noticed."

"Knew you hadn't. You've been too busy doing the same!" Amesley's eyes sparkled with mischief. "Been friends since that day at Eton when you saved me, Forry. You have my ear if you need it.

"What I obviously need is to better entertain my guests." Downing this brandy he rose to his feet. "Come, let us find the ladies and plan a divertissement. Are they in the front parlour?"

"Last I spied them, they were off to visit your children."

His lips almost curled into a rueful smile before he caught himself. What could be better than to confront the object of his torment than where it had begun in earnest!

The children were bored. They'd been confined to the house for the better part of a week, and a certain restlessness was leading them to tease each other. Georgina, despite her determination to put *him* from her mind, was more amused than indignant over the fact Vane had so carefully avoided her. Truth be told, she didn't want to see him either. And so she had told an inquisitive Amesley when he had remarked about his friend's odd behavior.

Of course, she had told no one, not even Tildie, the real reason she had not been herself since that night. Not even to herself did she wish to acknowledge the feelings that had burned through her blood in that moment they had swayed provocatively close. She had wished for his kiss as much as he had wanted to kiss her. It was deuced uncomfortable that they both were fully aware of it, and both fighting to pretend it had never happened.

Suddenly the ridiculous specter of two mature adults acting like green youngsters tickled her sense of humor, and she burst into laughter.

Leticia blinked up at her from the floor where she sat drawing designs on a sheet of parchment. "I'm so happy your eyes are smiling again."

Taking the child's hands, Georgina swung them to and fro. "You're right! We've been much too glum. I think we should do something truly delightful today, since you and Lawrence are so much better."

"What do you suggest, Georgina?" Tildie asked from the rocking chair where she mended linen just to have something to occupy her time.

"Lawrence and Leticia must decide," Georgina threw herself into the spirit of the moment, anything to take her mind off . . . "You must each decide what is your greatest wish right at this moment."

A wistful sigh escaped Leticia's lips as she glanced out the window at the misty day. "I wish it was summer, and we could have a picnic. I love picnics ever so much. Father only lets us go on them in the country."

Her twin hesitated, still seeming a trifle uncertain of the merriment they had tried to introduce into the sickroom. Finally, he looked up at her. "I would enjoy playing a game of hide-and-seek," he said slowly, as if the treat was beyond measure.

"Oh yes, yes!" Leticia bounced up and down on the rug, her gold-red curls flying. "A picnic and a game of hide-and-seek!"

"Then, so it shall be!" Georgina declared, standing and flicking out the folds of her favorite willow green satin day dress. "Follow me."

Laughing, Sabrina caught Leticia's hand and helped her from the floor.

"Lawrence, escort me please," Tildie demanded, and immediately he presented his curved arm.

They made a great processional down the front stairs, Sabrina making a mock trumpet with her hands and tooting, albeit softly. Foweley came into the front hall wide-eyed. He appeared shaken by her demands, but even he was not proof against the children's gasps of pleasure as they heard what she requested.

"At once, my lady!" he assured her, twirling on his heel to do her bidding.

By the time they arrived in the vast ballroom, two maids and three footmen were moving the heavy carved chairs against the walls and spreading a veritable mountain of coverlets and pillows upon the highly polished wooden floor. Another footmen built up a roaring fire in the enormous fireplaces at either end of the room.

Sabrina had retreated to her room and came now bearing hats or scarves for each to choose, "as protection from the blazing sun."

For some reason that pronouncement sent Lawrence into gales of laughter. Once they were all settled comfortably, a picnic was spread out before them. Vane's excellent French chef had outdone himself to create the fantasy. There was cold roast fowl, slabs of crusty bread, two kinds of cheese, the children's favorite shortbread, ripe red apples, and lemonade.

While they ate, Sabrina and Tildie took turns roasting the children with fantastic tales of picnics they had attended.

"That was ever so delicious," Leticia cooed, snuggling closer to Sabrina, when she was finished.

"Now can we . . . play?" Lawrence asked with a tentative smile.

"Of course we can!" Georgina declared, pushing to her feet. "Would you like to begin, Lawrence?"

Would his father's eyes blaze so brightly if he ever smiled like this, Georgina wondered absently. Refusing to concentrate on such an absurdity, she ruffled the boy's silky hair.

"The rules are: there are no rules! Everyone has to stay in this room, though, agreed? Now we shall all hide as you count very slowly to twenty."

Vane had counted on having his confrontation with *her* now and getting it over with. But the ladies were nowhere to be found, not in the morning room, or the children's rooms. He could feel his tension building, but attempted to remain very blasé as he observed.

"It appears the ladies have unwisely allowed the children to leave their rooms."

Amesley flicked him an uneasy glance. "I'm sure there was a good reason."

Not deigning to answer, Vane spun away. It was one matter for Georgina to throw his thoughts into chaos, but it was quite another for her to upset the well-ordered routine of his home and family!

Laughter, childish and other echoed from the third floor. Without consideration he thundered down the hall and took the stairs two at a time. He flung open the wide double doors of the ballroom, and to his surprise Sabrina spun past him, tripping prettily into Amesley's waiting arms.

"Oh." In a flash she appeared to conquer her shyness to meet Amesley's startled eyes. "I'm so sorry, my lord."

Incredibly, the rakish Amesley blushed, but recovered quickly to ask, "What delights have we interrupted?"

"We are playing hide-and-seek with the children," she replied simply.

Vane stood for a few moments, stiff with shock as his gaze took in the muddle in the middle of the ballroom, including the remains of their sumptuous spread. A thundering wave of anger washed over him as his son, wearing his night robe and slippers, crawled out from beneath a long trestle table at one end of the room. A moment later his sister, likewise dressed, followed him. Their faces were healthy and happy, but he managed to dismiss that thought at once.

"What is the meaning of this?" His roar caused the crystal drops on the chandelier to quiver; even the flames in the hearth appeared to cower.

In three long strides, he reached his stunned children and cupped their cheeks with his hands. At least their flushed cheeks were not due to a renewed fever! Before he could begin to question them, Tildie stepped from behind a long wine-colored drape at one of the tall window embrasures. Silently, she studied him for a long moment.

Her composure brought him up short. A loud creaking noise drew his attention to the large black walnut armoire where Georgina peeped out merrily.

"I guess I wi . . ." She stopped short when she saw him there.

He glared at her, letting go of his children to cross the room and tower over her, menacingly close.

"I can guess whose idea this is. I wish to speak with you in the library forthwith," he hissed through a tight jaw. Not waiting for her reply, he turned away. His retreat was blocked by Tildie, her knowing eyes demanding his indulgence.

"Sabrina and I shall accompany the children back to their rooms, Laurentian," she stated crisply.

Almost bewilderedly, he nodded then fled to the library. Emotion bit at his nerves and he vowed to settle this once and for all!

A long whistle escaped Amesley's pursed lips. "Never seen Forry like this."

"Father is . . ."

"Angry," Leticia finished for her twin. They stood with clasped hands, gazing around in fear.

"Father *never* gets angry," Lawrence uttered softly.

"Yes, it is quite interesting." Tildie declared, taking each child by the hand. She settled her dark piercing eyes on Georgina, who had stood immobile since Vane's attack. "What do you plan to do about it, my dear child?"

Georgina was stunned by this turn of events. Vane's whole air of detachment was gone, and decidedly so. He appeared vulnerable. This turn of events was infinitely more threatening to her fragile resolve to put him from her thoughts.

But she needs must remain strong, not only for herself but for the children. She looked Tildie squarely in the eyes. "I plan to have a long overdue talk with our host, and afterward I shall join you in the nursery."

She swept from the room with her chin thrust to the ceiling as armor. She wasn't sure quite how she'd end this nonsense once and for all, she just knew she had to.

She pulled the library door open peremptorily and locked it behind her. Vane stood at the hearth, the flickering firelight arcing a halo of red in his shiny auburn hair. His eyes had darkened to navy as though to mask the strength of his inner struggle.

She was suddenly frightened by what she was

172

about to do, but deep inside she knew it was the only course to follow. She needed answers, not only for herself, but for him.

She chose to start on the attack. "You have frightened your children over nothing. They have recovered sufficiently to be allowed from their rooms, and well you know it. Your anger is not about something as simple as a picnic and games to amuse your children. You are angry at yourself, and at me, for what seems to be happening between us against our will."

"Your boldness is, as always, charming." His drawl was decidedly pronounced. "But in this case, you are quite correct." He took a menacing step away from the fireplace and toward her. "What do you propose we do about it?"

Slightly unnerved, she took a step back and looked at him warily.

He crossed the room to stand over her. "I repeat, what do you propose we should do about it?"

She lifted her chin and glared up at him. "It seems obvious to everyone that something is going on. And it's the height of absurdity. We are not green youths, Vane. We are both five and thirty. If we wish to indulge this totally inappropriate fascination . . . and kiss, we should do so. It will no doubt be the cure for both of us." At the blaze in his eyes, her voice trailed off to a whisper.

"I'm tempted to put it to the test," he challenged.

"Then by all means let us do so." She gave back as good as she got, refusing to back down an inch.

He stared at her for a long moment until she stoically closed her eyelids. The touch of his hands on her shoulders burned right through to her skin, but she stood unresisting, and waited.

At last, his mouth met hers in a kiss that held her lips with mesmerizing power. It was the practiced kiss of a passionate man who controlled his emotions with an iron will. The pleasures he was capable of gifting with exquisite perfection were merely hinted at.

When he freed her, she stepped away and opened her eyes. Where was she? Panic unlike anything she had ever experienced cautioned her to go carefully. She dared not move, either toward him or away.

"Well, what did we discover?" His tone was a deliberate insult.

Suddenly she felt on much surer ground. It seemed he was as unnerved as she. "I discovered that you are afraid." Pointedly she turned away.

Strong hands at her waist stopped her flight and turned her back to face him. Abruptly his fingers caressed the mass of hair at the back of her neck, and forced her to look up into his glowing eyes.

"I fear nothing," he breathed.

Then he bent forward and captured her mouth in an intimate, open kiss. His lips searched before his tongue daringly stroked her mouth. His fingertips traced down her throat, over her shoulders, to the high curve of her breasts above her gown.

She met his kiss eagerly, and her skin swelled and warmed to his touch as a penetrating throb of pleasure raced through her. With the wall of detachment destroyed forever between them, she glimpsed the deep well of his passionate nature. She trembled, reacting as her own powerful needs were newly reborn.

This answer was so sweetly enticing, it terrified her!

# 6

He feared nothing. Not the incredible sweetness of Georgina's mouth, nor the passion spiraling through his blood when his hands moved to the slope of her back, pulling her lush softness even closer.

He whispered her name against her mouth, while his fingers stroked her luxuriant hair. He heard a soft gasp come from the back of her throat and exhilaration pounded through him.

Dragging his lips back and forth across hers, he coaxed her mouth open.

Her response as her lips met his eagerly and her small body melded into his much larger one, was the most exquisite gift he'd ever been given.

Stunned disbelief burned away his passion. Brusquely he freed her from the hot clinging kiss. Her sherry eyes were wide with shock above flushed rigid cheekbones. Shaking her head, she stepped back in denial.

So did he.

"Gracious me!" she breathed, her hands fluttering to her throat where a pulse throbbed.

He had the oddest desire to place his mouth on that very spot.

"This . . . this . . ." Suddenly she stopped, lifting her chin, and met his gaze with her old boldness. "This *attraction* is not enough to base a relationship upon. Even if we both wished it, which we don't. You and I view the world in quite different ways, my lord."

"So it would seem," he agreed, having learned long ago the most effective way to mask his true feelings.

"Then we shall simply acknowledge this for what it is and go on with our lives."

Go on! How dare she? She'd been nothing but a sword thrust to his peace of mind from the moment they'd met. How, after what they'd just shared, when long forgotten emotions poured through him with such force, could she casually dismiss him? He drew upon his most powerful defenses but could think of no appropriate answer. The nonesuch reduced to speechlessness by a woman, and a bold and sassy one at that.

"Now if you'll excuse me, I'm going to return to the children." She spun about, threw the bolt, pushed the door wide, and ascended the stairs, all as if nothing momentous had just occurred.

Bemused, he followed her with his eyes. After a moment's reflection, he too made for the nursery. With all his well-laid plans in ruin around him, it seemed like the right course of action.

Everyone waited, trying to appear busy. The children had books open in front of them, unfortunately Leticia's was upside down. Sabrina sorted silks with Amesley's desultory help. Only Tildie, rocking peacefully and mending, appeared to have any peace of mind. Georgina didn't even have the chance to prejudice them against him, he arrived directly on her heels.

So he was quite able to see Lawrence leap to his feet and rush to the door. "Are you all right?" he asked anxiously before seeing his father. Then a stuttered, "Oh, beg pardon, sir."

Leticia, ever the diplomat, threw herself into the breach. "Lady Georgina, your hair is ever so pretty falling down upon your shoulders. Isn't it pretty, Father?"

His sweet daughter's attempt to soothe the awkward situation made it all the worse. Georgina suddenly realized how she must look, and guiltily tried to restore her hair to a semblance of order. It was obvious to all, but the children, what had occurred in the library. He could sense their obvious confusion.

Amesley's and Sabrina's stunned looks could be dismissed, but Tildie's triumphant expression was a facer! He'd been a complete fool! Tildie's fine hand was evident in all that had happened. He was definitely at point-non-plus.

Lawrence had to tug on his hand to get his attention. When he turned to his son, Lawrence stepped back and squared his shoulders.

"Father, don't be angry with anyone but me. It was my idea to play hide-and-seek."

When had he become such an ogre to his own children? Pride in his son's fine sense of honor and an overwhelming perception of fatherly love caused him to kneel before Lawrence so their faces were on a level.

"I'm not angry with anyone, Lawrence. I'm very pleased that you and your sister are so much better. The doctor will be here in the morning to confirm your recovery. Perhaps it would be wise if you and Leticia rested a bit now."

The solemn little face cracked in a grin. "All right, Father. But I'm glad you aren't angry with Lady Sherbourne. She's made having the measles fun."

His son's new boldness could no doubt be laid at Georgina's door. He straightened and met her eyes. It appeared she'd not only disordered his thoughts, but his family's as well. Now he must decide what to do about it.

"Laurentian, I wish to speak with you in the library." Tildie's command broke into his thoughts. He watched her rise from the rocker and flick out the folds of her black skirt, a gesture he remembered seeing many times as a child. He had trusted her implicitly then. But now he was a man and must make his own decisions.

Nevertheless he dutifully followed in her wake, eager to confront his old governess with his new-found knowledge.

The lingering scent of the fragrance Georgina wore, a mixture of wild rose and jasmine, still permeated the library. Or perhaps he was becoming fanciful as well as emotional. He took a deep breath, holding it inside, before releasing it in a soundless sigh.

"So, Laurentian, what do you intend to do about this course of events?" As always Tildie was straightforward, her voice lined with steel.

For the first time he reminded himself that he was not her charge any longer. To prove it, he propped one shoulder lazily against the mantel.

"You mean the events that have been guided by your fine hand."

She eyed him with deep reproach. "I shall tell you what I told Georgina. *I* am doing nothing. You and Georgina seem capable of handling it all quite well yourselves."

Conflicting emotions burned in his chest, confusing him. "In this, Your Grace, I must disagree. Georgina and I find ourselves propelled into a situation that is uncomfortable for us and for everyone around us. You would have served us better by not trying to manage our lives." This, he realized, was as close as he'd ever come to criticizing her.

Nonplussed she stepped closer, and by habit he straightened to rigid attention.

"I suppose I managed to have your children come down with the measles so we were all thrown willy-nilly together! I have never *managed* you, Laurentian. I only presented opportunities for you to experience life more fully. My regret is that I left before you went to Eton. If I had been there, I'm sure things would have been different. I would have spared you whatever torment caused you to turn from the path I'd set you upon to this rigid, unyielding person you've become. It isn't right, Laurentian. You're missing all the good things life has to offer—and for what? For fear of failure? Criticism?"

Reaching one thin blue-veined hand, his old governess smoothed his hair off his forehead. "Almost I understood your mother's love of your beautiful ringlets, however inappropriate. I know they must have cost you dear." Stiffening her back, Tildie dropped her arm and stared at him.

Shrugging, he curled his mouth into a mocking smile. "Don't pity me, Tildie. I became exactly what I wished to be and have ordered my life the same way. There's much to be said for detachment and control. Look how far it's brought me. It serves me well, and I can't imagine changing now."

"But you have lost your sense of joy. And without change and growth, life becomes strangely flat." A gentle note crept into her voice. "That is what draws you to Georgina, you know. Her joyous, bold spirit. The way life just seems to sparkle around her. Yet, she had lost her ability to be in touch with her deeper feelings. And you. You are so in touch with yours, you must throw up barriers lest they break out and consume you! Together I should think you would both be more complete."

"I did not plan to ever fall in love!" The words spilled out unbidden. He made a prodigious effort to regain his disintegrating composure by lifting his brows in disdain. "Although I honored the children's mother, our arranged marriage fit into the well-ordered flow of my life. There is nothing well-ordered about the emotions Georgina inspires."

"Ah, Laurentian, I can tell you from experience one never plans to fall in love. The process is not well-ordered, but it is joyous beyond your wildest expectations. Would that both you and Georgina experience it!"

The children had settled down for a nap. Georgina had straightened the nursery while avoiding, as best she could, Sabrina's thinly disguised questions about what had happened in the library earlier. Amesley was either too well-bred, or he was trying to melt into the woodwork so she would so far forget herself as to let something slip. The longer Tildie and Forry's conference went on, the more nervous she became. She decided to take all the books off the nursery shelves, dust and alphabetize them. Anything to keep her mind off what was transpiring in the room below.

She was momentarily diverted as she watched her shy daughter blossoming under Amesley's kindness. They had settled, finally, on a hand of whist and were amicably battling over Amesley's new and unorthodox rules. Tildie had been right to suggest they acquaint Sabrina with some town bronze before her come out next spring. But was Tildie right about other things?

Common sense finally prevailed. She was not seventeen again, waiting for her father and Lord Sherbourne to decide her fate! It wasn't up to Tildie, or Forry, for that matter. She marched downstairs to the door where she took a deep breath before pushing it open.

"Would that both you and Georgina experience it," Tildie was saying, as she gazed solemnly into his face.

Georgina was momentarily stunned. "Experience . . . what?" she asked in a bright little voice that reflected nothing of the tumult taking place within her.

It seemed as if she had interrupted at a bad moment. Tildie appeared somewhat disconcerted, while Forry had his walls firmly back in place. Could this cool, apparently heartless, man be the one who had kissed her with such fire that she had been shaken to her very roots?

Stung by his reversal, her burning emotions twisted into one enormous mass of anger.

"I am a woman, of five and thirty, although I confess I haven't been conducting myself as such. However, I have come to my senses, at last. I feel I should be the one discussing this situation."

"Say no more!" Tildie smiled, gliding over to gently pinch Georgina's chin. "Wise child, remember it is never too late to embrace your feelings."

Again, they were alone in the library. The very walls seemed to shout at her, reminding her of their last encounter. And *he* was no help! His relaxed stance and air of quiet confidence disturbed her even more, for *her* body was betraying her by trembling with the remembered emotions he had ignited in this very room not an hour before.

"Georgina, I hold myself responsible for everything that has occurred between us. Although it is obvious I desire you, I bow to your wise observation that we are ill matched."

His voice was gentle, but there was a curious trace of sadness. A woman's instinct reassured her that his stronger emotions were being held firmly in check. Drat the man!

Her pulse suddenly pounded through her veins, one beat hot, the next cold, until it was difficult to order her breathing. Salty tears stung the back of her eyes. Blinking rapidly, she faced him squarely, giving no quarter and asking none.

"I fear, my lord, I am more curious than you to explore where these emotions could lead us." Half mocking, she laughed at herself. "I am not brave enough to hear what you find lacking in me, but I must tell you that were it not for the fact you live your life without a sense of joy . . ." She fought for words. "If you ever smiled, my lord, I might be so bold as to entice you to reconsider. So it is fortuitous that the doctor arrives tomorrow. He will no doubt release us. Then we shall bid one another farewell."

It seemed a great waste to leave him with so much unexplored between them, but she feared it would be tragic for them both if she did not. Common sense and newly awakened desire danced a strange waltz in Georgina's mind. Common sense won out, as it always had.

She quietly let herself out of the room. It was of course the wisest, most prudent course of action, she told herself as she trailed slowly up the stairs to her room.

Vane watched her walk away. With each step she took, her shoulders bent a little. By the time she reached the landing, all the joy seemed to have disappeared from around her. He allowed her to go, although the words to stop her nearly burst from him. But he held them in; that was his way.

Across the room was a small mirror where once a day so long ago his father had stood him. Examine your life he'd said. Are you learning all you can? He sought it out now.

Are you learning all you can? What did he really know of life. It seemed for thirty-five years he'd just been going through the motions. In the dim light his reflection hadn't changed much. But suddenly he knew, he had. It was time to let go of all that had happened in the past. It was time to forge a new beginning for himself. Did he have the courage to do it?

And more importantly, could he ever convince Georgina to be a part of it?

# 7

"Remember, it is never too late to embrace your feelings."

Although Tildie's words had been directed to Georgina, they now echoed through Vane's head. Georgina entered the morning room dressed in a particularly elegant cream cambric morning gown, and he felt as if the sun came in with her.

The doctor was abovestairs giving the children a clean bill of health, and instinctively they had gathered together to await his news.

Georgina glanced in his direction, and nodded a good morning, avoiding his eyes completely, then took a seat near Tildie, who was pouring coffee. That odd disquiet he always felt in her presence was recognizable at last as a deep yearning. With her bold and forthright manner, she had opened him and his children to an honest freedom of feeling. But the habits of a lifetime were impossible to change in a day. Although he could no longer deride that easy style, the vivacity she brought to bear on all she did, he was not yet at ease with acknowledging his own deep feelings.

At this moment, watching her animated face as she conversed with Tildie, catching the musical whisper of her laughter, his safe icy bower, from which he'd looked down on the rest of the world for so long, seemed meaningless. He wanted to be a part of things again.

He actually took two steps toward her when the doctor was announced, Leticia and Lawrence right behind him.

"My lord, I'm pleased to say the children have done extremely well due to your excellent care. On the morrow, the quarantine will be lifted."

The silence that followed his happy announcement appeared to bewilder the man. "Is something amiss, my lord?"

Vane could only wonder what the rest of the company was feeling. He, himself, felt a sense of urgency. Something must be done, and quickly, to keep Georgina here. "No. Thank you, doctor, for your happy news. Foweley will see you out."

Flicking a curious glance about the room, he bowed to the ladies and quickly departed.

"This will be our last night together!" Leticia wailed, breaking the heavy silence. She ran to Sabrina and clung to her skirts. "I'm going to miss you ever so much."

"Me, too!" Lawrence, always a model of deportment, forgot himself so far as to sit, uninvited, next to Georgina on the couch and lean into her confidingly.

"We have tonight! Let's make the best of it!" Amesley forced a hearty chuckle. "What say you, Forry? Shall we let the children decide on a bit of fun."

A light dawned. Perhaps Peter had inadvertently given him an opportunity. There was only one answer.

"I shall plan the festivities for tonight."

His pronouncement brought a range of reactions, none flattering: Sabrina and Amesley shared a speaking glance, the children appeared crestfallen, and even Tildie pursed her mouth in a moue of speculation. Georgina just stared at him wide-eyed, her expression an intriguing mixture of vulnerability and apprehension, but perhaps just a glimpse of hope.

"I shall plan the festivities," he repeated. "Lawrence and Leticia will assist me. We will summon you all when we are ready."

Both children squealed with pleasure. He held out his arms, and they rushed to his side. As they strolled hand in hand from the room, he could feel Georgina's warm gaze, and he could hear the faint crackling of his icy bower as it fell into pieces around him; freeing him.

"Egad, Forry surprises me!" Amesley looked as bewildered as she felt. "This is not in his style at all."

"Laurentian may surprise us all before this day is over," Tildie stated cryptically.

Sabrina's brilliant smile radiated delight. "I think it is marvelous he asked the children to help, don't you, Mama?"

Every one of them seemed determined to push her in a certain direction. She gazed at each rapt face in turn, hesitant to disappoint them, yet so uncertain of the future.

"I must confess I, too, am on pins and needles contemplating what may be in store for us. This Little Season has held nothing but surprises so far." There, she hoped that was optimistic enough without giving herself completely away.

"I think it has been wonderful!" Sabrina danced about the room, finally stopping in front of her. "London is not at all the terrifying place I imagined. And if everyone is as kind as Lord Amesley and Lord Vane, even for all his sternness, then I eagerly await my Season."

"I predict you shall be all the rage, Sabrina," Amesley replied with gallantry.

Beaming at him, Sabrina shrugged. "It matters

not, my lord. Regardless, I plan to enjoy myself to the fullest."

Admiration flared in his eyes. Unbelievably, Georgina watched Sabrina favor him with a dimpled smile. Her shy daughter had come a long way in these past few days, and no doubt the gallant young man across the room had everything to do with that. She caught a speculative glance in Tildie's dark eyes, and could nearly see the wheels turning in her active mind. But it was way too soon to be thinking of bridals for Sabrina. She had months to plot a happy ending for her, but only hours to make a decision about her own future.

She had practically worn a path in the cream carpet of her bedroom when the knock finally came on her door. Still it startled her, and she paused, not ready to face what came next.

She had declared them a mismatch—his stern correctness was annoying, his cool air of detachment too heavy a barrier to break through. Yet the tingling sensation of awareness she felt in his presence and the pleasure his mouth and hands had awakened in her could not be ignored. She considered herself a strong woman who had always known her own mind, but now she stood, buffeted by doubt.

What would be gained, what lost, by throwing her bonnet over the windmill, and following the dictates of her heart?

The second knock was louder and a childhood tattoo. Dum dah de dum dum. It couldn't be him! She rushed to the door and flung it open.

Lawrence stood at stiff attention, although his face was split in the widest grin she'd ever had the pleasure of seeing.

"Lady Sherbourne, I have come to escort you to our party."

He offered his arm, this miniature of his father, and she took it, glad for the moment of respite.

"What kind of party have you arranged?" she asked, burning with curiosity and a strange premonition.

Little flames of excitement lit his eyes to a brilliant blue. "It's a surprise!"

Surprise was mild compared to her feelings. She came up short in the ballroom doorway. Stunned, she gazed around the room in disbelief at the changes he had wrought. The others were already seated on thick coverlets spread upon the floor.

They were to picnic again, but tonight they would do so in a bower of loveliness. Trees in tubs from the greenhouse were placed strategically about the room; pots of flowers—roses, pinks, and cornflowers formed a meandering pathway through them.

Leticia had a lap full of yellow and white flowers. Somehow Vane had conjured up daisies! She was busily wreathing crowns for everyone.

Moonlight filtered in through the long windows bathing the room in fairy silver. She had eyes for no one but Forry. Tonight he wore no cravat and his shirt lay open at his throat. He stood under a young birch, propped in a characteristic pose, but his eyes were full of questions.

Instinctively she knew he had done this all for her. He wanted to prove he appreciated the life she had brought into his household, the joy she had restored to him and his children. She marveled at the depth of his understanding of her fears.

"Now that you have arrived, we can begin," he drawled, motioning her to sit beside Tildie, who was wearing an expression like a cat who had just licked clean a saucer of cream.

Georgina was content to watch him quietly orchestrate, by just a flick of his hand, a picnic feast beyond perfection. Each course was carried in on a silver platter—smoked salmon, roast partridge, sweetmeats. Champagne was served in the finest

crystal; Leticia and Lawrence drank their lemonade in a toast to many more picnics. Innumerable
removes followed, in fact she lost count, for she
found she wasn't really hungry at all. After a laugh-
filled hour, it was time for dessert.

A footman carried in an enormous covered platter. Even the children couldn't guess what delight
might be in store. He lifted away the cover to reveal a simple bowl of apples.

There was a collective breath of disappointment
from everyone but her. Looking at the red fruit, she
was reminded of the day he had saved the little
apple girl—perhaps that was the moment her feelings had first softened toward him. Had he felt
something special that day, too? It seemed so long
ago.

She lifted her eyes and found his gaze resting on
her face. More relaxed than she'd ever seen him,
sprawled across a blanket on his side, he looked so
vital, so desirable, she felt her heart skip a beat.

Without a glance at the others, he said softly,
"Now the games shall begin," never taking his eyes
off her face.

A great wash of pleasure crashed over her, causing her limbs to feel like loose strings. If Lawrence
hadn't helped her to her feet, she wasn't certain she
could have stood.

"We are playing hide-and-seek," Lawrence announced importantly. "I choose Lady Sherbourne to
hide."

"And Father will seek!" Leticia chimed in, nearly
quivering with excitement.

He covered his eyes, with a great show of reluctance, and began to count.

Her heart was pounding, her insides a whirl of
fearful anticipations. Bemused, she could think of
nowhere but the cabinet where she had hidden once
before.

Between his spread fingers, he watched Georgina step into the cabinet.

"Father has a surprise for Lady Sherbourne, so we must leave them alone now," Lawrence whispered with great importance.

"Yes, we must wait for them in the parlor," Leticia added, urging Tildie and Sabrina and Amesley out.

Although Amesley appeared nearly overcome with laughter, something he would pay dearly for later, Vane realized his plan was working to perfection. He met Tildie's dark eyes, and she nodded approvingly.

He heard Leticia whisper, "Do you think you might become my real sister, Lady Sabrina? I'd like that ever so much," before the ballroom doors were securely shut.

His daughter's fledgling female instinct had honed in on his own desire. It might not be easy to capture this new zest for living, but he would try. No, for the prize Georgina presented, he would do anything and succeed! It seemed incredible, but there the thought was clear in his mind—there was nothing he would not do to win her. Love, he discovered, *was* the most powerful emotion after all.

He picked up an apple and weighed it in his fingers. Juggling it carefully in one palm, he strolled to the cabinet and slowly opened the door.

Georgina's heart leapt to her throat and stayed there, sending hot excitement coursing through her at his appearance in the narrow opening. He was haloed by the firelight. She couldn't help but notice what beautiful coloring he had; the vibrant auburn of his hair, his gold skin where it disappeared enticingly into his open shirt, the brilliant blue of his eyes, and his dusky sensuous mouth. There were no barriers between them now.

Suddenly he lifted the apple to his mouth and bit into it.

"Forry, what is going on?" Was that really her voice, so sparked with fearful delight?

"As Adam said to Eve. Take a bite and discover for yourself," he drawled and offered the apple to her.

"It was Eve to Adam, as you very well know!"

In this instance, she fully understood what Tildie had tried to tell her. She looked at him and knew she loved him. She loved him, and she would not waste another precious moment!

Trying vainly to control a strong inner trembling, she took the apple from his hand and bit into it. Licking the sweet juice from her lips, she slowly placed the apple back into his hand.

With a bark of laughter, he tossed it over his shoulder. Then he stepped into the cabinet with her.

There was room for two only as they stood so closely her body ached with the contact and her tense muscles yielded eagerly to his. Desire sprang up between them like a palpable force. She had wondered what his mouth would be like if the long sensuous lines ever deepened at the corners in a real smile. Now witnessing it, pleasure burst like bubbles through her veins, making her giddy.

Raising her hand, she ran her fingertips over his warm lips. "You have a beautiful smile," she breathed in a dreamy voice that sounded scarcely like her own.

"You make me want to smile, Georgina. What do you think we should do about that?"

There was only one answer.

She reached both arms around him and pulled the cabinet door closed.

# PETTICOAT HALL

## by
## Joan Smith

# 1

Lord DeSale tossed the latest copy of the *Morning Observer* aside in disgust and rang for his butler, Hawker.

"Send Lord Rawden to me, at once," he said grimly.

The butler scuttled upstairs to inform his lordship that his papa was in a rare pelter, and if he knew what was good for him, he would mind his *P*'s and *Q*'s. Hawker found Lord Rawden just finishing his morning toilette. Half a dozen spoiled cravats were tossed on the bed. Young Rawden was a high stickler where his toilette was concerned.

His barbering was a veritable work of art. A cap of sable hair was brushed artfully forward in the stylish Brutus hairdo. Faint smudges beneath the dark eyes marred an otherwise handsome face. There was nothing rugged in its fine sculpturing, yet his broad shoulders and athletic build spoke of the Corinthian.

Undismayed by his papa's summons, Lord Rawden allowed his valet to assist him into a superbly tailored jacket of blue Bath cloth. He gave a final pat to his Oriental cravat before glancing down at his highly polished Hessians. Unless he could see his own reflection in their glistening toes, they would be returned to his valet for further application of Kelly's boot black. They passed inspection on this occasion. Rawden concurred with Beau

Brummell that a gentleman should make his toilette with the greatest care, that he might forget it once he left his dressing room.

"Have you any notion what is to be the subject of this morning's scold, Hawker?" Rawden asked the butler.

"His lordship was reading an account of the curricle race to Brighton in the journal, along with the size of the bets."

"Did it mention that I *won* five hundred pounds?"

"You might as easily have lost. There was a full account of the carriage you overturned as well."

"*I* overturned?" Rawden asked, his eyes wide in astonishment. "You wrong me, Hawker. Every way you wrong me. It was Devlin who overturned the ladies' rig. If that cowhanded Lady Montrose had not been handling the ribbons herself, it would not have happened. The lady was not much damaged. I saw her at the theater last night."

"Be that as it may, your name is included among the participants. His lordship particularly wanted you to attend Parliament yesterday afternoon. They were voting on his bill."

"Damme, so they were. It slipped my mind. No matter, Hawker. I shall turn him up sweet." The butler turned to leave. Lord Rawden called after him, "Thank you, Hawker. It is kind of you to have warned me."

Hawker just shook his head. He had been keeping an eye on young Rawden for so long, it was second nature to him. There was good stuff in the lad; it was just his high spirits that led him astray. If only his Papa would be a little patient. Naturally a young buck wanted to sow a few oats before settling down. Mind you, Rawden had been sowing his wild oats for some few years now. He was nudging thirty. Small wonder that his papa was becoming impatient.

When Lord Rawden entered his father's study, he knew instinctively that the usual paternal impatience had given way to fury. He was not greeted by the customary fiery eye or hot tongue, but by a new coldness. He was not even invited to sit down, but received his scold standing up.

"It is time you settle down, Charles," Lord De-Sale said.

"I am sorry I missed the vote yesterday, Papa."

His father waved his hand dismissingly. "One vote more would have made no difference. The Tories were bound to vote my bill down. No, I am referring to this curricle race, which you considered more important than the affairs of the country. I have been too lenient with you, Charles. I have decided it is time you marry. There is nothing like a wife and family to settle a man down."

"You know I have been looking about for a wife, Papa."

"You are not likely to find a suitable one at Lady Oxford's place," he snapped. "A divorcee!"

"A *Whig* divorcee!" his son reminded him.

DeSale ignored this piece of impertinence. "I met a suitable young lady at Bath last winter. The Campbells are connections of ours on your late mama's side, God rest her soul."

"Campbell? I do not recognize the name."

"Nor did I, but I met the ladies at a rout party and was struck with their eligibility. It transpired during the course of conversation that we are connected. They reside at Petty Coomb Hall, in Berkshire. The elder gel would be the better match. Miss Campbell inherited the Hall, as there is no son. The younger chit would be more in your line, however. Quite a beauty, I promise you, but not one of these wayward misses. She is well behaved, wellborn, and has a dot of ten thousand. You will marry her."

His son stared in disbelief. "Sight unseen?" he asked.

"*I* have seen her. She is suitable. You have loitered long enough, Charles. I have this morning written to Miss Campbell informing her that you will pay them a visit within the fortnight. She is clever enough to know why you are going. I expect you to make the younger gel an offer. Miss Bonnie, and a bonnie lass she is, too."

Lord Rawden felt the first stirring of panic. There was no arguing with his papa when he was in this mood. It was the mood that had sent him to Oxford when he wanted to attend Cambridge. It was the mood that had prevented him from joining the army to fight Bonaparte, and it was the mood that would see him married to a lady he loathed, unless he kept his wits about him.

"I think you should know, sir, that it was not I who overturned Lady Montrose's rig yesterday," he said.

"No matter, Charles. You were there, taking part in the shameful affair when you should have been in the House. I have let you talk me out of all the excellent matches I have been at pains to arrange for you. If you end up with a provincial miss, it is your own doing."

"But I can arrange my own match. Miss Lombard—"

A scathing eye raked Lord Rawden. "Miss Lombard has made herself a byword for shameless carrying on. I swear the hussy was tipsy at Sir Giles Mason's dinner last week. No, I have decided you will marry Miss Bonnie Campbell. They will be expecting you in mid-October. Prepare yourself for the trip."

"You are quite right, Papa. Miss Lombard would not do. Lady Anne Tilson is much more—"

"Lady Anne accepted an offer from Southam last

week. Of course, *you* would not know what is going forth in *polite* society. Good day, Charles."

Lord DeSale picked up a pen and pulled forward a sheet of paper. Lord Rawden opened his lips to issue further objections, then closed them again. He would wait until Papa was in a better mood. There was no talking to him when he sat like a gargoyle, shuffling papers.

Rawden went to the saloon to pace to and fro. Miss Bonnie Campbell. He thoroughly disliked the lady even before laying an eye on her. She would be one of those redheaded Scottish antidotes with spots and butter teeth. A provincial in a round bonnet and dowdy gown. Good God! He'd be the laughingstock of London.

Over the next week, he tried various ruses to change his papa's mind. Two boring afternoons in the House, listening to the childish goings-on there, did him no good. Staying home one evening and asking his papa if he would like a game of chess was met with a lowering brow.

"Should you not be preparing for your trip to Petty Coomb Hall?" was the cool reply. "I have received a reply from Miss Campbell. She looks forward to seeing you at Petty Coomb soon."

It was on Saturday of that same week that Soper, Rawden's sharp-eyed valet, spotted an advertisement in the journal for a butler for Petty Coomb Hall in Berkshire. "Ain't that where we're going?" he asked.

Rawden scanned the advertisement, and as he read, an unholy scheme entered his inventive head. "That is where *you* are going, Soper. You see the ladies are not coming to London to interview prospective butlers, yet they want a man with experience in a noble household. They'll not find many willing to remove to the wilds of Berkshire. They will leap at such a fine fellow as yourself. Lord Devlin will give you an excellent character."

"I've never buttled!"

"You were born and bred in my father's house. You know Hawker's duties. It will only be for two weeks."

Rawden studied his valet and saw no reason why a butler could not be a well-built fellow with a sharp nose and snuff-colored hair.

"What is the point of my going as butler?" Soper asked. "I could help you pull off your pranks as well in my natural position of valet."

"You misconstrue the matter, Soper. I shall not be there for most of the time. I shall be delayed until late October, and in the meanwhile, it will be your foremost duty to give the ladies a disgust of me. I shall hire a room at Minden, the closest village to Petty Coomb Hall, to keep in touch with you. Blacken my character until no sane female would let me within her door. Then, when you have dyed me in deepest pitch, I shall appear in person, behave obnoxiously, and make my offer for Miss Bonnie. What can Papa say when I have made an offer and been rejected?"

"Damn-all," Soper said, his lips stretching to a grin.

"I shall write the letter for you, along with my own note to Petty Coomb delaying my visit. I shall tip Devlin the clue he must give you a character if Miss Campbell applies to him. We shall use a pseudonym for you. Who would you like to be?"

"I'd like to be you. Seems to me you have a good time."

"Lord Rawden is not likely to be applying for the position of butler, however. Use your noggin, Soper."

"Call me Mr. Charles, then. Your Christian name."

"Very well, if it amuses you."

"I foresee one problem," Soper said. "Who is to tend your wardrobe in the meanwhile?"

Rawden shrugged. "The inn at Minden will do my laundry and polish my boots. No one who matters will see me, so I need not worry for my reputation. I can write to Papa from there, and you, as butler, will intercept any letter Papa might write to me at Petty Coomb."

"I'll give her a go if you say so," Soper said reluctantly, "but something is bound to go amiss."

"Nonsense! The plan is foolproof. Now, let us write your letter of application."

Soper was hired as butler. Miss Campbell wrote Rawden a note agreeing to the postponement of the visit. Nothing went amiss with the scheme until Rawden had checked into the Hind and Hound, a cozy Elizabethan inn at Minden. He had decided he must use an alias, too, and chose the name Soper, as Soper had purloined his. Soper went with him to the inn to unpack his master's bags and receive some last-minute instructions before continuing to Petty Coomb Hall.

It was Soper's trip to the inn's cellar to search out a good vintage for his master that did the mischief. The stairs were ill lighted. Soper tripped over a cat who accompanied him, and wrenched his ankle so badly that he had to be carried up to his bedchamber. The swollen ankle required the services of a sawbones, who decreed that Mr. Charles would be bedridden for a week, bound up the ankle, and left.

Soper said grimly, "I told you something would go amiss."

"Damme, and it was a perfect plan! I wonder if I could hire someone else to impersonate a butler."

"Not in these parts. The locals would be known to Miss Campbell. And you've not time to send to

London. The butler is to arrive today. You must go and make yourself disagreeable without me, your lordship. You won't have any trouble," he added with a gimlet glance.

Rawden sat beating the side of Soper's bed with his fingers. He disliked very much to give up his plan. Where could he get someone to fill in for Soper? Damme, there was no one—except himself! *Why not himself?* He knew a butler's duties. Soper's black suit would fit him. And it would be only for two weeks. But then, how could he appear later as Lord Rawden when he had given the Campbells a disgust of him?

The answer was not long in coming to him. Devlin, of course. He loved a caper of this sort. He would be Lord Rawden, when the time came for that gentleman's brief appearance. Rawden wrote the letter to Devlin and was so confident of his friend's help that he did not feel it necessary to await a reply.

"If you are quite comfortable, Soper, I shall leave at once for Petty Coomb Hall. Ask the servants for whatever you require here. I shall nip in to see you from time to time."

"How will you get there?" Soper asked.

"In my carriage, of course— Oh. A butler would not have a post chaise. I must hire a hansom cab."

"He'd not be wearing a nifty blue jacket with yaller trousers either. You must change into my black suit. Take my bag with you. You'll find all you need there in the way of linens." A wide smile split Soper's lips. "I'll make do with your things, Mr. Charles, seeing as you'll be using mine."

This was Rawden's first intimation that being a butler might not be so amusing as he had first thought. In fact, he was much of a mind that clothes made the man, when he stood in Soper's poorly cut suit. And when he was sunk to hiring a donkey cart for the trip to Petty Coomb Hall—no proper carriage was available at Minden—he had grave misgivings that he could stick it out for two weeks. It was only the alternative of being shackled for life to a redheaded provincial miss that gave him the fortitude to carry on.

# 2

Petty Coomb Hall was a miniature stone castle set in the flank of the Berkshire downs. In mid-October, the park grass was still green; the trees had turned to gold, with silver fields of dried stubble stretching into the distance beyond. A pair of swallows circled in the azure sky above. A perfect autumn day!

It was the castle that was petit, not the coomb, but it was the castle's small size that had given birth to the Petty in its name. It boasted matching squared towers at either end of the facade, with a crenellated roofline between. What had once been a moat was now a garden of wildflowers encircling the house. It was one of the chief pleasures of Miss Campbell to go for rides on the downs and gaze from afar at her domain. As her parents had had no sons, she, as the eldest daughter, had inherited the estate. With a female running things, and running them very well, too, it was not long before the locals had dubbed her estate Petticoat Hall. Whatever they chose to call it, it was all hers, and she was queen of the castle.

The only thing that could have pleased her more was if it were in Scotland, from whence her forebears had come some centuries before. But this was mere romancing. She had been born and reared in Berkshire, and, in fact, had never been farther afield than her one trip to Bath to visit Uncle Angus when he was bedridden with gout last winter. There she had met Lord DeSale, and that meeting had led to Rawden's visit.

Since receiving DeSale's letter, she had been a very busy queen, with no regal staff to do her bidding. Her butler had recently retired, but she still had servants enough, and now that she had a fine London butler coming to lend the household a touch of town bronze, she felt Lord Rawden would not be disappointed. She had not been entirely disappointed either to receive word from Lord Rawden that his visit would be delayed until the end of October. It gave her time to refurbish a few items.

The main item requiring refurbishing was Bonnie's wardrobe, for it was, of course, of paramount importance that Bonnie turn out in a style to please a city buck. Neither her face nor figure needed any enhancing. How this raven-haired beauty had been born into a family of redheads was a matter of conjecture. Papa used to say that Bonnie favored her mama, but even Mama had not had jet black hair, though she had had Bonnie's blue eyes.

Miss Campbell was not so well favored physically. Her red hair had a sad tendency to frizz in humid weather. Her green eyes were not attractively tilted like a cat's, nor did they have the mile-long lashes of Bonnie's. They were merely adequately fringed. She took some care to wear a wide-brimmed bonnet, and had succeeded fairly well in keeping the freckles to a minimum this year. Her figure she knew to be past redemption. No matter how much she ate, it remained thin, with no fulsome thrust of breasts or flare of hips.

Her fair skin was neither lined nor faded, however. No one ever mistook her for Bonnie's mama. If her manner was a little bossy, well she was the mistress of Petty Coomb Hall. And it was such a delightful position that she was in no hurry to exchange it for being some man's wife. She knew her nature did not take kindly to the sort of simpering that was apparently necessary to nab a husband. She liked her independence too well. She had but one dream, and that was to travel. Scotland was first on her agenda, of course, to tour Drummossie Moor and see those places where Bonnie Prince Charlie had roamed. After that, a leisurely tour of Italy, then home to Petty Coomb, to resume her reign.

None of this could be done until Bonnie was bounced off. Miss Campbell, Felicity, had intended to present Bonnie in London next Season, and was extremely happy to have been spared the bother of this expensive affair. The money she had been saving would finance her travels instead. She had planned to bear all the cost of Bonnie's Season, to leave her sister's dowry intact. Ten thousand would buy her a baronet, according to Mrs. Legg, the local Solomon. How she would stare to hear Bonnie had nabbed a viscount, heir to an earldom, without stirring from home!

As Felicity stood on a hilltop overlooking her domain, she spotted a donkey cart approaching, and hastened homeward. It would be Mr. Charles, the butler. Felicity was a little shy of meeting him. No doubt he would find their ways provincial. The best plan would be to take him into her confidence. He was only a superior servant after all, even if he was accustomed to noble households. There was no need to feel embarrassed at her ignorance of lordly customs.

She had time to brush her hair into place and be sitting at her leisure in the saloon when the door knocker sounded. She had alerted Mary, the downstairs maid, to answer it and show Charles in. He seemed to be a forthright man, to judge by his firm handling of the door knocker.

Within half a minute, he was at the doorway, bowing and smiling. "It's the new butler, mum," Mary said, and curtsied herself out of the doorway. Behind Charles's back, she gave a saucy grin. Mary took the palm for beauty in the kitchen. Her blond curls and dimples made her a favorite with the footmen and grooms. Felicity judged it was the butler's appearance that caused that bold smile. She had not expected such a young man, and certainly not one so handsome. This lad would cause havoc with the maids. He was too handsome by half! He had a bold eye in his head. She disliked the way he examined her, as if he were her equal.

"Have I the pleasure of addressing Miss Campbell?" he asked in a well-modulated voice, with no trace of servility in it.

"That is correct. Pray have a seat, and we shall discuss your duties, Mr. Charles. Charles," she amended. One did not call her butler "Mr." Yet there was some air of breeding in the man that made it seem natural.

Charles sat down and arranged a friendly smile. "I expect you have written to Lord Devlin, my latest employer?"

"Certainly I did, Charles, and he gave you an excellent recommendation. I did not inquire why you had left his services?"

Her tone made it a question, and Rawden had his answer ready. "Truth to tell, madam, I was unhappy there. One dislikes to speak ill of his friends—er, employer—but the fact is, I found his household somewhat irregular."

"I see," she said, not seeing at all. "In what way?"

Rawden gave a dismissing shrug. "He is a bachelor. It is no secret that Devlin runs with a wild pack of Corinthians. Somerset, McLaughlin, Rawden," he added, taking this early opportunity to blacken his own name. "I prefer a more settled sort of life, which is why I wish to remove to the countryside."

Felicity came to sharp attention. "Rawden!" she exclaimed. "You are acquainted with Lord Rawden?"

"Indeed, I am." He would say no more without prodding. He was too wise to rush his fences.

Felicity hesitated only a moment before charging on. "You seem a nice, sensible fellow, Charles." She wished his last name were not a man's first name. This "Charles" lent a touch of intimacy to the conversation that she would happily have done without. "The fact is, we are expecting a visit from Lord Rawden."

"Oh, dear!" he exclaimed. "I hope I have not unwittingly maligned a close friend."

"I have never met the gentleman. The fact is, he is coming to look over my little sister, Bonnie—with a view to matrimony, I mean."

"No doubt you know what you are about, madam," he replied, with an air of disapproval. "Lord Rawden is considered an excellent parti, I believe."

"He is rich as Croesus. The family is good, too," she pointed out. "His papa admitted his son is restless. It seems horrid to be quizzing you like this when we have just met, but you understand my position. Naturally, I would be extremely reluctant to urge the match forward if Lord Rawden is actually dissipated. Is he a lecher?" she asked frankly.

"That would not be my place to say, madam. He has some reputation with the ladies. He lives high— horses, gambling."

"But he is well to grass."

"True. How long he will hold on to his fortune is another matter."

"He will also inherit DeSale's fortune. Let us hope he grows up before that happens."

"One can but hope, madam," Rawden said doubtfully.

Felicity drew a troubled sigh. "Well, enough about that. Perhaps we shall speak of it again later. You know your duties. We shall have a longer coze after dinner. I want your advice as to the proper way to entertain a gentleman like Lord Rawden. We live quietly here in the country. You will tell me what will amuse him."

Charles said stiffly, "I doubt you would be willing to provide the sort of entertainment that would amuse Lord Rawden, but I shall tell you how the nobility disport themselves, if that is what you wish."

"Yes, that is exactly what I wish. Good day, Charles. Mary will show you to your rooms. I am happy to welcome you to Petty Coomb Hall. I think we will get on well together. You seem very—sensible," she said, hesitating over the word to describe him. A little stuffy, perhaps, but his high morals would at least prevent him from trifling with the female servants.

He rose and made his bow to Miss Campbell. Before he got out the doorway, Miss Bonnie came bouncing in. She carried her blue gown, to which she had been adding a lace flounce to impress Lord Rawden. She stopped when she saw Rawden. Rawden also came to a dead halt. Who was this fair charmer? He had made his estimate of Miss Bonnie from her elder sister, who was about what he expected—a bran-faced redheaded provincial from the tip of her matronly coiffure to the toes of her shagreen slippers. But this one! He had never seen such heavenly blue eyes, and such a sweet expression. Her hair was like black silk, all shimmering with echoes of peacock and purple and gold in the light from the windows. Her lithe form was not entirely concealed beneath a simple dimity gown.

"You must be the new butler," she said, in the sweet accents of a young lady. "I am Miss Bonnie."

"I am Charles," he said, with a becoming bow. He quite forgot that Charles was the butler, however, and continued on to shock his mistress. "Well named, Miss Bonnie, but I would never take you for a Scotch lass. You do not much resemble your sister."

From her seat by the window, Miss Campbell said, "Thank you, Charles. That will be all for now."

He recalled himself to a sense of duty and bowed in her direction. "I shall find Mary myself, madam. No need to disturb you. Good day." But he could not resist one last look over his shoulder at Miss Bonnie.

He found her smiling—or to put it bluntly—laughing at him. The minx was well aware of her powers with the gents. His answering smile was not a shade short of outright flirtation.

"He's handsome!" Bonnie said, when Rawden had left.

"A regular Adonis! I dread to think of that hawk in our dovecote. And I took him for such a sensible fellow. He did not try his flirting tricks with me."

"He would have to be brave to do that," Bonnie exclaimed.

"Why, you make me sound like a harpy."

"Oh no, not a harpy, Felicity. Just a little shrewish."

"He knows Lord Rawden," Felicity said.

"Does he really! What is Rawden like? Is he handsome?"

"I did not ask. His papa called him a handsome pup. As he has the reputation of a womanizer, one assumes he is not ugly."

"Oh, I hope he likes me! I have added the flounce to my gown. What do you think?" Bonnie asked, holding up the gown for approval.

Felicity took one look at the rough stitches and said, "I think you had best marry a very rich gentleman, my dear. You are not good for anything but an ornament. Where did I go wrong? Fetch my sewing box. I must pull out this mess and put the flounce on properly."

While Bonnie ran off to fetch the sewing basket, Felicity went to the kitchen to speak to Cook about dinner. From the servants' stairway, she heard a familiar voice, though it was nearly buried beneath the servants' loud giggles.

"Good God, you offer a man cooking sherry after a hot ride in a donkey cart!" Charles was saying. "Fetch me up a bottle of your mistress's claret, Mary."

"That ain't for us servants," Mary said sassily.

"Your mistress wants a tony London butler. We fine gents do not drink cooking sherry. Now, off with you, wench."

Miss Campbell's blood was on the boil as she quietly opened the door and stared at the scene of dissipation going forth in her usually well-run kitchen. She was just in time to see Charles give Mary a playful tap on her bottom. Mary turned and grabbed his hand. A little tussle ensued.

"I'll speak to you in my office, Charles, at once," she said in icy accents.

All heads turned at her commanding voice, then the playful scene froze, as if the participants were involved in a game of statues.

Charles was the first to come to life. He straightened up, removed his hand from Mary's bottom, and said in a choked voice, "At once, madam. I am entirely at your disposal."

209

# 3

Despite his long legs, Rawden had difficulty keeping pace with Miss Campbell as she strode angrily toward her study. She did not sit down, nor did she invite him to do so. She stood arms akimbo and lit into him. "Raked my hair with the footstool. She reminded me of Papa," was the way he described the dressing down to Soper when they met later that week.

"I do not expect my butler to fraternize with the housemaids," she said, fire darting from her green eyes. "Nor do I expect him to make a mockery of me behind my back. A tony London butler, indeed! You flatter yourself, sir! Your behavior might pass muster in such a rackety house as Lord Devlin's. It will not do here. I am paying you twice what I paid my last butler, and *he* did not expect to be supplied with the best claret in the house, I might add."

"I am sorry if I transgressed, madam," Rawden said, in such an uppity manner that Felicity felt sure he was going to quit her services on the spot.

After one leap of anger at her tone, Rawden quickly reminded himself that he was only playing a role here. Should he tug his forelock to show his audience that she was mistress, he a lowly serf? No, that would be doing it too brown.

"That was ill done of me," he said. "I have found that a little levity smooths the wheels of congress between the butler and the lower servants."

"I find it quite the opposite. One in charge is better advised to keep his distance, or you will find you gain no respect from the housemaids and footmen. As to congress between butler and maids, that is best kept to business congress. In short, you are to keep your hands off the maids, Charles."

"A friendly pat," he said, blushing at his folly.

"You had not been in the house ten minutes! Such swift friendship leads me to fear you picked up some bad habits at your last place of employment. Now, while we are about it, I would like you to comb your hair properly. Why is it all brushed down about your forehead? It looks very odd."

Rawden had forgotten this detail. "It is called the Brutus hairdo, madam. All the crack in London." As she apparently did not recognize it at all, he added, "Among the butlers, I mean. Naturally, we do not ape our betters."

"Well, it is not the crack in Berkshire." She sensed some devilry in his mock mildness. Was he making fun of her? As she was paying this fellow an inordinate sum to bring them up to spec, however, she added, "It does not matter about the hair. Wear it as you wish, but keep a civil tongue in your head." Actually, she rather liked the hairdo. It reminded her of some Grecian hero—Apollo, was it? If it was a city style, then she wished Charles to keep it, to impress Rawden.

"I am very sorry, madam. I only went to the kitchen to inquire about my quarters."

"Your rooms are on the top floor, overlooking the front road. You will find the door open. It is the blue suite."

"Thank you, madam."

"You will also find a bottle of excellent claret there," she added. "We do not expect our butler to drink cooking sherry. On those occasions when he feels the need of a sustaining nip—and I trust these

211

occasions will not arise too frequently—he is free to help himself to a bottle from the cellar. You will find the household keys in your room."

"Thank you, madam. If there is nothing else, I shall go and unpack now."

She nodded her dismissal. "I shall wish a word with you this evening."

"I am completely at madam's disposal."

Rawden bowed and escaped into the hallway. Witch! By God, he would have to look sharp or he would find himself turfed out before he had accomplished his aim. He wiped his brow with his handkerchief and darted up to his bedchamber. It was about what he expected. A cubbyhole, but with its own drawing room, and the promised bottle of wine. The label told him it was not what he would call excellent claret, but it was certainly better than the cooking sherry. He sat in the armchair by the window, raised his feet to the table, and drew the cork.

He drank one glass, then another. This masquerade was going to be more difficult than he had foreseen, but there were compensations. Bonnie was a darling, and Mary was by no means an antidote either. Best not annoy the shrew by pestering the servants, however. He looked out over the unfamiliar countryside, judging not its prosperous cornfields nor the sheep grazing contentedly, but its terrain for riding potential. Then he remembered that he would not be riding. He would be standing like an automaton to open doors and do the shrew's bidding.

What else did Hawker do at home? As he thought about it, Rawden decided Hawker had a pretty soft touch. The wine cellar was his major concern. He ordered the servants about, and kept the household accounts. He counted the silver after dinner parties to see no one had run off with the spoons. He toured the house at night to see the doors were locked.

Rawden poured a third glass of claret and relaxed. He'd nip into Minden tomorrow—probably in a dogcart—to buy some books to pass the next few weeks without being bored to tears. What else would he need? Some decent wine. The harpy would probably keep a check on how many bottles of her "excellent claret" disappeared from the cellar. Perhaps he could arrange to hire a mount and keep it at the Hind and Hound for his weekly afternoon off duty. As there were only females at Petty Coomb, it was unlikely they'd have any horseflesh up to a man's weight. The nags would not be for the butler's use in any case.

He was dawdling over his third glass of wine when he heard the rush of footfalls on the stairway. A footman appeared at the doorway.

"Miss Campbell wants to know if you ain't unpacked yet, Charles. She's had company, and is sore as a gumboil that you wasn't there to let Mrs. Legg in."

"I shall be down presently," Rawden replied, quelling down his annoyance.

He rose and straightened his jacket, then descended the stairs at a stately gait. He had taken Hawker as his model of a perfect butler. Charles may not have been present to show Mrs. Legg in, but he was there to show her out, and he did it with such condescension that Miss Campbell was almost inclined to think he was worth his salary. How Mrs. Legg stared at his Brutus hairdo, and his handsome face, composed into a perfect mask of superiority. There was no butler to touch him in the neighborhood.

When Mrs. Legg had been shown out, Rawden thought it might be wise to tender an apology for his tardiness. He came to the doorway of the saloon and coughed discreetly.

"Oh, Charles! There you are," Miss Campbell said. She was actually wearing a smile. "You found your room to your liking?"

"Very handsome, madam."

"I am glad. Now I would like you to have a look at the gold guest suite, and see if you think it would suit Lord Rawden. If you have any suggestions as to how we might make it more suitable, don't hesitate to say so. We want Rawden to be happy here." She took up her sewing. "Bonnie will show you the suite," she said. "You will find her in the garden, I expect. I would like to speak to her when she comes down."

Rawden was not tardy to nip out into the sunshine of a golden autumn day. As he had seen no gardens upon his arrival, he assumed they would be at the rear of the house. He eventually espied a tiered garden with a gardener taking a load of compost to encourage blooms. He followed him and spent a few moments strolling through rows of flowers.

"G'day, sir," the gardener said. "You'd be new butler?" Rawden nodded. "I be Higgins, a junior man. Does mistress want Cappin?"

"I beg your pardon?"

"Head gardener. Does mistress want 'un?"

"No, I am looking for Miss Bonnie."

"Home garden," the man said, and resumed his work.

Charles wended his way back toward the house. He eventually found Miss Bonnie in the midst of a row of tall clay pots, examining the remains of sea kale.

"Miss Campbell said you would show me the gold guest suite, Miss Bonnie," he said. "She wishes me to look it over."

Bonnie looked up at him with a pair of laughing blue eyes, made more romantic by a broad-brimmed hat. "I hear you have just had your first scold, Charles," she said.

"You have large ears!"

"Oh no, I was just outside the open window, and heard the whole thing." She pointed to her sister's study. "You must not take my sister's little rants too seriously. She has a hot head, but she is really very kind."

They returned to the front of the house. "It is Lord Rawden's visit that upsets her," Bonnie confided. "We are not at all accustomed to such grand visitors. That is why she hired you, to tell us how to go on. Is he very handsome?"

"He is considered tolerably handsome," Rawden replied, with a twitching of his lips.

Bonnie stared at him. "Why are you laughing? Is he ugly? I shan't have him if he is ugly."

"He is not ugly, but he is not good enough for you, Miss Bonnie," he replied, with a flirtatious smile.

"Felicity would not like you to flirt with me, Charles," she said, trying for a note of severity, and failing miserably.

Charles held the door, and Miss Bonnie scampered in. They mounted the staircase, then down the hall to a Gothic chamber with gold brocade tapestries and bed hangings. The room was not tatty, but its grandeur was fatigued. There was a massive desk, a toilet table, a *bergère* chair.

"The drawing room is in here," Bonnie said, leading the way to another room of faded elegance.

Rawden looked about, trying to think of some sensible comment to make. "It looks adequate," he said.

Miss Bonnie pointed out the view from the window and returned to the bedchamber, where Rawden tried the mattress with his hand. It felt hard as a rock, but he did not wish the ladies to go to the expense of buying a new mattress. "Perhaps a feather tick could be added on top of this," he said.

"I told Felicity so, but she felt a man would like a hard mattress. We moved this carpet up from the dining room. It is hardly worn since Felicity and I take most of our meals in the breakfast room. Just for two, you know, it is not worthwhile using the dining room, but of course we shall use it when *he* comes, so it has a new carpet. Are the pictures all right? Felicity moved the Canaletto from her own room in here."

He looked at a scene of Venice, featuring a bridge and the Grand Canal. "Felicity plans to go to Italy," Bonnie said.

"The pictures are fine." He felt guilty, all this work being done to impress him when he had no intention of offering for Bonnie. He said, "Actually, Rawden will spend very little time in his room, if he follows his usual behavior. He likes riding, good company, good wine."

"My sister wants to consult you about wine. I expect Rawden will bring his own mount. I do not care for riding," she said. "Pity. It would be something we could do together."

Rawden gazed at her, and said softly, "I shouldn't worry about that, Miss Bonnie. No doubt Rawden will find other things for you two to do together. After all, he is not coming to assess Petty Coomb Hall; he is coming to meet you."

"Oh, I am being smartened up, too," she assured him with childish candor. "I am having a new ball gown made up specially to impress him. And we are going to give a grand ball, with a hundred guests and champagne and everything. We count on you to tell us how to do it up brown, Charles."

216

The more she talked, the more guilty he felt. "Rawden does not much care for balls," he lied.

Bonnie's face assumed an air of tragedy. "You must not tell Felicity so! I am especially looking forward to the ball. We have not had a ball at Petty Coomb since Papa died six years ago. In fact, we cannot cancel it now, for we have been talking it up to the neighbors for weeks. It would be too shabby to rob us of our ball. Why does Rawden not like balls?"

"I spoke too strongly. I meant it was not necessary to have a ball to impress him. He prefers outdoor activities. Riding in particular."

"I hate riding!" she exclaimed. "In fact, I am beginning to think Rawden and I would not suit at all. I thought I would be going to all the smart balls in London if I married him."

It was a perfect opportunity to give Miss Bonnie a hint that Rawden would be amusing himself with other ladies, but he could not bring himself to say it to this child. That was what the beautiful Miss Bonnie was; a child who had some dreamy notion of marriage being a long party with a handsome prince.

"Marriage is more than a ball, Miss Bonnie," he said. "It is running a house, having children, and visiting relatives who are dead bores. I think what you want is a Season, to get this mania for balls out of your system."

"Felicity was going to give me a Season, until Lord DeSale said his son was coming to visit us. If I don't care for him, I shan't have him, whatever Felicity says."

Rawden at once felt a surge of protective instinct. "Surely she would not force you—"

"She has said a dozen times what a wonderful opportunity it is for me. I would not dare to suggest refusing him. I daresay it would be pleasant to be a countess, and get to wear a tiara and go to Court."

"A tiara can be heavy, and Court can be a dead bore."

Bonnie looked at him as if he were Solomon, uttering the wisdom of the ages. "That is very true, Charles. I daresay a tiara could be heavy, especially if one had to learn to ride. I am happy you came to us. And about Mary—if you truly love her, Felicity would not mind your keeping company with her. It is just that she dislikes low carrying on in the house. You understand," she said, with a condescending smile.

"It is early days to speak of true love. If I find, with time, that Mary and I suit, I shall do the thing up properly, never fear."

"I am glad we had this little chat. You can always confide in me if you run amok with my sister. I have some influence in that quarter," she said. He knew by her accents and her noble mien that she was quoting some older lady. Miss Bonnie was a delightful child; she might even make a delightful bride for some young pup, but she was too young and ingenuous to appeal to Rawden at the moment.

They returned belowstairs. "I shall show you the pattern for my new gown this evening, Charles," she said. "You will tell me whether it is stylish enough to please Rawden."

"But I thought you had decided against the match!"

She looked at him as if he were a simpleton. "No, indeed! I am merely thinking of it more realistically. A tiara can be heavy," she said, "but still it would be rather nice to wear a tiara." Then she floated off down the stairs to meet her sister, with her head held at a lofty angle that suited a heavy tiara.

Rawden saw he must step up his blackening of

Lord Rawden's character. With no very sure notion of his duties, he retired to the butler's room to await any chance callers. He found a comfortable chair and a rag-eared copy of *Pamela*. He sat down and was soon deep in the machinations of Mr. B.

Bonnie went to the saloon to mysteriously inform her sister that Charles was very wise, and he thought Lord Rawden would like a feather tick on his bed. A little further questioning gave Felicity the notion that Charles had been trying to turn Bonnie against the idea of marrying Rawden. This would not do!

# 4

"Your duty in this house is to serve the family and advise the servants, Charles. Not vice versa," was Miss Campbell's chilly advice to her new butler when she discovered him with his nose buried deep in the pages of Richardson's *Pamela*.

He leapt to his feet, embarrassed to be caught in his idleness. "I have not been serving the servants, madam."

"Well, you have been advising my sister against marrying Lord Rawden. Don't do it again," she said, and turned to leave. At the doorway she turned back. "I did not come here to check up on you, Charles. I am happy to see you enjoy good literature. Feel free to use the library in your spare time."

"Thank you," he said. What a strange lady this Miss Campbell was. Scolding out of one side of her mouth, while more or less apologizing out of the other. He was happy to have the run of the library.

Another little altercation arose between mistress and butler in the saloon after dinner when Miss Campbell discovered the fire had not been prepared. She had been impressed with his manner of announcing dinner. It had not been entirely comfortable with him lurking behind her all the time she ate, whisking covers off dishes and handing them to Poole, the footman, to serve. Such niceties were not observed at Petty Coomb, but as she had been subjected to this uncomfortable procedure at Lord Halton's table, she thought it was just as well to become accustomed to it before Rawden's arrival.

She was on sure ground with the unlaid fire, however. She summoned Charles and pointed to the empty grate. "We have a fire in the evening, Charles. It is chilly in October."

"I shall speak to Poole at once, madam," he said.

"Surely it is the butler's place to prepare the fires!"

He looked at her askance. He had no idea how to lay a fire. Fires might have made themselves for all he knew about it. "Perhaps in smaller households such as Petty Coomb. It was not the butler's duty to lay the fires at Lord Devlin's establishment, but I daresay I could learn if madam wishes."

"Good gracious, what is to learn? Higgins has left us a basket of chopped wood from the cherry tree that came down in the last storm. Put it in the grate, put some journals under it, and light them."

Rawden did as she requested, but the journals had an obstinate way of burning for an instant, then guttering out. When he had been at his job for several minutes, Miss Campbell came to see what caused the delay. Charles had laid a flat pile of paper beneath the grate.

"You have to separate the journals and squash them up, Charles," she said, shaking her head at his obtuseness.

This proved marvelously effective, and in no time a great blaze was roaring up the chimney. "You can damp the fire down now," she said. Again he looked at her in bewilderment. "The flue, Charles! Adjust the flue."

"Ah, just so. And where might the flue be, madam?"

She hopped up and twisted the knob herself. The roaring flames subsided to a more gentle roar.

"In future, the fires will be your responsibility," Miss Campbell said. "Always keep the grates clean and a fire laid here, in the library, and the breakfast room, in my and Miss Bonnie's chamber. And your own, if you wish," she added.

This sounded like a full-time job to Rawden. But it was not the end of his new duties by a long shot.

"I would like you to make an inventory of the wine cellar tomorrow," she continued. "We will want some special wines for Lord Rawden's visit. I have paid the cellar little heed since Papa's death. I count on your expertise to assist me. Oh, and I would like you to get me a turtle from London."

"A turtle, madam?" he asked, his head reeling.

"For turtle soup, Charles. Mrs. Legg tells me it is all the crack. There is not a green turtle to be had in Berkshire. I believe they are bought live, and have to be transported somehow. I daresay it will cost a fortune, but I begrudge no expense. I want this visit to be a success."

"Would Cook not be the one . . ."

"Cook has never been to London. I thought you might do this for us. Lord Devlin's cook must know where to buy a turtle."

"Certainly, she makes an excellent turtle soup."

"Good, then you will write and get her receipt for it. Now, about entertaining Lord Rawden. I daresay he would like to ride and shoot a few afternoons. One cannot expect a swell like Rawden to spend his whole time meandering through the village with Bonnie, though that would suit her down to the heels."

"I happen to know Rawden is a keen rider," he admitted.

"I thought as much." She noticed Charles was still standing, and motioned him to sit down. "A pity Bonnie has no knack with horses. She will occasionally get on the donkey's back, but it is four pence to a groat she will even fall off Maisie if she goes faster than one step a minute. *I* could ride with him, but that would hardly help the romance along."

"Are there no gentlemen in the neighborhood who might accompany him?" he asked eagerly.

"We do not follow city practices here, Charles. Our neighbors are hardworking farmers, as we are ourselves. The gentlemen might take one or two afternoons off to ride or hunt, but Lord Rawden must be entertained on a daily basis. It is really a great nuisance," she said with a tsk. "One would think a gentleman of property like Rawden would take some interest in more serious things, but I fear it is not the case."

Rawden felt a sting at her condemnation, but leapt at the opportunity to turn her from her goal. "One really wonders if he would make a proper husband for Miss Bonnie," he said, with a well-simulated frown.

"He would suit her very well. She hasn't a serious thought in her head either. She is very pretty, and she is expensive. She will enjoy a life of idleness and frivolity, helping him squander his fortune. And she will get to wear a tiara. She has always wanted that. She is not likely to find one among the locals. I am quite determined to bring this match off, Charles, and I look to you for help in doing it. You *did* say Rawden is not actually a lecher?"

"He likes high-flyers," Rawden prevaricated. "I fear Miss Bonnie is too young and innocent to suit him."

"Oh, but surely you are mistaken there. Those fast gentlemen never marry the dashers they run around with. When it comes to making a match, they always choose a young innocent."

"That is a common misunderstanding. It has been

my experience that they more often than not become caught in the toils of some experienced lady."

"He would be better off with a well-behaved lady like Bonnie. And she is so pretty, you know, that he might even fall in love with her, and settle down. That is what his papa and I hope. Bonnie really is something out of the ordinary, do you not agree? It is not just my partiality that makes me think so?"

"She is an incomparable," he admitted.

"Well then, perhaps all will work out for the best. Ah, here she is now. Speak of the devil," Miss Campbell said, as Bonnie appeared at the doorway.

She was carrying a pattern book and a length of pale blue silk. "I am going to show Charles the pattern for my ball gown, Felicity," she said. "He will know whether it will do."

Rawden rose and bowed as she entered. Felicity thought it a little odd. Their old butler did not bow when they entered a room, but only inclined his head. Perhaps this, too, was a city trick of which she was unaware.

"Yes, Charles will know all the latest fashions," Felicity agreed, and handed him the book. "Do sit down, Charles. As we are treating you as our mentor, we shall not insist on the niceties of our formal relationship."

Rawden's wayward nature rose, and he heard himself say, "After being reprimanded for neglecting the distance due between superiors and their inferiors, I wonder if I dare to have a seat, ma'am."

He expected to receive a blast from his mistress, and was surprised that she laughed good-naturedly. Miss Campbell was rather attractive when she laughed. "Touché, Charles," she said. "But I shall keep you in place, never fear."

Rawden's eyebrow rose in surprise. Felicity, looking at him, thought she read a challenge in that bold dark eye. A warmth invaded her cheek. He sat down, and she handed him the pattern book. "This is the gown Bonnie has chosen," she said.

Rawden examined a gown lavishly garnished with ribbon and lace. He looked at the blue silk Bonnie handed him and thought she would look like every other deb. He had only one comment.

"In London, the debs wear white their first Season."

"Here in the country we are more lenient," Miss Campbell replied. "The young girls wear pastel shades—pink, jonquil, pale blue. This will just match Bonnie's eyes." Rawden's lack of enthusiasm was evident. "We have already bought the blue silk," she said testily, "and paid a stiff price for it, too. The gown will be blue; it is the pattern we are discussing."

"I would leave off the ribbons," he said.

"Oh no!" Bonnie pouted. "The little bows are so sweet."

"Too sweet by half," Felicity said. "The ribbons go, Bonnie. As we have asked for Charles's advice, we shall take it. I happen to agree with him."

Bonnie pouted and flipped the page. "This is what Felicity plans to wear," she said to Charles. Her voice urged him to condemn it.

He looked at a severely cut gown, lower at the bodice than Miss Bonnie's, and with a deal more dash to it. "In green, to match your eyes, miss—ma'am?" he asked, and looked to verify the shade of her eyes. They looked darker in the evening than he had first thought. Not peridot, but emerald.

"Just so," she said, and felt her cheeks become uncommonly warm. It was the fire; she had not damped it enough. "Cabbage green, to match my eyes."

"You do yourself an injustice, madam, if I may be forgiven for making a personal comment," Raw-

225

den said. "They are not cabbage green; they are closer to emeralds."

Felicity racked her brain for some reply that forgave the bold fellow without encouraging him. She knew perfectly well she was not keeping a proper distance from her butler, but she was only twenty-four, not fifty. She had enjoyed very few flirtations, and none with such a handsome specimen as Charles.

"I wish they were blue, like Bonnie's," she said, and closed the book. "In any case, it is not my *beaux yeux* nor my gown that will be of interest to Lord Rawden. You may return to your duties now, Charles. Bonnie and I shall work on our list for the ball. Get the notebook, Bonnie." Why had she felt it necessary to give Charles an explanation for his dismissal? She must not think of her butler as a friend and confidant.

Rawden retired to his cubbyhole to consider what duties his mistress was referring to. She was not expecting any callers that evening. It was too early to extinguish the lamps and lock the doors. He was to begin the inventory of the wine cellar in the morning. Ordering the wine, at least, was a duty he would relish. It would mean trips into Minden.

As for the rest of it, this masquerade was not only a dead bore, it badgered his conscience. Miss Campbell was going to a deal of useless bother and expense on his behalf. Really it was a shameful thing he was doing. He had no idea the shifts and shams ladies were put to in order to nab a husband. Rearranging the entire household, buying wine and a turtle, making new gowns. It was an infamous stunt he was pulling off. It had seemed a good joke before he knew the Campbells.

Now that he knew how much the match meant to them, he felt wretched. And he knew that despite Bonnie's undeniable beauty, he cared no more for her than he cared for any of the other nubile ladies his papa had paraded before him. Why did Papa think he wanted a pretty nitwit for a wife? When he married, it would be to some sensible lady with more than a pretty face to recommend her. In fact, what he actually required was a strong-willed lady who would keep him in line. Yet she must not be a shrew, and, of course, she must have some small claim to beauty.

When he found his cubbyhole becoming chilly, he remembered the fires to be laid, and went above-stairs to do the ladies' rooms. Higgins had left a plentiful supply of logs. The grates were clean. He had only to put on the wood and scrunch the journals up as Miss Campbell had shown him. Fancy his not knowing that! What a useless creature he was, when all was said and done. What were his accomplishments? He had got a gentleman's C at university. He was a renowned whip. He could go several rounds with Gentleman Jackson, and he could culp a wafer at Manton's Shooting Gallery with the best of them. And, of course, he was judged to have a way with the ladies.

These seemed small accomplishments for a man of thirty years, who had had every advantage and opportunity. Papa was right; he was a useless fribble. But he could and would change his ways without being shackled for life to Miss Bonnie Campbell. He had begun this tiresome masquerade, and the best he could do now was execute his role in a satisfactory manner, while trying to turn the ladies against Rawden. Devlin would impersonate him when the time came, and he would disappear from Petty Coomb Hall. He only hoped his papa never learned of the charade—or Miss Campbell either. Would she not deliver him a rare bear garden jaw if she knew!

In Miss Campbell's bedchamber, he saw a rect-

227

angle of lighter paper on the wall where she had removed the Canaletto. On the wall facing her bed was a Stubbs painting of a bay mare. Miss Campbell liked horses. There was one thing they had in common. He glanced around at heavy mahogany furnishings. On the desk sat a ledger in which she kept track of expenditures. No doubt heavy ones due to his visit. Her toilet table held no lavish display of cream pots and perfumes such as he saw in other ladies' boudoirs.

He went on to Miss Bonnie's room. It was much as he expected—a riot of pink canopy and curtains, with girlish white furnishings, gilt-trimmed. The walls held French paintings in the style of Watteau and Fragonard. *Fête champêtre* scenes of ladies in flower-garlanded swings, under ethereal trees. A marble-covered gothic novel rested on top of the counterpane. Her desk held a vase with one rose, and a very poor sketch of a young man. Perhaps her idea of Lord Rawden.

He really was behaving like a scoundrel. He should go down and confess to Miss Campbell at once. She was not so stern as he had first thought. She had a sense of humor. She might understand . . . But as he remembered her reaction to his playful pat on Mary's derriere, he decided against it. Instead he would try to turn her against Rawden, but do it in a manner that caused her as little work and expenditure as possible. And in two weeks he would leave, a free man.

# 5

Charles proved so able a butler over the next week that he was soon considered an indispensable part of the household. His occasional lapses in knowledge were ascribed to the differences between running a grand noble house and a merely genteel provincial one. He did not take it amiss when Miss Campbell told him his duties included helping the footmen lift the rugs to take them out for a beating on the clothesline, though he knew perfectly well Hawker did not perform such lowly chores at his papa's house. Nor did Miss Campbell hit the roof when he occasionally shared a wink or joke with Mary.

She knew he spent longer in Minden than the ordering of wine called for. Surely three trips were excessive? Mrs. Legg reported having seen him in the Hind and Hound, but overall he performed his household duties so well, and got on so well with her other servants (despite his friendly way with them) that she did not call him to account.

Under the unusual circumstance of Lord Rawden's impending visit, Charles and Miss Campbell spent much time together. She was happy for his advice on such matters as wine, food preparations, gowns for Bonnie, and especially on details for the one large ball she planned. Charles did not think it necessary to turn the ballroom into a Persian tent. She was happy to hear Rawden disliked such lavish displays.

She was also told that Rawden disliked turtle soup, or indeed any such troublesome dishes. Rawden was determined to keep Miss Campbell's investment of time and money in this pending visit to a very minimum. As the days wore on, and he saw that every detail of the household was being scrutinized for improvement to please him, he felt perfectly wretched.

"I begin to think Lord Rawden is a more sensible gentleman than his papa led me to believe," Felicity said, upon hearing that she must on no account hire twelve musicians for the ball.

"Rawden really prefers smaller parties," Charles explained. "A few neighbors and a piano player would suffice."

"But the ball is not only for Rawden," Felicity said. "Bonnie has convinced me I am not doing my social duty vis-à-vis our neighbors. The ball is as much for her as for Rawden."

"Then I shall say no more. My life would not be worth a Birmingham farthing if I deprived Miss Bonnie of her ball."

Other duties not usually ascribed to a butler fell in his way as well. The matter of Lord Rawden's being a devoted sportsman made it imperative that suitable rides be found for him. "Suitable," Miss Campbell was given to understand, included fences, water, ditches, and any other challenges she could think of. As Miss Campbell was a keen rider, she offered to show Charles her usual routes.

"You can ride papa's mount," she said. "Belle is still capable of giving a good ride. Papa bought her just before he died. I could not bear to part with her, and it is always convenient to have a spare mount for company. I try to ride her myself as often as I can, to keep her in shape."

"I would be very happy to help," Rawden said at once. "I can always spare an hour at some time during the day. I should enjoy the exercise."

"Excellent!" Felicity exclaimed. "It will kill two birds with one stone. Both the nag and you get your exercise. Dear me! What an unfortunate way to put it!" she laughed.

"I did think your butler might take precedence over a nag," Rawden said, smiling.

"Oh, is that what you thought? I'll have you know horses come very near the top of my priorities. I thought it was your being called a bird that you might object to. Of course, I did not mean a hedge bird."

"What did you mean?"

"Why I meant a peacock, to be sure," she replied, without even realizing she was flirting her head off. She had noticed that Rawden's linens and shoes were of excellent quality. His suit was about what one would expect, but his Brutus hairdo suggested a touch of dandyism. "But what will you wear for riding, Charles? I wonder if Papa's—"

"Actually, I have a trunk of clothes I left in Minden, as I did not want you to think me a clothes-horse," he explained. "Reach-me-downs from Lord Devlin. We are about the same size. I shall have them brought here."

He dashed Soper off a note to send his riding boots and a suitable jacket and trousers for riding.

When he appeared the next morning dressed in a blue superfine jacket and buckskins, with a shining pair of top boots, Felicity nearly fell over in astonishment.

Bonnie was with her, and it was the younger lady who exclaimed, "Oh, Charles! Felicity, does he not look fine as nine pence? The neighbors will think you have got a beau!"

"Very nice, Charles," Felicity said, in a strangely choked voice. "Very nice, indeed."

When Charles held the door for her and assisted her onto her mount in a very civil way, she did indeed feel she was with a beau. She hardly knew how to treat him, but she soon reminded herself that he was her butler, and naturally she would continue to treat him as such, even if he looked and behaved like a gentleman.

Rawden was more interested in the horses than in the impression he was making. He noticed that Miss Campbell rode a bang-up bay mare. She set a slow pace until she was convinced Charles knew what he was about, then the pace quickened to a full gallop as they rode hard over difficult terrain. She was an excellent horsewoman. Seated on her dashing mount, with a stylish beaver hat tilted over her eye and the wind tinting her cheeks pink, she looked very attractive. She was also considerate of her riding companion, always giving him ample warning of any approaching obstacle.

"You ride very well, Charles," she complimented him. "Where did you learn?"

"I spent my younger days hanging about stables," he replied. For some reason he could not quite comprehend, he had taken to telling the truth about details, as much as possible, while still living the bigger lie.

"There is a ditch ahead, just beyond the elm trees," she cautioned. "Do you think our rides will please Lord Rawden?" Before he could reply, she was sailing over a ditch, with Charles beside her. They shared a moment of perfect exultation, with the wind in their faces, a powerful steed under them, and no thought but guiding the animal over the ditch.

When they were both safely landed on the other side, he said, "He would be hard to please if he demanded more than this!" Felicity did not reply, but she nodded her agreement. The only thing that could have added to her own pleasure would be if Charles were indeed her beau. She admitted to herself that her pleasure in his company was getting out of hand.

Yet it was so enjoyable to have a riding companion that they went out together often, much to Mrs. Legg's consternation. "A lady does not ride with her butler!" she declared.

"I must exercise Papa's mount" was the weak reply.

On another outing, they stopped on the crest of a hill and looked down on Petty Coomb Hall.

"It looks like a little fairy castle, does it not?" she asked softly. "I love the way the wildflowers have taken over the moat. They encircle the house in a garden." Beyond the moat, the park spread, with the cornfields beyond it. To the east, black-faced sheep grazed contentedly. To the north, the tenant farms spread along the bank of a stream. The whole looked not only pretty, but prosperous. A smile of rare contentment curved her lips and lit her green eyes. The wind pulled a curl loose from her hat, to play about her cheek.

"Indeed, it does," Rawden replied. He, too, felt a sense of peace settle around him. "You are a good landlord, Miss Campbell. I compliment you."

She spoke in a knowledgeable way about her crops, her farmers, and her sheep. "I do not like to boast," she said, "but I have raised the farm's income since taking over from Papa. He was a little old-fashioned, you must know. I hired a more scientific bailiff when our old one retired, and he has increased the yield by ten percent. The tenants found me a little too managing at first. I had to let them know I was in charge, or they would walk all over me. That is when they began calling my estate

Petticoat Hall. I take it as a compliment that they realize a lady can run a farm successfully."

"I believe you could run the country," Rawden said.

"Oh, I am not that ambitious. Running Petticoat Hall satisfies me. I have no desire to take on any more duties."

"But you will marry one day, I expect?"

Her heart beat faster. "No, that will not be necessary. I already have what ladies marry for—a home of which I am mistress. Why should I hand the control of it over to some jackanapes who will in all likelihood not run it as well as I do myself? There is a good deal to be said for independence."

"Indeed, there is," he said, with a thought of his papa. "I envy you, Mis Campbell."

Felicity naturally assumed her butler felt the chafe of being a servant, when his natural abilities were capable of worthier endeavors. Indeed, she had felt for some few days that Charles's talents were wasted in running a small establishment like Petty Coomb. Yet she hesitated to urge him to better himself, for she had come to rely on not only his advice, but his companionship. It was time to begin severing the connection. She must not indulge herself at the expense of another.

She said, "There is no reason you should not be independent, too. You are intelligent and hardworking. Why do you not try to better yourself? You might find a position at Whitehall, and a patron who would get you a seat in Parliament. There is no saying what doors might open to a young man with your abilities."

Rawden's papa frequently urged him to make a career for himself in the House. On every occasion, Rawden felt the greatest reluctance. Yet when Miss Campbell suggested it, he felt not annoyed but flattered. He had no idea she thought so well of him.

He decided to make a joke of it. "Are you trying to get rid of me, ma'am?" he asked.

"Certainly not. I should miss you, Charles." Their eyes just met, then both looked quickly away. "I am thinking of your own good. A man should put his abilities to their full use."

He turned to her and said, "Should not a lady do the same? In that case, surely you will want to have children, ma'am?"

"I practically raised Bonnie," she replied. "That is enough mothering to suit me. No, when I get her bounced off, I plan to travel. Scotland first, then Italy. I want to ride in a gondola and see Saint Marks. I want to view the Roman Forum by moonlight and see the Sistine Chapel. I want to tour Tuscany and drink wine under the trees. And after a few years of travel, I shall return and settle down here to grow old."

Rawden listened, with a smile growing in his eyes. "You are a fraud, Miss Campbell. Here you have been passing yourself off as a shrew, when you are a full-blown romantic. Gondola rides and the Forum by moonlight, indeed! That would be more enjoyable with a lover, would it not? As you are a well-reared young lady, one assumes the lover would be your husband."

It was true she had envisaged these romantic scenes being enacted with a gentleman, but her mysterious companion had never had a face, nor a precise relationship to her. He was a dream lover. She felt that in future he might wear the face of her butler. In her confusion, she did not know what to reply, and resorted to railery. "Do you find me a shrew, Charles? What a facer. I thought we got on uncommonly well."

"Perhaps—too well," he murmured. He drew a step closer. Their eyes met and held as his hand reached for hers.

Felicity felt a wild pounding in her heart. Good God! He is going to kiss me! She pulled her hand away and began chattering mindlessly. "My only other aim is to become Mistress of the Hunt. I see no reason why a lady should not do it."

"I have no doubt you would do an admirable job, ma'am."

The moment passed. They spoke of other things, but Felicity knew it had become impossible to go on living with Charles under her roof. Something had changed irrevocably that afternoon. She feared she had fallen in love with her butler.

Charles brought her tea to the saloon that evening. She did not ask him to sit down on that occasion. She said, "After Rawden has left, we shall discuss a more suitable position for you, Charles."

"I left London because I wanted a simple, regular life, ma'am."

"Being my butler is too simple. I have noticed you make good use of the library at the Hall. I daresay it is your wide reading that gives you the air of an educated man. With a better position, and your good looks, you might make quite an advantageous marriage. With a little money behind you, there is no saying how far you might go. Look at Lord Eldon—his papa was in the coal business, he made a runaway match to Gretna Green, and now he is Lord Chancellor, if you please."

"Far removed from a simple, settled life," he pointed out. "You are very ambitious for *me*; why not for yourself? I understand your not wanting to marry some local farmer. As you were kind enough to call me good-looking, I shall venture to say that a handsome lady like yourself might marry as high as she pleases. An earl, even a duke."

"I never shared Bonnie's hankering after a title," she said simply. "I *did* think, when Lord DeSale mentioned his son's requiring a firm hand,

236

that he meant I should throw my bonnet at him, but—"

"You would make him a better bride than Bonnie would," Rawden said. Where had that notion come from? Having said it, he realized it was true. Red hair had begun to take precedence over blond or black. A smattering of freckles was attractive, and he had always preferred an outspoken lady over a Bath Miss.

Miss Campbell just shook her head. "Let us remain within the purlieus of reality, Charles. Bonnie is the only one with any claims to a face. He will want an incomparable, not an ape-leader, and I promise you I have no use for a fashionable fribble. I got the Hall. One cannot have everything. *Entre nous*, I believe I got the better of the bargain, but I do not intend to abandon Bonnie completely. I shall keep an eye on young Rawden, and if he shows signs of running amok, his papa and I shall bring him to heel, never fear."

"You are the lady who could do it," he said pensively.

But did he really want to be brought to heel? A gentleman with Rawden's experience of ladies knew Miss Campbell was falling in love with him. He feared he was becoming a little too fond of her as well. Any possibility of a match had been destroyed by his foolish masquerade. He must bring it to a halt at once. He was within Ame's ace of confessing his sin that moment, but surely there was a less brutal way of doing it.

He would write to Felicity, as Lord Rawden, delaying the trip indefinitely, to bring the preparations at Petty Coomb to a stop. Then he, as Charles the butler, would receive a letter making some excuse for him to leave Petty Coomb. A peaceful parting. He would tell Papa what he had done; receive a thundering scold, and then win back his father's respect by reforming himself.

Miss Campbell need never know he had made a fool of her. That seemed the kindest way. He returned to his cubbyhole; Miss Campbell sat on alone, thinking over her teacup.

# 6

"Pest of a man!" Felicity exclaimed, when Charles brought her the letter from Lord Rawden, forwarded through the courtesy of Lord Devlin in London. "It is from Rawden, Charles. He has put the visit off *again*. He finds he cannot come on the thirtieth of October, as planned. The ball is arranged for Halloween night. I have told my friends he will be here."

"What excuse does he give?" Rawden asked.

"He does not even honor me with an excuse," she railed. "No doubt the exigencies of racetrack or gaming hell make it impossible for him to come on that day. I shall look a fool."

"Rag-mannered! If I were you, I would reply that the exigencies of life in Berkshire make it impossible for you to receive him at any other time." He looked for her reaction.

"It is what he deserves. If it were not for Bonnie I would do it, but she has her heart set on him."

"She has not even met him. It cannot break her heart to lose out on a stranger. Indeed, I do not think him suitable for her in any case." Again he watched and waited.

Felicity gave a tsk of annoyance. "No, I cannot refuse him permission to come, but he will do without his ball. I shall not arrange any other lavish entertainment for him. The ball is all arranged. It will go forward without Lord Rawden. We do not need him to enjoy ourselves."

Yet she was not really looking forward to it much. Charles would be standing at the doorway, not standing up with her. It irked her that Lord Rawden, who had no character, no concern for others—nothing but a title and a fortune—should be placed so highly in society, while worthier men like Charles must be relegated to the serving class.

Bonnie had to be told of Rawden's delay when she returned from a trip to Minden. "But you won't cancel the ball, Felicity!" was her comment.

Felicity assumed her heart was not entirely shattered. "Indeed, I shall not."

"Good!" She rushed on with the news from the village. "A new millinery shop has opened. Very dear, but the sweetest bonnets. It is run by a Mam'selle Drouin, a Frenchie. Oh, and there is some mysterious stranger staying at the Hind and Hound. They say he is a grand gentleman, with a crest on his dressing gown, and not less than five jackets. How I should love to meet him. He does not leave the inn, for he is crippled, and can only walk with a cane. Mr. Soper, he calls himself. Of course, it is in an alias. I think he is an English spy—a lord, obviously—keeping an eye on Mam'selle Drouin. There is no saying what she is up to."

"I cannot think she is up to any nefarious doings in Minden, except charging an inordinate sum of her bonnets," Felicity said. "Nor can this mysterious stranger keep much of an eye on her if he does not leave the inn."

"He could be watching her with a spyglass. The new millinery shop is just across the road from the inn. Have you ever met Mr. Soper, Charles? Mrs. Legg mentioned seeing you in the inn a few times."

"I do not know any spies," he replied vaguely. He had no comment to make on this mysterious

240

stranger, but he would quiz Soper about the crested dressing gown when next they met.

Felicity said, "Did you speak to Mrs. Sangster about helping out with the serving for the ball, Bonnie?"

"Yes, she was thrilled to death to be in on it, and wants to know if you could use Annie as well. I said yes, so I did not have to bother asking Mrs. Perkins if she would help."

"That is fine. I must answer Lord Rawden's letter now. I shall try to get a firm date for his visit. He only says he will be delayed, and no idea of whether he will come a week late or a month."

Felicity left, and Bonnie said to Charles, "I hope he does not come at all."

"This is a new wrinkle!"

"Yes, I have been talking to Miss Hopper in Minden. She is to make her curtsy at St. James's next spring, and if I do not get an offer from Rawden, then Felicity will have to take me to London, too, for there are no partis hereabouts. Miss Hopper says there are hundreds of balls and routs and water parties and plays! I shan't accept Rawden's offer, but don't tell Felicity so. I mean to make Rawden fall in love with me and break his heart. That will show him a lesson, brute!"

The plans for the ball continued apace. There was a pleasant air of excitement about the house as the maids plied their beeswax and turpentine, Cook baked up her dainties, and the ladies labored over their toilettes. On the day before the ball, Felicity decided to apply a mask of lemon juice and cornstarch, in an effort to bleach her freckles. She had applied the mask and sat in her chamber, looking like a clown at Astley's Circus with her white face, when she heard a knock at her door.

Expecting a servant, she went to answer and

found herself staring at Charles. Her hands flew to her cheeks in dismay.

"Good God! What has happened to you!" he exclaimed.

"Charles, you wretch, catching me out in this state!" she laughed. "I am bleaching my freckles. The cornstarch makes a paste to hold on the lemon juice. What do you want?" It was unusual for Charles to come to her door. She feared some catastrophe had befallen the ball.

"I have had a letter, special delivery, from Mama," he said, holding out the letter he had had Devlin forward.

"Not bad news, I hope?"

"Bad news and good news. My uncle has died. I must attend the funeral, as he has made me his heir."

"An inheritance!" she exclaimed. "But that is wonderful!" Then she remembered the proprieties and expressed the proper concern for his loss.

"It is not a large inheritance. A small farm in the north," he explained.

"You could sell it! It is enough to get you started on the path to independence, as we discussed the other day."

A sparkle invaded her eyes. Charles would set up a business; he would become a vastly successful merchant. Several young ladies were marrying into the merchant class . . .

"I do not plan to sell it. I shall be independent on my own little farm, raising a few cows and chickens. As my home is so far away, it would be very difficult for me to go for the funeral and return. I had hoped to get away immediately. I—I would not be coming back," he added reluctantly.

A sob caught in her throat. "Oh, Charles! You cannot leave me!" Her hands instinctively reached to his, to hold him from leaving. When she noticed what she had done, and heard the anguish in her voice, she was ashamed of her lack of control. "With the ball tomorrow night—I—I quite counted on you," she added. She released his hands, but he grabbed onto hers in a crippling grip.

"I am truly sorry, Felicity." When he heard what had slipped out, he continued, "I shall call you so, this once. You don't mind?"

She just shook her head, too distraught for words. She knew the tears gathering in her eyes would soon fall. She reached up to brush them away, and felt the cornstarch congealing on her cheeks. It was the last straw, that Charles should see her like this, when he was leaving forever. He must not see her acting like a ninnyhammer. She lifted her chin proudly and asked, "When must you leave?"

"I plan to pack and leave immediately, but I shall not leave you in the lurch. I know a butler who will be happy to stand in for me until you can make other arrangements. An excellent fellow. He lives nearby. He can be here by tomorrow."

"That is very thoughtful of you," she said. "We shall have a word before you leave—settle up your salary and so on. I shall await you in my office downstairs. Oh, and you must take my carriage to the coach stop, of course."

Rawden wore a broad smile as he darted up to his rooms and threw his—mostly Soper's—belongings into a case. Had it been infamous of him to announce his departure before the ball? Would Felicity have been so emotional if he had waited until after? He wanted the element of surprise. A lady was more likely to blurt out the truth if she were caught unawares. The meeting in her study would tell the tale.

It was a very businesslike meeting. Felicity gave him a generous pourboire. She wished him well in his new life, and said she had enjoyed having him work for her. And all the while her face was white with unhappiness; her eyes were dark and troubled. It was only pride that held back the tears.

"Will—will you write to me?" she asked. Then rattled on nervously, "To let me know how you are going on, I mean. I cannot picture you on a small farm, somehow."

"How *do* you picture me?" he asked.

"Oh, as a man of affairs. I don't know. A successful politician or even merchant." She looked at him hopefully, wondering if he would grasp her meaning: she envisaged him as a man a lady could marry.

"I shall be picturing you in Italy, having that wine under the trees in Tuscany," he said softly.

"I shall let you know whether I get Bonnie bounced off on Rawden."

Felicity realized she was making idle conversation to keep Charles a little longer, when he must be on thorns to begin his long trip. "Good-bye, Charles," she said, and shook his hand.

He accepted her hand, then daringly placed a light kiss on her cheek. "We have been more than mistress and servant. Let us part as friends," he said. Then he hurried out of the office, out of the house, into the waiting carriage.

Felicity rushed to the window to see him leave. She let the tears come when she was alone. The congenial life she had enjoyed before meeting Charles lay in shatters. She knew it would be many years before Petty Coomb Hall gave her any pleasure. Even Italy no longer glimmered with its former allure. Her dream lover had a face now, but that face would be on some little farm in northern England. It would not be 'entirely at her disposal,' as she was accustomed to.

The house was like a tomb without Charles. A dozen, a hundred times over the remainder of that day and the next busy day preparing for the ball, Felicity wished she could consult him on some detail. Everything went wrong. The servants were mopey and undisciplined without the butler to guide them. The maids made a frightful job of setting up the refreshment parlor. The table looked like a church bazaar, with too many flowers and glasses scattered around it at random. Cook could not find the receipt for punch that Charles had left with her. Mary did not dust the chairs before arranging them around the edge of the ballroom.

The new butler arrived as promised, but he was unfamiliar with the house and was of little help. Besides, he had a slight limp, that made it difficult for him to dart around as his job demanded—though it was kind of Charles to have sent him.

The ball, that was to have been the highlight of the season, was rapidly sinking into a debacle. And Felicity did not even care. She took no pleasure in donning her new green gown. She had known she could not dance with Charles, but at least she wanted him to see her in her finery. As she had invited a dozen neighbors in for dinner before the ball, she tried to keep up her spirits. She wanted Bonnie to enjoy herself. Somehow the ballroom was ready in time; the dinner went off with no major disasters.

At eight-thirty, Felicity and Bonnie stood at the door of the ballroom to greet their guests as Soper, the replacement butler, announced them. One hundred people crowded the small ballroom, but it might as well have been empty for all the pleasure Felicity took in the soiree. Sir Henry FitzGibbons, a local squire who had his eye on Petty Coomb Hall, led off the opening minuet with Miss Campbell, and congratulated her on her ball. She smiled a wooden smile and thanked him. She danced with other guests. Bonnie seemed to be enjoying herself.

Most of her guests did not know why Miss Campbell had taken into her head to have a grand ball, and were only happy she had done so. Mrs. Legg and a few other crones knew the ball had been planned to entertain Lord Rawden, and were very much disappointed that the guest of honor was not present.

"What happened to Lord Rawden?" Mrs. Legg demanded during a pause in the music.

"He was delayed." ·

"Will he be coming later tonight?"

"Oh no."

"When can we expect to meet him?"

"He did not say, Mrs. Legg. He only said he would be delayed. He was to have come yesterday. I hope we will not have to wait too long for his visit."

"Perhaps he will arrive later this evening."

This had not even occurred to Felicity; she did not think it very likely Rawden would come that night.

Suddenly Soper mounted the little platform from which he had been announcing callers earlier. As the guests spotted him, they fell silent, waiting to hear who was arriving so late.

"Lord Rawden," he announced, and Charles, the butler, entered. He was outfitted in an impeccably tailored evening suit. A ruby as big as a cherry sparkled in the immaculate folds of his cravat. But it was not the clothing that made the man. He looked every inch the gentleman, and always had, even in his dowdy butler's suit.

Felicity felt she should pinch herself to see if she was dreaming. What freakish notion had Charles taken into his head? She had complained that Rawden's defection was making her look foolish, and he was trying to save her by this masquerade, in a suit no doubt given to him by Devlin. But he was only making things worse. Mrs. Legg recognized him at once.

"Why, that is not Lord Rawden. It is your butler," she said to Felicity. A few other neighbors recognized him as well and set up a clamor.

Rawden walked forward to meet Felicity. As he drew near, she saw the wicked twinkle in his eyes.

"Miss Campbell," he said, bowing to her and Miss Legg. "I daresay you have been explaining to Mrs. Legg the little charade we have been carrying on here at Petty Coomb."

Felicity just stared at him, with an expression between chagrin, amusement, and trembling joy.

"It was a matter of the utmost secrecy," he confided, ostensibly for Mrs. Legg's benefit. "I was sent here incognito by the Foreign Office to keep an eye on a certain suspicious character in the neighborhood. The—person proved innocent."

"Mam'selle Drouin!" Mrs. Legg exclaimed. "You are a spy, and that fellow at the inn was your colleague! Is he a lord, too?" She looked doubtfully at the unprepossessing Soper.

"He is my valet, who is giving Miss Campbell a hand with her ball this evening."

"So that is why you were so often seen in Minden." Mrs. Legg turned to Felicity. "And you, sly puss, making excuses for him, saying he was doing errands for you. You cozened us completely—though I *did* wonder about those rides with your supposed butler." She looked archly at Lord Rawden. "I quite understand. A matter of such national importance . . ."

"Just so," Rawden said somberly. "And now, if you will excuse us, ma'am, I have a most important matter to discuss with Miss Campbell." He led Felicity to the morning parlor and closed the door behind them.

"I have wanted to do this for two weeks," he said, and drew her into his arms for a long, heady kiss.

Felicity knew she was mad; it was the only thing that could possibly account for her allowing her butler to tell her guest such wild lies, and to kiss her in this wanton way, with his arms crushing her against him until she could scarcely breathe. Yet if it was madness, she must have this one moment of it to sustain her a lifetime. She might die a spinster, but at least she would know what she was missing. So this was love; this reeling in the head, this tingling along the senses, this deep, burning ache of need for someone.

Before she quite succumbed to a swoon, she pulled away and gazed at him with wild, bewildered eyes.

"Charles, you're mad!" she exclaimed.

"Mad with love for you."

"You should be on your way to the funeral. How do you expect to pull off this stunt when Lord Rawden might be arriving any day?"

"Lord Rawden has arrived, Felicity. He arrived two weeks ago. It is a long, unedifying tale, I fear."

*"You?"*

"Precisely. Papa ordered me to come and propose to Bonnie. I—disliked the idea, and after a few mishaps, came as your new butler, to give you a disgust of Rawden, hoping you would turn him off. My friend, Devlin, was to have come in my place when Rawden eventually made his appearance. There is no Charles, no uncle, no funeral. It was all a ruse."

"What changed your mind?" she asked suspiciously. Yet the story was easy enough to believe. She had always sensed Charles was a gentleman, and had some idea Rawden was a rogue.

"Falling in love with you," he said, seizing her two hands. "You are worlds too good for me. I am— or was—as I described Rawden to you. A ne'er-do-well, a wastrel—but I have changed. You have made me realize that true happiness is not found at a card table, or a horse race. I have been happier here with you, making your fires and beating your rugs, than I ever was in my life before. It is my intention to become a reformed character. With you to keep me in line, I know I can do it. Give me a chance, darling."

"But you were supposed to offer for Bonnie," she said, in a weak voice.

"She has already told me she plans to turn me down. She prefers a Season. That is easily arranged. The more important point is—can *you* ever forgive me?"

A smile of dizzying delight softened her dark eyes as she gazed on Rawden. "It may take awhile," she said.

He folded her in his arms. "Take all the time you want, my dear. I am entirely at your disposal."

raturing him. I daresay it would be difficult to be
a countess, and get to weat ... Standing as ... Court
... Actions can be heavy, an ... Court can be ... doe ...